See No Evil
A Psychic Eye Mystery

Victoria Laurie

DEDICATION

For my podcaster in crime, Sandy.

Love you to the moon and back, sistah!

CONTENTS

ACKNOWLEDGMENTS

I would like the thank the following people for assisting with the production of this book: My sister, Sandy; Trish Long; and Muad Ezza

PROLOGUE – TAKEN FROM THE FINAL PAGES OF *FATED FOR FELONY*

Arriving at Toscano's office, I was ushered down a narrow corridor to a cramped room with soundproofed walls and a large picture window where Ball Cap stood on the other side hovering over a control panel.

I took a seat in the chair facing a laptop and a thick file, and the assistant who'd led me to the room adjusted the microphone boom to a few inches in front of my mouth. She also pointed to a set of headphones and a glass of water and said, "Mike will be here in a minute to go over the show's layout with you. We're live in twenty."

I waited for Toscano with my phone on silent but parked right next to me. My knee bounced as the minutes ticked down, and my gaze kept reverting to the phone's display, but it remained black.

A tapping sound startled me, and I jumped, only to see Candice wave from behind the glass. She offered me a thumbs-up with raised brows as if to ask if I was okay?

I nodded and forced a smile, even though on the inside, I was still on pins and needles.

Toscano came in just then, carrying a giant mug of coffee and a yellow legal pad. He touched me warmly on the back

1

and took his seat. "Wow," he said with a big grin. "You clean up nice, Abby."

I dipped my chin. "I thought it important to look professional today."

"I bet," Toscano said with a wink. "Any word?"

"No."

Toscano sighed. "Plan B?"

"Maybe," I said, lifting my watch to look at the time. We were three minutes to air.

"Okay, I'll let you take the lead and follow your cue. Oh, and I should tell you there's been a *big* spike in subscribers since the news broke about Scott's confession. Especially that last bit."

I felt myself grinning. "The irony, huh?"

Toscano laughed. "Yeah. Wait until my fans hear that the reason Scott took so many measures to cover his tracks and change his appearance—"

"The brown contacts were a bit extreme," I interrupted.

"Truth," Toscano said. "But it just goes to the paranoia he felt after he stopped in to see a psychic when he couldn't locate his father all those years ago. She told him to look for the color blue in his father's name, which we now know was the correction of Blueford from Beauford, *and* she pointed out that, if he were to ever commit a crime like murder, he'd eventually be discovered by another psychic, one who would bring national attention to him."

"Crazy how full circle this all was, right?"

"It is," he said, shaking his head. "Here's a case that a psychic helped make impossible for me to solve until I got the help of another psychic."

"At least it leaves you with a little more respect for people like me," I said.

I grinned ruefully. "You, I have the utmost respect for. The others out there . . ." he paused meaningfully. "Let's just say the jury's still out."

"Mike," came a voice over the intercom. I turned and saw that Ball Cap was talking to us. "We're on in sixty."

"Thanks, Ray," he said, and donned his headphones.

Taking Toscano's cue, I put mine on as well.

"Can you hear me okay, Abby?" he asked into the microphone.

I leaned in a little to speak into my own mic. "I can, Mike, thanks."

"Great. Any word?"

I looked at my phone again and shook my head.

"What do you want to do?"

"Twenty seconds," said Mike from the control room.

I sighed and checked in with my intuition. "We'll need to stall. Start with the case and work through the investigation. We'll wrap up with a thumbs-up or a thumbs-down for me and the Austin bureau."

"Good. And you're still okay to take a few calls at the end?"

"I am."

"Five seconds," Mike said, and then he counted down on his fingers.

My headphones filled with the sound of Mike's signature intro and background music, and I tried to appear engaged and happy to be there, but the truth was my stomach was twisting itself into knots, and, aware that I was on camera, I had to work hard not to glance at my phone every three seconds.

Mike introduced me again, and I waved to the camera in front of me, then waited as he explained the case we'd just solved to listeners who were joining the podcast for the first time.

As I sat there, a bad feeling started to creep up my spine. It was like a foreshadowing that I couldn't quite explain, and I gave into the impulse to glance at my phone, which was still dark. I tapped at it just to be sure I hadn't missed the message, but the text box was empty of new alerts.

Focusing again on Mike, I tried to put the feeling out of my mind, but it wouldn't let go. It hovered there like a foul smell, lingering in the background and distracting me with its insistence that something was about to go very, very wrong.

For reassurance, I looked over and through the glass of the control room, spotting Candice, sitting in a chair watching the show. She smiled at me and offered a nod. It helped to have her there, but still, I couldn't let go of this mounting anxiety.

And then my phone lit up, and my attention diverted there. A simple emoji met my gaze, and I felt my stomach muscles clench because I'd now have to do something I didn't want to do.

"Abby," Mike said, and my attention switched again to him. I realized he was holding up the notes I'd made from our first podcast together. "Would you like to translate these for the audience?"

"Sure, Mike, but let me first begin by saying that, the real hero of this investigation was Executive Assistant Director Simon Nash."

"Yes," Mike said, nodding enthusiastically. "Nash was crucial to the case. After all, he's the one that convinced me to let you have a go at it."

"He was. His belief in innovative solutions, like using me, is just what the bureau needs right now, and I think we all work harder and are made the better for his leadership."

"Great guy," Mike said, like he meant it.

"Okay, enough gushing about Nash," I said with a lighthearted laugh. "He's a humble man, and I'm sure he'd shrug off our praise and suggest we put the focus on the steps taken to solve the case, so, as to your question about my notes . . ."

Mike and I continued to tell the listeners about how the investigation unfolded, and I actually enjoyed participating in the podcast, much to my surprise. It'd also allowed me the leverage I'd needed to save our jobs, which should've brought me a huge sigh of relief, but something was still nagging at me. Some awful thing was lurking just around the corner, and I didn't know what it was about. I just knew it was bad.

Finally, we finished speaking about the case, and Mike

said, "Okay, we'll take a few calls from fans who want to ask Abby a question about the case or her abilities." Mike then looked at Ray, and he nodded and held up two fingers, then a piece of paper with the name Jason on it.

Mike pressed the button for line two on a gadget that looked like a speakerphone in the middle of the table between us. "Hi Jason, you're on the Toscano Files. What's your question for Abby?"

"Hey, Mike, so my question for Abby is, what're the winning lottery numbers?"

I chuckled, but inwardly, I was rolling my eyes. If I had a dime for every person that asked me that question, I'd be wealthier than most lottery winners. "Your guess is as good as mine," I told him simply.

"No, I'm serious," he said.

"I know you are, Jason, but intuition isn't that specific. To get a sequence of numbers that will land on a specific day for a specific lottery just isn't something we can do." No way was I going to mention that I'd once flippantly given a dear friend a series of numbers that *had* actually hit the lottery. The *last* thing I needed was a client list full of people who wanted me to repeat that magic.

"Oh," Jason said. He sounded like he was between fifteen and eighteen. "Can you tell me, though, if *I'm* going to win the lotto?"

"You are not," I said. "But that won't stop you from playing, and I see quite a bit of money being spent on gambling in your future. If that's enjoyable to you, and you have the money to spend, great, but I suspect that you'll wind up with more debt than you'd anticipated due to a streak of bad luck, so I'd be careful of allowing the gambling to get out of hand, okay?"

There was a lengthy pause, then a meek, "Okay."

Jason hung up, and Mike pressed line four. "Simone, you're on the Toscano Files. What question do you have for Abby?"

"Hi, Mike," Simone said, her voice pitchy, as if she was

extremely nervous. "I wanted to know . . ." Simone's voice started to shake, and then she paused for so long I thought we'd lost her.

"I wanted to know . . ." she tried again, and this time it was evident that she was crying.

Mike and I looked at each other, and that really, really bad feeling of foreshadowing enveloped me like an inky cloud. A series of images began to fill my mind as I reached out and connected with Simone's energy, all of them familiar. All of them awful.

"Simone!" I said sharply. "Are you in trouble?"

"I wanted . . . to know . . ." she said again, ignoring my question. This time her words were almost indistinguishable through her sobs.

I stood up and looked at the control booth, not for Ray, but for Candice. She got up from her chair and came to the glass. *What's wrong?* she mouthed.

I could hardly form words, and all I could do was point to the speaker and shake my head. Candice seemed to understand, and she spoke to Ray who looked down at his panel and shook his own head.

Meanwhile, Simone's crying was filling my ears while a terrible feeling was filling up my intuitive senses. "Where are you calling from?" I demanded. "Simone! Where are you?"

There was a sudden hitch in her voice, as if she'd just experienced something painful, and then she said, "I wanted to know . . . if you can solve . . ."

I stood there frozen, hovering above the microphone while Mike and I exchanged wide-eyed looks. He seemed to sense the tension in the background of Simone's voice too, and he was obviously alarmed by the fact that I was so agitated.

"Solve what, Simone?" Mike finally asked.

"My . . . my . . ." she whispered. And then with a long sigh she added the last word. "Murder."

And then there was a terrible *BANG*, and the sound of a body, crumpling to the floor.

CHAPTER 1

For a long, long moment, no one moved. I don't think anyone even breathed. After the shot and the unmistakable thud of a body hitting the floor, the only sounds that followed had been a soft, sinister laugh and three beeps, indicating the murderer had hung up.

And then, almost in unison, my phone vibrated at the same time Toscano's did, and he paused only to hit the center control to mute our mics before pulling his cell out of his back pocket. In the control booth, I saw Candice also lift her phone to her ear.

My gaze fixed on her for several long seconds. I didn't feel capable of reaching over to lift my own phone. The shock of what'd just happened was simply too much to fully comprehend, and I needed a moment. Watching Candice, who was always the calmest person in the room, helped.

As I focused on trying to read her lips, one of the only thoughts I was able to form was how pale she looked. The blood had drained from her face, and it made her beautiful features appear ghostly and distorted. But her gaze was sharply focused, and as I keyed in on that, I came back to myself a little.

"I don't know *what* the fuck that was!" Toscano shouted, running a shaking hand through his thinning hair. "Jesus Christ, Marty. I mean . . . Jesus Christ!"

I didn't know who Marty was, but I was guessing he was someone who was demanding answers and probably high up the food chain. Toscano's gaze landed briefly on me, and he also looked pale and ghostly, but a sheen of sweat had broken out across his face, and he appeared to be trembling. "Can we trace the call?" he asked the caller.

A sinking feeling in my gut suggested we couldn't. It was immediately obvious to me that this sick fuck had meticulously planned the live murder, on-air.

"She could be anywhere," Toscano said next. Then he looked at the control booth, where his producer sat staring at his equipment, a haunted look in his eyes.

Toscano waved, but Ray, his producer, didn't move. So Toscano got up, walked over to the glass, and pounded on it.

His poor producer jumped right out of his chair. "Get us off the air!" Toscano barked. "And open your mic!"

Ray reached over and flicked a switch. "I don't know what happened," he said in a quavering voice. "I screened her, Mike! I swear! She didn't sound like that when I talked to her! I never would've put her on if she had!"

"Where was she calling from?" Toscano demanded. "What area code?"

Ray looked at a pad of paper next to him. "She was local."

"Bullshit," I muttered. My voice had come back to me along with the rest of my senses—including the sixth. "She wasn't local."

I had a sick feeling forming in the pit of my stomach— more than I already had—about where Simone had been murdered. Her death felt personal. It felt like it was orchestrated to publicly torment, torture, and taunt me and Mike.

"You getting a bead on her, Abby?" Toscano asked.

I nodded, but then shook my head.

Toscano's brow furrowed, and he said, "Marty, hold on a sec." Lowering his cell and staring intently at me, he asked, "Which is it?"

"I'm getting a bead on *him*, Mike," I whispered.

"Who's him? The killer?"

"Yeah."

"What kind of a bead are we talkin' here?"

I swallowed hard, feeling on the verge of both panic and

fury. "He's in Austin," I whispered.

"He's where?" Candice's voice through the speaker asked.

I glanced at her behind the glass.

"How do you know he's in Austin?" Toscano said, answering Candice's question in the process.

"I just . . . do."

"Abby, I've got Brice on the phone," Candice said. "He's telling me that Dutch is already making some local calls to the APD."

I allowed my gaze to soften, and I stared out into space, while I focused on what my intuition was trying to tell me. I saw the Frost Bank Tower—an iconic landmark building in central downtown—and I knew that the crime had taken place somewhere in the area.

To go a little deeper, I closed my eyes, and that's when my intuition plonked my awareness into a dimly lit room. In front of me, I saw a desk, like the kind you'd see in a classroom, but all around the desk were discarded items like erasers, crumpled paper, pencils, and chalk. Most tellingly, however, was the pool of blood at the base of the desk, indicating this was a place of violence. My mind's eye lifted away from the desk to look for other focal points, and the only other one I found was on the far wall, which displayed a dusty chalkboard, cementing the idea that the place where Simone had been murdered was an abandoned classroom.

I took a deep breath and tried to block out the noise of my own surroundings, just focusing on trying to get as clear a picture as my intuitive mind could form. That's when I seemed to become acutely aware of a sinister sense within the classroom. Something felt like it was on the prowl. And then, in my mind, I heard a low rumble which seemed to reverberate all around the classroom. My mind's eye moved to the shadows in the corner, and something there stirred. Something sinister. Another low rumble sent the dust on the floor reverberating, and that's when I realized the rumble was a growl.

My heart was beating hard, but it'd been beating hard ever

since Simone had come on the air. Still, there seemed to be an extra note of fear that came with that growl. Something wicked was waiting and watching from the shadows.

My view hovered there, next to the desk as if I was actually in the room. Goosebumps lined my arms, and I could *feel* the threat within that room. I tried to calm myself from the mounting panic that seemed to waft all around me like the smell of something decomposing. And then, from the shadows, stepped a beast. It somewhat resembled a lion, but most of its features were distorted in a way to make the thing look nightmarish. Its fur was white but dotted with blood, and it had large, protruding fangs. There was blood around its muzzle, and it seemed to smile sinisterly when it stepped out of the shadows, like it knew I was there to psychically connect to it.

The most disturbing part of the beast's appearance, however, were its eyes. They glowed the color of blood, and there was an evil glint in them.

The appearance of the beast didn't necessarily scare me, but it did alarm me, mostly because the beast seemed able to stare right into my soul. Like it could tell what I was thinking, and for a moment, I felt caught in that gaze, spellbound by it. It began to approach me, and I knew it wanted to kill me just like it'd killed Simone.

"Abby," I heard Candice say, a moment before I felt her hand on my shoulder.

I jerked, and my eyes flew open, the vision unfolding in my mind's eye, melting away.

"You okay?" she asked me.

I shook my head, trying to clear it, and said, "Yeah. I was trying to get a feel for the killer."

Her gaze traveled to the notepad in front of me. "Did you?"

"I . . . I don't know, Candice."

She squatted down to eye level. "You're pale, Sundance. You might be going into shock."

I rubbed my arms. I felt cold to the bone. "I think he shot

Simone in an abandoned school. Somewhere in Austin."

Candice nodded. "I'll pass that info on to the boys. Sit tight. I'm gonna get you something to eat."

Candice got up and headed out of the recording studio, and I was left to stare at the notepad. It felt difficult to pull my thoughts together, but I managed to take up the pen and scribble down what I'd seen in my mind's eye.

And then I flipped the page and began to sketch out the beast. I just felt compelled to get the image of the beast out of my mind and down onto paper, and I'm no artist, but I was able to roughly flesh it out.

"Here," Candice said. I looked up and saw that she was holding out a protein bar. I took it greedily. I hadn't eaten a thing since the night before, and I'd been so nervous about this morning that I'd barely eaten any of my dinner.

While I devoured the protein bar, Candice swiveled the pad of paper around so that she could see what I'd drawn. "Yikes," she said. "What's this?"

I swallowed and reached for the bottle of water that'd been set out for me by one of Toscano's crew. After taking a sip, I said, "It's the image of the killer that came into my mind's eye."

Candice's brow furrowed. "That looks like something out of a nightmare."

"It is. Or maybe a better term might be a daymare."

Her gaze lifted to me. "I'm assuming this thing is just a metaphor?"

I shrugged. "If you're asking if I think an *actual* beast murdered Simone, no. Her killer was definitely human, but there are clues in that sketch that can help pinpoint the sick fuck who pulled the trigger."

She studied the sketch again. "I can't imagine what those clues could be, Sundance. I mean . . ." She tapped the notepad for emphasis, and I couldn't argue with her. There seemed to be nothing even remotely useable from what I'd drawn. But then I went back to the previous page where I'd described the classroom, and again I said, "He took her to a school. It felt abandoned."

"Any sense of what area in Austin?" Candice asked.

I sighed and closed my eyes for a brief moment. In my mind's eye, I saw a bullseye dead center to the city. "Somewhere downtown."

Opening my eyes again, I saw the frown on Candice's face. "Not a whole lot of abandoned schools in downtown Austin, my friend. I'd be surprised if there was even one. Real estate downtown is at a premium. No way would the city allow the footprint as big as a school to remain unused."

It was my turn to frown. "I think I need Oscar," I told her. "These clues aren't making any sense to me right now, and I think I'm too jolted by what just happened to cipher out their meanings."

"Call him," Candace suggested.

I shook my head. "I need to *see* him, Candace. In person."

Candice stared at me, her lips pressed into a thin line. "On it," she said, and lifted out her phone to tap at the screen.

"Can I see?" Toscano asked, pointing to my small notepad.

It was then that I realized he was off the call with whoever Marty was. "Sure," I said, sliding the notepad toward him.

He studied the first page, then flipped to the second, and I watched his brow furrow. "I don't get it," he finally admitted.

I nodded. "Me either, Mike. But there's something there. I gotta get home and toss this stuff at Oscar to see what he thinks."

"Do you think Simone was young enough to be in school?" he asked me next.

I thought back to the sound of her voice. There was an articulate, mature essence to it. "No," I said. "She seemed to me to be anywhere from her early twenties to her early thirties."

He nodded. "Then the school was just a place to commit the act."

"I think so. If I'm right and it's an abandoned school, then there wouldn't be a lot of people around who could've heard the shot."

Toscano scowled. "Except for the hundred thousand or so who were tuning in to my podcast live today."

I winced. "Who's Marty?" I asked next.

"My executive producer. He's the guy that handles distribution and ad revenue. He's losing his shit over this."

"I think most of us are," I confessed.

Candice came in from the control booth and said, "We're booked on a flight through Delta. Wheels up at five p.m."

I stood and held out my hand for the notepad. Toscano gave it to me, and I moved toward the door. "Are you coming to Austin or staying here?" I asked.

"I'll be there by tomorrow," he told me. "How long should I plan on staying?"

I checked my intuition, extending my sense carefully out, trying to find the point at which Toscano would head back here to DC. "Two weeks. Give or take."

Toscano nodded, but his expression mirrored my worried thoughts.

Two weeks is a long time to roam free and murder more victims. And murder more victims wasn't even something I questioned. I knew this guy was out to make a statement— bigger, maybe even far bigger than the one he'd already made.

And that worried me to the core.

We got back to Austin around seven p.m., and Dutch was there to greet us at baggage claim. "Hey, dollface," he said, wrapping me in his arms.

I squeezed him tightly, and took a deep steadying breath, which was something I didn't feel I'd done since Simone's murder that morning. "You smell so good," I told him, burying my face in his chest.

He chuckled. It was a new joke between us. I'd given Dutch a bottle of Gio Armani cologne for his birthday the month before, and he'd only recently started wearing it. The scent by itself was pleasant enough, but when he wore it, the cologne was transformed into something greater than the sum of its parts, and I found the scent absolutely irresistible.

Dutch squeezed me tight, and whispered, "I put on a little extra just for you, Edgar."

Edgar is the first nickname Dutch ever assigned to me, and he gave it to me after reading a book on Edgar Cayce. He also calls me cupcake, dollface, and, occasionally, "Oh great, beautiful goddess of my body, heart, and mind. Capturer of my soul. Binder of my essence. Giver of all my dreams come true."

Okay, so I'm fibbing on that last one. Let's just say it's the unvocalized nickname in the group.

"Oscar's at the house," he said.

"Is there dinner also at the house?" I asked.

Dutch chuckled again, letting go of me and taking up my hand. "What do I look like? An amateur? Of course there's dinner at the house."

"Pizza?"

"Thai. We haven't had it in a while."

My stomach gurgled with anticipation. "You're too good to me, cowboy."

Dutch grabbed my bag off the baggage carousel, then grabbed Candice's too. "And don't you forget it."

Candice, who'd moved off to make a call, came back to us and took the handle of her luggage when Dutch offered it. "Brice says he's headed out to pick up the Thai food you ordered, Dutch. He'll meet us at your house."

My stomach gurgled again. It was a thirty-five-minute drive from the airport to our house on the northwest side of Austin.

Candice smirked. "We should get going. Abby's stomach is about to get hangry."

I narrowed my eyes at her. "Ha, ha. Sooo funny, Candice."

"Too late," Dutch muttered, winking at her. Digging into his jacket, he pulled out a bite-size, peanut butter and chocolate Larabar. Handing it to me, he said, "I plan ahead."

I took the bar, peeling back the wrapper while grumbling a little, but, secretly, I was grateful to him for providing me a little amuse-bouche for the ride.

When we arrived at our house, I noted with a bit of excitement that Dave—my former handyman and now business partner to my husband—had parked his truck at the curb. Dave had been looking after my two beloved dachshunds, Eggy and Tuttle.

I'd had Eggy since before I'd met Dutch. He was getting up there in years now and was as chill a pup as you'd ever meet.

Tuttle is the opposite. She's three years younger than Eggy, and full of exuberant energy. Dutch had brought her home as a present to me, and she'd been one of the great gifts of my life. I couldn't wait to wrap my arms around both pups.

After getting out of Dutch's car and grabbing our luggage to make our way up the walkway, the door opened and Dave stood in the entry. "There you are!" he said. "I was about to dive into the food without you."

I had a smart comeback on the tip of my tongue, but the urge to say it fled my mind when, out from around Dave, bounded both my pups.

Seeing me, they began to bark and wriggle excitedly. I dropped my purse and the handle to my suitcase, squatting down to catch them as they leapt into my arms, covering me with kisses, whimpers, wiggling bodies, and more excited yapping.

"I guess I'm chopped liver," Candice said, looking down at us with that same smirk on her face.

"If you were chopped liver, they'd be all over you," I said, cuddling Tuttle as she pressed her nose against my neck.

Eggy glanced up and seemed to just realize Candice was there. He switched his attention from me to her. She bent down and scooped him up, allowing him to cover her face in kisses.

"I'll take the bags inside," Dutch said, grabbing our luggage, and heading inside.

"They were very good dogs," Dave said.

I kissed the dimple between Tuttle's eyes a dozen times, then lifted her under her front legs to look at her appraisingly. "I see you didn't hold back on the treats."

Tuttle was definitely chunkier than when I'd left.

"Like I said, they were good."

Candice and I each carried our furry bundle into the house, which was more crowded than expected.

Besides Oscar and Brice, three other agents from the Austin FBI bureau were there. Agent John Williams—a rookie to the Austin bureau but someone who'd already come in very handy on the previous big case we'd worked; Agents Kevin Cox and Scott Baldwin, who were longtime members of the Austin office, and who were always quick to back me up against any naysayers, and Director Gaston.

Gaston's appearance was the most surprising because he'd also just been in DC.

I smiled at each agent as I came through the door, my gaze pausing on Gaston.

"Director," I said with a nod.

"Abigail," he replied in that soft almost whispery voice he has.

"How'd you beat us home?"

A tiny smirk quirked at the edges of his mouth. "I know people."

I grinned. "You know people? Like, the kind of people with private jets?"

"Perhaps," was all he'd concede.

"Come and grab it," Brice called from the kitchen.

Gaston stepped to the side and waved me ahead. "After you," he said.

A glance around the room told me that everyone else also seemed to be waiting for me to go first. "Gee," I said when it was obvious that no one was going to dare step in front of me at the chow line. "It's like I've got a reputation or something."

"Or something," Oscar said with a chuckle. I scowled at him, but that only made the whole team start laughing.

Rolling my eyes while trying to suppress my own laugh, I headed toward the kitchen.

Brice had set out all the food buffet-style, and I picked up a plate to load it up. I'm known for my fast metabolism and inability to go overly long without sustenance. And, by sustenance, I usually mean junk food.

We gathered at the large dining room table Dutch and I had picked out from a local furniture store that specialized in creating furniture out of reclaimed timber. The table was large enough to seat eight comfortably, ten if we wanted to push it.

I'd almost protested when Dutch suggested we get it because I was afraid it was too large. Neither one of us had family here in Texas, and the only people we usually had over were Candice and Brice, but tonight I was grateful for the extra room.

No one spoke about the murder while we ate, and for that, I was grateful. Every time I thought about poor Simone, I lost my appetite. I could easily picture how terrifying her final moments had been—I've been on the receiving end of a killer's murderous intent a number of times now—and the fact that the poor girl had both known that she was reaching out for help, and that it wasn't going to matter anyway, because she was still going to die, was a sadistic twist that ratcheted up the level of cruelty and inhumanity to her murder. It had been a horrible, horrible way to die.

Still, the team seemed intent on distracting me enough to allow me to eat my meal. Gaston talked about the deal he'd struck with Simon Nash, the Executive Assistant Director at the FBI, (and Gaston's boss) to keep the Austin bureau open . . . for now.

"He's put us on probation for the next twelve months. If we generate any bad press during that time, he'll close the office, but for now, we've gotten a pass."

"We'll have to make sure to generate some good press then," Candice said. "And we'll have to make sure that we continue to give Nash the credit for believing in our nontraditional approach." Her gaze slid to me, and I smiled gratefully, glad to have her on my team.

Gaston nodded. "I'm going to talk to Mike Toscano and ask him if it's all right to have Abby on his podcast from time to time."

My mood immediately changed, and I stabbed at my pad Thai noodles with a fork. "Yes, because that's worked out so well already. I wonder how many more women I can have murdered on air?"

The table fell into stunned silence, and everyone stared at me. I'd said the quiet part out loud.

"Abigail," Gaston said into the tense silence. "You're not responsible for what happened today."

I twirled my fork, staring down at my plate, my eyes brimming with tears. "It sure feels like I'm responsible. Would Simone have been murdered if I wasn't a guest on Toscano's show?"

"Yes," Candice said firmly.

I looked over at her. "How can you be sure?"

"Because, someone sick enough to do that to a poor woman on air, put some planning and forethought into the deed. Your presence on Mike's show only made it more enjoyable to that sadistic piece of shit—you weren't the catalyst for the event, you were just part of the scenery."

"I agree with Candice," Dutch said. And all around the table, each person present nodded their heads.

I weighed what she'd said in my mind for a minute, finally nodding too. "Okay," I said. "I guess I can see that side of it."

"You ready to talk about it?" Oscar asked.

I set down my fork with a sigh. "Yeah. Let me get my notes."

I got up from the table, headed to my purse, and retrieved the notebook where I'd rewritten my impressions about the killer. Handing the pad to Oscar, I said, "It's not much, but it was a pretty sharp vision."

"Got it," Oscar said.

"Can we all take a look?" Brice asked. "Eight heads are

better than one."

"What are we looking at?" Dave asked.

"A woman was murdered on air today when Abby was a guest on a popular podcast," Candice told him. "Abby has written out her impressions of the killer and other things surrounding the girl's murder."

Dave's eyes widened. "Oh, jeesh! Guys, I'm just here for the food."

"Gimme," I said to Oscar, motioning toward the notepad. After taking a screenshot of the notes and the sketch, I said, "I'll text it to all of you, except for Dave."

"Thanks," he said, gobbling down the last few bites of his food before pushing his plate away. "I should get going and leave you all to your business."

"Thank you, Dave," I said. "I really appreciate you looking after the pups while Candice came out to help me in DC."

"Anytime," he said, carrying his plate to the kitchen sink. He then made his way to the front door, and I heard it close at the same time I hit the send button on the photo shots I'd taken of my notes and the text to all the cells around the table.

Almost in unison, each person lifted their phones and tapped at the screen. The room was silent while everyone looked the photos of my notes over.

Brice was the first to finish, and he set his phone down with a frown. "I don't think I get it, Abby."

I nodded. "I know that some of my visions can be really cryptic, but I think there're several clues in there that'll become evident once we investigate this a little more."

"Is this a werewolf?" Williams said. "Or some kind of rabid lion?"

"It looked more like an evil lion in my mind's eye," I told him.

"The abandoned school is interesting," Oscar said. "But you've noted that it's somewhere downtown?"

"Correct."

Oscar and Candice exchanged a pair of knowing looks. "I

doubt there're any abandoned schools in downtown Austin," he said.

"I know, I know," I told him. "But we should look anyway. Maybe there's a school that's recently been shut down."

"Elementary, middle school, or high school?" Dutch asked.

I sighed. "I couldn't tell you. All I saw was the desk, some debris, and the dusty chalkboard."

"It's more likely to be an elementary school," Candice said. "Elementary schools typically have fewer students, so they're smaller, and when they get shut down, they're not leaving as big a footprint as a middle school or a high school."

"Or, it could be a private school," Brice offered. "If the land is privately owned and closed, then the city wouldn't be able to sell it off to the highest bidder."

"Was there anything from APD?" I asked him. "Have they gotten back to you about a woman murdered today?"

"No," he said. "I spoke with Grayson about an hour ago, and there's been no call about any woman being murdered today."

Nikki Grayson was an APD detective, and Oscar's soon-to-be fiancée. That is if he ever got around to proposing to her.

At the mention of her name, when I looked at Oscar, his face reddened. I rolled my eyes at him, letting him know I thought he was being silly for stalling the proposal. But then my attention shifted back to Brice. "It's likely that no one's reported her missing yet."

"Are you sure she was murdered here in Austin?" Agent Baldwin asked me.

"Yes, Scott. I'm sure."

"The reason I'm asking is, do you think that she might've been from Austin, but was murdered someplace else?"

I considered that for a moment, weighing it in my solar plexus, where it felt heavy. A heavy feeling usually indicates the answer to a yes/no question is no. "My gut says she was murdered in downtown Austin. Her killer would've been careful though, he wouldn't have wanted to risk any potential witnesses, so he might've had her in a location where there was no one within hearing distance, or where the sound of a gunshot wouldn't be out of the ordinary."

"Then our first task is to try and find out who she was, and where she was murdered," said Agent Baldwin.

"Yes," Brice said. Turning to Oscar he added, "Hernandez, get me a list of any shuttered schools, either public or private, first thing in the morning."

"On it, boss."

"What about also doing a search on her first name?" I asked. "It's not like the name Simone is super common."

"It's more common than you think," Dutch said. "I already ran a search, and it came back with a little over four hundred and seventy women with the first name Simone, living in the Austin metro area."

"Yikes," I said. "That's more than I would've thought."

"We could start calling each of them," Agent Williams said. "If we reach anyone that answers to that name, we know it's not her."

"That's as good a place as any to start," Brice said. "You mind taking point on that, Williams?"

Williams nodded, but I could tell by the rookie's expression that he definitely minded. Phone polling is so dull, and it can also be super frustrating when no leads developed. Plus, four hundred and seventy phone calls is *a lot* of calls to make.

Brice then turned back to me. "Are you sure this was all your radar was able to key in on?"

I sighed heavily. My radar is super handy for almost everything you'd need it to be handy for, but sometimes, when something is particularly complex, or upsetting, my intuition speaks to me only in pictures, and it can be quite a challenge to decipher. "It is," I told Brice. "I'm sorry it's not clearer."

"Don't be," Gaston said. "The clues are here, Abigail. We'll just need to bring some good old-fashioned detective work to the table, and we'll figure it out."

"If you want to tune in again at any point to try and pull more out of the ether, go for it," Agent Cox said with a slight chuckle.

I winced. My radar can easily be triggered, and, just by asking me to tune in, Cox had inadvertently flipped the switch, and my intuition called up the same classroom vision to my mind's eye. But triggering my intuition when I'm already exhausted is akin to igniting an instant migraine.

Still, as the vision formed, I couldn't avoid looking at any detail my radar offered up.

Staring at our dining room table, I allowed my gaze to once again go unfocused, and as I looked at the vision in my mind's eye, I actually *did* notice something different.

On the desk in the center of the room were now four random items: a rock—about the size of a fist, a flashlight that was turned on and shining brightly, a small pail of water, and a stuffed animal in the shape of a bunny.

The arrangement was so odd that I lingered on it for several moments, waiting to see if the four objects would morph into something else.

"Coop?" Oscar said. "You okay?"

I blinked, focusing my vision again and looked up at him. "I just saw something else."

"What?" Brice asked.

I shook my head slightly, feeling foolish at the thought of even mentioning what I'd just seen, but I knew they were important clues, even if they were simple, everyday objects. Pointing to my notepad which was still in front of Oscar I said, "Can I have that back?"

He reached it out to me, and I took it. Flipping the page, I began to draw another rough sketch. This time, however, I only focused on the desk and the odd assortment of objects on it.

When I was finished, I turned it toward the group, and

almost in unison, they leaned in to look at what I'd drawn. Pointing to each object, in case my artistic skills weren't the sharpest, I said, "A rock, a flashlight, a pail of water, and a stuffed bunny."

Looking up at the group again, I could see more than one person who seemed to be waiting for me to deliver a punchline, but I kept my expression serious, so that they all knew this wasn't a joke.

"I don't get it," Baldwin said.

"Me either," I replied. "But there's no way my radar would've offered these objects up if there weren't another important clue in them."

"Could they represent the location of the school where Simone was murdered?" Dutch asked me.

I thought about that for a moment before shaking my head. "I think they represent something else. They're metaphors, that I think point to Simone's identity, but how to glean their usefulness isn't something I can suss out right now. I mean, it's been a hell of a day."

Dutch reached over and squeezed my hand. "Sorry," he said.

I shook my head. "Don't be, love. I'll be okay, I just need some sleep."

"You need a bit more than that," Gaston said. "If the political climate were different, I'd order you to take some time off, Abigail."

"I know, sir. And, after this case is over, Dutch and I plan to take a good long vacation."

Gaston nodded, then he tucked his phone away and stood up. "We'll wait to hear if APD learns about any women missing or murdered, but I also want us to contact some of the surrounding law enforcement agencies. Let's reach out to the sheriff's departments in Williamson, Hays, Bastrop, and Caldwell counties and let them know we're searching for a female gunshot victim or a recently filed missing person's report of a female age . . ."

Gaston looked at me, and I realized I hadn't offered any

description of our victim yet. Pinching the bridge of my nose, because the headache was starting to get sharp, I closed my eyes and pointed my very tired radar at Simone.

"I'd put her in her early twenties," I said. "Dark hair and possibly dark complected. I feel like she drove a light-colored car—possibly white or silver. She feels like she was slight of build, but not necessarily short, and there's something about the mountains with her. She might've been a transplant from someplace like Colorado." I opened my eyes again, and looked at the group, who were once again staring intently at me. "Sorry," I said sheepishly. "That's all I can manage to pull out of the ether tonight."

"That's more than enough," Gaston said. To the group he added, "Call the county sheriffs and give them that description. Tell them we're looking for anyone that might fit that profile."

"Yes, sir," many of those gathered said.

The group began to get up and take their plates to the kitchen. I followed behind Candice and was a bit impressed that Agent Baldwin had taken it upon himself to be the dishwasher in the group. He took everyone's plate, rinsed it off and put it in the dishwasher.

Oscar and Cox busied themselves by closing all the cartons on the leftover Thai food, and putting each one in the refrigerator, while Brice mopped up the counter after them.

I looked at Dutch who had a twinkle in his eye. We were just about the only two people not doing anything to clean up, mostly because the rest of the group had it covered. "We should invite them over for takeout more often," I whispered.

He chuckled. "I wonder if they're available for parties."

I laughed and leaned into him. He wrapped his arms around me, and I once again buried my face in his chest. Hugging my husband felt like coming home. There was no more reassuring, calming, or safe feeling in the world to me than to feel his strong arms encircle me and hold me tight.

"Love you," I mumbled.

"Back atcha, Edgar," he said, resting his chin on the top of my head. "Let's try to wrap this one up quick so we can take off on that vacation, eh?"

"Are you still thinking someplace out West?"

"I am," he said. "Montana's beautiful. So are Idaho and Wyoming."

"What would we do out there?" I asked, still holding him tight.

"Anything we want. I could teach you how to fly fish. Or we could go for a long hike. Or we could just cuddle around a nice big fire."

"I love all of that," I said, lifting my chin to look up at him. "Let's do it."

He grinned. "I'll start looking into rentals, and get a few options for us."

"Thanks for dinner," I heard Oscar say.

Letting go of Dutch, I moved to Oscar and gave him a hug. He seemed startled by the move. "Cooper," he said. "Watch the PDAs, or your husband's gonna get suspicious."

I laughed and squeezed him tighter. "Shut up," I said. "I'm just grateful we get to continue to work together."

"Yeah, yeah," he said, patting my back, but I could tell he was pleased that I'd hugged him.

Stepping back from him, I found Candice moving in for a hug. "Can I get one of those?" she asked.

"Of course!"

We hugged and when she let go, there was Brice, holding his arms out to me, which was really a shock because that man is not a hugger. "Get some rest," he whispered as he squeezed me once and let go.

After he'd let go Agent Cox stepped forward, gave me an awkward half hug with a pat on the back and said, "See you tomorrow, Cooper. And don't worry. We'll get this son of a bitch."

"Thanks, Kevin," I told him.

Then Agent Baldwin wrapped me in his arms, and I was shocked at how warm his hug was. "Baldwin!" I mocked.

"Who knew you were a good hugger?"

He chuckled and let me go. "Take care of yourself, kid," he said. "The team needs you."

I will admit that my eyes misted a little. "Thank you, Scott."

He nodded and moved off. That left Agent Williams and Director Gaston. Gaston stepped forward first and laid a gentle hand on my shoulder. "Thank you for all you do for this bureau, Abigail. I know it sometimes comes at significant personal cost to you, and I'm grateful."

"Of course, sir," I said, my eyes getting misty all over again.

Once Gaston had moved on, Agent Williams stood awkwardly in front of me. I could tell he was probably wishing he'd just headed for the door the minute things started to get mushy, but he was sort of stuck now.

He eyed me with a bit of terror in his eyes. I mean, here was this rookie who'd caused me and our office so much trouble, but whom I'd actually grown a little fond of in recent weeks.

Still, there was no way I was going to make him feel pressured into any public display of affection. So I extended my fist and said, "Gimme a fist bump, Williams, and call it a night."

He let go of the breath he'd so obviously been holding and extended his own fist out to touch mine. "Goodnight, Ms. Cooper."

"Goodnight, Mr. Williams," I replied.

He began to walk past me toward the door but then stopped himself, and said, "I haven't told you this yet, but I'm glad I was assigned to the Austin bureau, and I really regret ever making trouble for you. I had no idea what an asset you were to the cause."

I offered him a gentle smile and felt the shift of energy between us move from barely veiled tolerance, to respect. "Thank you, John. That means a lot."

And it really, really did.

CHAPTER 2

Dutch and I got to the office super early, stopping to pick up coffee and doughnuts for the crew. Even though we walked in just before seven a.m., we still weren't the first people there.

"Morning, Sundance," Candice said after I set down two of the boxes of doughnuts on the counter near the coffee maker.

"Morning, Cassidy." Looking around I added, "Wow. I didn't expect for Baldwin and Cox to be here so early."

"They got here about ten minutes ago. They're reaching out to all the local surrounding sheriffs' departments to get the word out about Simone and see if anyone fitting her description has been reported missing yet."

"Still no word from Nikki on that?"

"Nope. I just called her. She's on her way into the office herself, but when she woke up, she checked dispatch first thing, and there weren't any women reported missing or murdered overnight."

I sighed. "Dammit. We need to learn who she was, so that we can start tracking a suspect."

"Do you think she knew her killer?" Candice asked.

I'd had a full night's sleep and was feeling much better mentally, so I checked in with my radar and said, "There was a connection, but it feels loose."

"How loose?"

I shrugged. "To my mind, they may have met at some point prior to yesterday, but it wasn't like they were on a first name basis."

"Hmmm, interesting," Candice said, like that was important.

"What?" I asked.

"If it's true that they knew of each other but weren't actually acquainted, then it's quite likely they lived or worked in the same area."

I pointed a finger gun at her. "That's true. So, once we know Simone's full identity, we hopefully won't have to look far to find a person of interest."

She tipped an imaginary hat at me. "Bingo."

"Hey," Agent Cox said, walking up to us while eyeing the boxes of doughnuts.

"Good morning," I said, waving at the morning snack. "Help yourself. There's plenty."

"Any bear claws?" he asked hopefully.

"Please, Kevin. What do you take me for, an amateur?" I opened the lid of one of the boxes with a flourish to reveal an assortment of doughy deliciousness including three bear claws in the center.

"You're too good to me," he said, reaching for a napkin and loading it up with two of the treats.

Cox is a guy in his early fifties who, despite his unhealthy proclivity for sugary pastry, keeps himself in remarkably good physically fit shape.

"Anything interesting come in from the calls you've already made?" Candice asked him.

He took a bite of the bear claw, then thumbed over his shoulder. "Baldwin just got a hit that could be something."

"Oh?" I asked. "What'd he get?"

"A nineteen-year-old girl went missing three days ago. She fits the description you sketched out, but her name is different."

I cocked my head at him. "What was her name?"

"Elena Navarro. She's from South Austin, but she and her boyfriend live in Cedar Rapids. She went missing from work after she and the boyfriend had a fight." Cox bounced his brow in a look that suggested he wasn't buying the boyfriend's story.

"Can you get me the report?" I asked.

"Sure. I'll tell Baldwin to forward it to you as soon as the Cedar Rapids deputy sends it to us."

"Morning," someone behind me said.

I turned to see Oscar, also eyeing the box of doughnuts. "Oscar," I said.

"That last bear claw is spoken for," Cox told him sharply. He'd already plowed through half of one claw and was holding tightly to the second.

I tried to suppress a giggle but couldn't. The warning in Cox's expression was too funny not to giggle at.

And of course, Oscar being Oscar, immediately took the bait. "This bear claw?" he asked, stepping forward to pick up the pastry.

"I'm serious, Hernandez," Cox said, glaring at Oscar like he'd just asked a perp to drop his weapon.

"Relax," Oscar said, chuckling himself. "I'm not going to eat it," and he made like he was going to set it back in the box when he suddenly pulled it back to lift it to his mouth and lick it all over before setting it back in the box.

"Dude!" I gasped.

"Oscar!" Candice exclaimed.

And poor Agent Cox . . . The man looked like he'd just been kicked in the gut. "Not cool," he growled.

But Oscar thought he was being hilarious. He carried on laughing as he selected a chocolate frosted doughnut with sprinkles, then headed to his desk to gobble it down.

Meanwhile Cox continued to stare at him with narrowed eyes and a flinty expression. I could see the wheels of revenge already turning.

"I can go out and get you another bear claw," I suggested. I wanted peace in the office, not contention, and a doughnut was a stupid thing to pick a fight over.

Cox's gaze cut to me. "Don't worry about it," he said, and headed back to his desk.

I sighed, and Candice and I exchanged twin "Boys are

stupid!" eye rolls.

She then laid a hand on my shoulder, and said, "This is where I leave you for the day."

"Leave me? Why? Where're you off to?"

"I've got a case."

"What's the case?"

"Running a background check on the boyfriend of the daughter of a wealthy client."

"I'm guessing the boyfriend comes from more humble beginnings?"

"Yep. And it wouldn't be hard to come from more humble beginnings than these people. Their net worth is in the hundreds."

I smirked. "I'm assuming that's hundreds of *millions?*"

She winked at me. "It's like you're psychic or something."

I grinned. "Or something."

Candice sashayed by me, heading to the door, and I had a moment of regret where I wished for simpler times when it'd just been me, with my private practice, and her, with hers, and we'd often collaborate together on her cases that were so tame compared to the ones I was working now.

I was heartened a little when my own intuition suggested that she and I would be working on something together soon.

"Cooper!" someone called.

I turned to see Agent Baldwin waving at me. "I just forwarded that missing person's report to your email. Check it out, and let me know if you want me to head over to start some interviews."

I nodded and moved to my desk, booting up my laptop and waiting for my email to load. I saw the email from Baldwin near the top of the stack of new mail, but what really caught my eye was the one right above it. The timestamp on that email showed that it'd come in maybe only a minute ago.

The sender was unknown, and the email address of the sender was simply, 666@guerrillamail.com.

A chill went straight up my spine when I read the subject header. *Did you enjoy that?*

I knew from working with the FBI that Guerrilla Mail was used to send emails without the ability to trace where they came from. The mail server offered "disposable email", or email generated through an encrypted server that would allow for email to be delivered completely anonymously. A reply could only be sent for an hour before it vanished and was no longer a valid address.

Seeing the email provider was reason enough for concern, but that subject line hit me like a gut punch. I knew immediately that it was connected to Simone's murderer.

There was also a PDF attachment to the email that I knew I'd see when I opened it, and, because this guy was a sick and twisted fucker, I knew that it'd definitely be something shocking.

"Dutch!" I called, loud enough for him to hear me in his glass-enclosed office at the opposite end of the open-floor plan.

He was behind his desk, on the phone, but he didn't hesitate to get to his feet when he heard the tone of my voice. I watched as he said something to the caller, then hung up and came out of his office toward me.

"What's happened?" he asked, closing the distance between us.

I waited until he was next to me to point to the email. "This just came in."

He squinted at it, read it then flattened his lips into a thin line. He knew it was trouble just like I did. "Open it," he said softly.

Baldwin, Cox, and Oscar had all gotten up from their desks and were gathering around us. I waited until they were right behind me to click on the email.

It opened, and there was no text written, just a grainy photograph of a woman, lying face down on a concrete floor with a large pool of blood around her head.

I hissed at the sight, closed my eyes and turned away. "It's Simone."

"Abby," Dutch said, laying a hand on my shoulder. "Move

over a little so I can forward that to the team."

I scooted to the side without looking back at my inbox and heard his fingers clicking on my keyboard. Then he said, "Done. And I deleted it from your email."

I nodded and looked back, feeling shaky and nearly on the verge of tears. I'd seen dead bodies before—far too many, actually—so I should be used to such images, but I'd been the last person Simone had ever spoken to, so her murder felt personal. Like I was partly responsible.

"Hey," Dutch said to get my attention.

I looked up at him, trying to pull myself together. "I'm okay," I whispered, but even my whisper quavered a little.

"Go get a coffee," he said, cupping my chin to look at me intently.

My gaze slid to the large dispenser of coffee we'd brought with us from the doughnut shop.

"Get a fancy coffee," he insisted. "One with foam and lots of sugar."

"Okay," I said. I got to my feet, and Dutch squeezed my shoulder. I knew he actually wanted to give me a hug, but it'd be a little weird in this setting, and I knew he wanted to keep things on the professional side for the moment.

"I'll be okay," I repeated. "Promise."

"I know." Dutch then turned to look at Oscar. "Hernandez," he said.

"Yes, boss?"

"Go with her."

Oscar went back to his desk and grabbed his keys and his jacket. Walking quickly past us, he said, "Come on, Coop. Foamy, sugary coffee awaits!"

I offered Dutch what I hoped was a grateful smile and trotted after Oscar.

Hernandez led the way down the stairs, but he turned toward the parking structure attached to our building, rather than continuing on to the front door and the street. There was a coffee shop right next door, so I didn't understand why we were headed to the garage.

"Where're we going?"

"Across town," he said. "There's a better coffee place near my house, and the drive will do you some good."

He wasn't wrong. I did need a minute or twenty to collect myself.

We got in Oscar's SUV, and as he drove, he said, "I'm in a bad way, Coop."

"Bad way how?"

"With Nikki. I spent the last two days at her place, trying to work up the courage to propose, and I just couldn't do it."

The tension in my shoulders relaxed a little. Casual conversation with my buddy was just what I needed. "Why do you think that is, Oscar?"

He shook his head. "Dunno."

"Have you ever proposed to anyone else?"

"Nope."

I sighed. "Well no wonder you're paralyzed with fear."

Oscar looked sharply at me. "I'm not—"

"I mean, it's totally understandable why asking a simple question would leave you a quivering, scared mess."

"Coop—"

"It's *much* better not to ask her and forever wonder rather than dig deep, deep, *deep* within yourself to find the ounce of courage to say four little words. I completely understand your total reticence and willingness to remain a little babyman, pouting in the corner because he'd rather suck on his binky than take a chance at lasting happiness."

Oscar offered me a level look. "Will you stop?"

"Tell me how I'm wrong," I challenged.

It was his turn to sigh. "If she says no, then it's over, and I don't know that I want to risk that. She's the best thing to ever happen to me, Coop. I don't want to lose her."

I rolled my eyes. "Why would you think it'd be over if she said no?"

He blinked at me and gave me a look like it should be obvious. "Wouldn't we *have* to break up?"

"*No!* Oscar, my dude, if she says no, she'd probably be

turning you down because she's not ready. You guys have only been dating . . . what? Nine or ten months, right?"

Oscar nodded, and there was a hopeful look in his eyes.

"Listen, if she turns you down, she's only doing it because she needs more time to make sure that, if and when she *does* say yes, she's sure she wants to commit to you for the rest of her life."

Oscar seemed to mull that over for a minute, his anxiety readily apparent.

"Listen," I told him. "Nikki's a smart, independent, confident cookie. She knows her mind, and she knows her heart. She's not going to make an impulsive decision, and it's *because* you guys have been seeing each other for the past ten months that you should feel encouraged. No way would a woman like that waste time on a relationship she didn't see potential in."

Oscar sat with that for another beat or two, but, eventually, he nodded. "Okay," he finally said. "Thanks, Coop."

"Anytime, my friend. Now propose to your girl, so we can get started planning your wedding."

His brow shot up. "Your radar telling you she'll say yes?"

I scowled at him. He'd asked me this once before, and I'd steadfastly refused to give him any insight, because I wanted him to work through his fear of rejection on his own, not use me like a safety blanket. But now I'd gone ahead and let the cat out of the damn bag.

"I haven't tuned in on her decision, buddy," I lied. "I'm only offering you some incentive and encouragement."

Oscar's shoulders sagged. "Really wish you'd cut me a break and look, Coop."

"I know, buddy. I know." I patted him on the shoulder. "But this is *your* summit to climb. All on your own. You can do it!"

He chuckled. "Yeah, yeah."

We pulled into the lot of a little coffee shop with a light-yellow awning, chartreuse stucco, and a bright orange door.

"Cute," I said.

"They have great pastries here too," Oscar said, as he parked and we got out of the car.

"I've already had two doughnuts," I told him.

He snorted. "Like that's ever kept you from sampling another something delicious."

I grinned. "Truth."

We headed inside the coffee shop, which was a bit crowded, but Oscar found us a two-top, and put his jacket over one of the chairs to indicate the table was taken. We then got in line, and I looked over the menu. "Ooo, that lavender, honey latte sounds amazing."

"Every coffee here is good," he said. "Nikki and I come here all the time. She's gotten that one before, and I think she really liked it."

"Sold," I said, poking him with my elbow. "And that hazelnut crème, chocolate chip scone has my name written all over it."

"That's the spirit," Oscar said, elbowing me back.

We got our treats and our coffees and sat at the table Oscar had claimed. "Ohmigod," I said, biting into the scone. "This is amahgazmic."

"Amahgazmic?" Oscar said. "Amazingly orgasmic?"

I pointed my trusty finger gun at him and clicked my tongue. "I love that you get me."

"I wish I got more of that vision you had," he said. "I thought about it all night, Coop, and I can't figure it out."

"It's one of the trickier visions I've had," I agreed. "But the complexity of it tells me this case is going to have more than just one moving part."

"What's that mean?"

I shrugged. "It feels complex in a way that we're only just finding out. Simone was the first, but she sure as hell won't be the last, which is frustrating and upsetting. I wish I could just point to someone on the street and say, 'that guy' and have you guys take him down."

"You mean take him *in*," he said.

I frowned. "Trust me, Oscar, by the time this is all over, you'll want to put him down like a rabid animal. He'd be someone who'd be just as dangerous in prison as out."

"That's what prisons are for, Coop. They lock up the dangerous types."

"Yeah, but there's something about the energy of this guy—it's different. He has the power of persuasion about him. He'd be someone that, if he went to prison, he'd recruit other inmates to his way of thinking. He'd radicalize them and make them even more dangerous."

"There's already a lot of that going on," Oscar said. "You look at any maximum-security prison, and they're all radicalized in one way or another. Each gang has its own culture, and radical belief system. It's part of the way they survive the violence of living in a tribal society."

"I hear ya," I said. "But this guy's different. Trust me. If he gives you a reason, you take him out, okay?"

Oscar looked at me with a furrowed brow. "I've never heard you say something like that, Coop. You're the one who's usually arguing the opposite—giving the criminal his fair share in court."

"Our last case changed me," I told him, knowing it had. "I thought I'd seen the worst humanity could offer, until we faced that sick, son of a bitch."

Oscar nodded. "The torture chamber," he said, commenting on just one of the horror show discoveries we'd stumbled across as we worked to chase down a truly demented and depraved serial killer.

"Yeah, the torture chamber," I agreed with a shudder. "That guy deserves the death penalty if ever anyone did."

"He'll get it," he said. "Both Oklahoma and Texas have capital punishment at their disposal."

"Good."

"But back to this guy, Coop. Now that you've had a good night's sleep, is there anything else you can pull out of the ether about him?"

I finished chewing the bite of scone I'd just taken and then inhaled a deep cleansing breath before closing my eyes and focusing in on the man in question. "He's young," I said, surprised that that was the first thing to come to my mind. "I hadn't anticipated that he'd feel so young."

"How young?" Oscar asked softly.

"I'd say the same age as Simone. But he's influential, just like I said before. He's got this power to sway other minds. I'd bet my savings that he has a following of some kind."

"Is he religious? Could he be a cult leader?"

I sat with that for a moment. "It's so odd, Oscar, because I feel in a way his *is* religious, but it's not in an established way. I feel like he's contorted some other belief system, twisting it in a way to suit his needs."

"What's his motivation?" Oscar asked next.

The answer hit me hard. "He hates women," I said simply. "There's this sense that he sees us as less than human, like we're some kind of feral animal, to either be tamed, or put down."

"Which is how you described dealing with him," Oscar reminded me.

I opened my eyes. "You know how these malignant narcissists are. They project onto others what they're most guilty of."

"So he's a malignant narcissist now, too?"

"I'd say he most definitely is. I can see the narcissism clearly in his energy, along with the other requirements; the antisocial behavior, aggression, and sadism."

"Most serial killers are malignant narcissists, though, Coop."

"This one's different," I insisted. "He feels successful outside of his sadistic pursuits. He feels self-made, and confident in a way that tells me he's used to taking chances and having them work out for him."

"All of that might make him easier to find," Oscar said.

"Agreed."

"Anything else about him, like maybe his physical appearance?"

I focused my radar one more time. "He's tall. Good looking," I said, feeling a sense of beauty about his features. "He's charismatic, skilled with numbers and strategy. I think he's got blond hair, and it feels light blond over dirty blond. His eyes are light too. Blue, or gray, or green."

"That's great," Oscar said, jotting all I was saying down in the note app on his phone.

"We still need our corner piece," I said. "We need to find Simone."

"Check your email, Coop. See if that report on Elena Navarro gives you an intuitive bing."

I took my phone out of my purse and pulled up my email. My breath caught when I saw that another email had come in from Guerrilla Mail—this time from a different set of numbers and letters before the @.

But that wasn't what caught my attention. It was the subject header, which read, *Ha, ha! Made you look!* And there was only one line of text in the email, and it read; *Watching you, seeing you squirm, just like Simone.*

And he had. And I hated him for it. I turned my phone so Oscar could see the screen. "He's taunting us," I said.

Oscar's expression was hard. "No, Coop," he said. "He's taunting *you*."

CHAPTER 3

We left the coffee shop almost immediately. On the way, I complained—a lot—about the fact that I seemed to be the favorite plaything on the serial-killer-du-jour menu.

Oscar—bless his heart—mostly just listened.

"I mean, seriously!" I yelled, all worked up from an overload of caffeine, sugar, and love notes from a monster. "What the actual *fuck* is with these sick, sadistic, pieces of shit? Like, what is it about *me* that they think is so much fun to toy with?"

"I don't know, Coop. It's messed up."

"*Messed up*?" I yelled. "I *wish* it was just 'messed up'!" I used air quotes for that last bit, and this was Oscar's cue to comment no further, nod silently, and drive a *lot* faster.

"It's not like I go *looking* for trouble!" I continued, waving my arms around as I spoke. "I mean, why don't they target one of *you* idiots for a change?"

Oscar nodded and added a shrug.

"I mean what is *with* these twisted psychos?! It's like I'm putting out some sort of 'come hither-killer' vibe!"

My air quotes were getting a workout this morning.

"*How did he even get my email?!*" I screeched next.

Oscar continued to simply nod without reply, so I pushed on his shoulder a little to let him know he needed to.

He made a face like he was reluctant to get involved in my rant again, but at least he answered. "It's not hard to suss out, Coop. All of our email addresses are our last names plus the at Austin FBI dot com."

"*Well then I want a new email address!*"

Oscar went back to nodding. Vigorously.

"And you *know* how Dutch is gonna react to this, right?"

Oscar's nod paused for a moment . . . we were entering dangerous territory here.

"He's gonna ground me or assign one of you fools to follow me all over town! Who wants *that* detail?"

Oscar held very, *very* still.

"No one!" I shouted. "*No one* wants to babysit my sorry ass!"

Oscar let out the breath he'd been holding.

"And you know what? I don't want the hassle of having to explain why I need to go where I want to go when I want to go there!"

"Maybe Rivers won't overreact this time, Coop," he said gently.

I crossed my arms, scowled hard, and stared out the passenger window. "Oh, please! Someone so much as stumbles near me, and my husband covers me in bubble wrap. That man is stupidly overprotective."

Silence followed, and I could feel the tension wafting off Oscar, so I turned my head to look at him. He seemed on the verge of wanting to say something but was holding back.

I didn't blame him.

"What?" I asked curtly.

Perhaps my tone wasn't the most inviting, because Oscar continued to hesitate.

"Oscar, *what?!*"

"I don't disagree about that protective protocol, Coop." I opened my mouth wide to start yelling again when Oscar put his hand up defensively and said, "As much as you don't like it, this fucker has a thing for you. He's willing to toy with you from a distance for now, but that could change in a second."

Oscar snapped his fingers for emphasis.

"If we don't take some precautions for your safety, then you could end up like Simone, and no way could any of us live with that."

And just like that I calmed down.

"Dammit," I muttered, conceding the point. "Fine. But I'm *not* going to be locked inside some panic room while you guys get to enjoy your freedom. I'm sick of living like *I'm* the prisoner."

"Understood," he said. Then he added, "I'll volunteer for protective duty, Coop. You and I make a good team, and together I think we'll make the most progress on this case."

I sighed heavily and laid a hand on his elbow. "Sorry, buddy. Didn't mean to get all worked up there."

Oscar turned left to pull into the parking garage at the bureau, and said, "It's okay. I get it."

We headed inside, and when we came through the door, I was a little surprised to see Toscano there. "Mike," I called. His back was to me, and he was talking with Brice and Dutch.

He turned and smiled when he saw me. "There you are," he said.

I smiled in return. Mike and I had gotten off to a very bad start when we'd first met, but after working the last case together, we'd developed a genuine respect for each other, and perhaps even a friendship was sprouting up between us.

He's a giant of a man, six five if he's an inch, broad in the shoulders and chest, and bearded and mustached, with mostly salt-and-pepper hair. He's gotta be in his late sixties, but he still looked good, more youthful in appearance and manner than I'd guess his actual age to be.

Toscano used to head the DC bureau, and he even mentored Brice for a period of time. He retired not long ago, and on his way out the FBI door, he took dozens of cold case files with him, which he featured on his weekly podcast, the *Toscano Files,* which was insanely popular with the true-crime crowd. Before his last podcast aired, Mike had over a million regular followers, and I'd heard that number had doubled recently, probably thanks to the "controversy" of having someone of my profession on board.

I eyed my watch as I approached him. It was just after nine thirty a.m. "When did you get in?"

"I took the five-forty-five a.m. shuttle," he said. "Just

came from the airport."

"Ah," I said, laying a hand on his arm. "Glad you're here."

Oscar held out his hand to Toscano. "Sir," he said. "Welcome back."

"Agent Hernandez," Toscano replied warmly. "Glad to be back, but I wish it could be under better circumstances. Any luck finding Simone?"

Oscar and I shook our heads. "Not yet," Oscar said. "But we're monitoring all the area's missing persons' reports, so we're hopeful that we'll get a lead on her soon."

"What about Elena Navarro?" Baldwin called from his desk. "Cooper, did you have a chance to look at that report I emailed you?"

"Not yet, Scott," I replied with a frown. Pointing to Oscar I added, "We've been dealing with other emails this morning."

"Emails?" Dutch asked, emphasizing the plural.

I blanched. Shit. I'd let the cat out of the bag. Then again, he was bound to hear about it soon anyway. "I got another email," I confessed.

Dutch's expression turned to granite, which I've come to learn is his way of shutting down all emotion, lest it get in the way of logically solving the problem. "Show me," he said softly.

I brought out my phone, pulled up the email, and handed it to him. "There's a simple message, and that subject header, but no attachment this time."

He eyed the email for a long moment. "You need to stick by my side and stay here at the office until we catch this son of a bitch," he said, handing my phone to Brice, who looked at it and scowled.

I offered Oscar a pointed look and mouthed, *See?*

He cleared his throat, and said, "Sir, your wife and I spoke about this on our way back from grabbing coffee, and if it's all right with you, I'd like to partner with her as we move forward with this case. I can watch over her while we work."

Dutch's expression didn't change, but he did pivot his

gaze back and forth between me and Oscar. "Fine," he said, but then he settled that steely gaze on me and added, "You need to carry a weapon at all times, Edgar."

I rolled my eyes dramatically. "You boys and your guns."

I hate guns. Like *hate* them. Dutch had given me one as a present once, and I thought it one of the most insulting presents I'd ever gotten. Still, I'd learned to shoot it, but it mostly stayed in its pearl-white gun safe at home.

"I'm serious, Abby," Dutch growled. "Where's your gun?"

"At home. Under the bed. Behind a bunch of shoe boxes. Collecting dust."

"Oscar," Dutch said. "Take her home to retrieve her weapon. And I want her to wear it on her person. Her holster is in the front hall closet."

"You're kidding me, right?" I snapped, anger brimming at my lowered brow. "First of all, cowboy, I'm standing *right here*! Second, I'm *not a child* who needs you to give instructions to the babysitter! Third, driving home and back is a *giant* waste of time when we have a case to solve!"

Dutch handed me back my phone, but still refused to address me. Instead, he called over his shoulder, "Agent Baldwin. Print out a copy of that missing person's report for my wife. She can look at it in the car on the way to retrieve her weapon."

"Yes, sir," he said.

I glared at Baldwin like he'd just joined the conspiracy against me, and he quickly lowered his gaze to his computer.

"You can't make me, you know," I told my husband.

"You're right. But I can *insist* that you remain here, locked away in this office during the day, and under my protection at all other times."

I shook my head and balled my hands into fists. I *hate* being treated like a child.

"Coop," Oscar said gently. "It's okay. Let's just get your gun so that your husband doesn't worry about you so much that you end up being more of a distraction than an asset."

I was breathing hard with frustration, but listened to

Oscar's logic, and suddenly, I understood Dutch's point.

"*Fine*," I said.

"Thank you," Dutch replied, his tone softening. He also reached out to grab my hand and squeeze it to show me that he wasn't mad, just concerned. I sighed, but relaxed my posture, and my expression.

Baldwin approached us then, and handed me a thin, blue file. "I'll keep monitoring the area to see if any more reports come in. Text me if you want me to pursue that lead." He pointed to the file in my hand, nodded at me in a show of support, then moved back toward his desk.

"You ready?" Oscar asked.

"Yep," I said, and once more we headed out the door.

On the way to the house, I opened up the Elena Navarro case file, and read the short report there.

Elena was a nineteen-year-old woman who worked at the large grocery chain, H-E-B, as a cashier. She'd apparently left work in the middle of her shift, and hadn't shown up for work since. Her coworkers and supervisor had grown concerned, as this was very out of character for the earnest, hardworking young lady.

Her backstory was that she lived mostly with her boyfriend, but she would often stay at her parents' house when things were strained between them, and lately, according to her supervisor who'd also been Elena's confidant, things had been especially strained.

The boyfriend, Mark Gutierrez, claimed that he and Elena had had an argument the night before she went missing, and he said that she had grabbed some extra clothes on her way to work the next morning. He assumed she'd be staying with her parents, and when she didn't come home or answer his texts, he figured she was still mad.

He claimed to have had no connection to her disappearance, and, interestingly, my radar agreed with him, which was troubling, because it was almost always the significant other. When my intuition hinted that it was someone else, it always complicated things.

According to the report, Elena had shown up for her shift, and had been working in the back, helping to unpack and sort inventory from the corporate truck delivery, when she announced to her coworker that she had to take a break to answer a personal call, and then asked her coworker to cover for her.

The coworker, a man identified only as Patrick, agreed, and he covered for Elena for the next hour and a half, but when she didn't return, he became angry at all the extra work he had to do without her and went in search of their supervisor.

Hearing that Elena hadn't come back from break after an hour and a half, her supervisor put a call out on the store's PA system asking that Elena report to her office, but the young woman never showed up. Thinking she might've taken ill and gone home, her supervisor texted her a message that said she wasn't mad that Elena had left in the middle of her shift, but they would need to talk about it.

Elena never answered the text, but the supervisor did note that her text to Elena showed "read" in the late evening hours, meaning that Elena had seen the message and had chosen not to respond.

The next day, Elena was a no call/no show to work, and again her supervisor reached out, going so far as to contact the girl's parents, who then reached out to her boyfriend, but no one had seen Elena since she disappeared out the back door of the grocery store.

I finished reading the report right when Oscar pulled into my driveway. I closed the file, my mind and my intuition already buzzing. "Come on in for a minute, would you?" I asked. "There're some things about Elena that I want to get down on paper before I lose them."

"Sure, Coop," he said.

We headed up the walk to the home Dutch and I had built together, and when I opened the door, there was Tuttle, bouncing and barking with joy. Eggy trotted into the front foyer much less enthusiastically, and by the massive yawn he offered me in greeting, I guessed that we'd woken him from a good nap.

After saying my hellos to the two pups, I led the way to the kitchen and waved at the counter. "Have a seat while I get my stupid gun."

"Can I get something to drink?" Oscar called to me, just as I headed into the master suite off the kitchen.

"Of course. There's Dr. Pepper in the fridge, and I think some juice or water if you want it."

Oscar didn't reply, but I heard the refrigerator door open as I walked over to the bed. Keeping my focus on Elena's case, I got down on the floor and lay on my stomach, inching toward the edge of the bed to look underneath the bedskirt at all the clutter I kept there, which was quite a bit.

Mostly, there were shoes. I love shoes. Gorgeous footwear of every kind is my kryptonite. And I spent a fair portion of what should've been a retirement account on the collection.

To avoid having any commentary from the peanut gallery—and, by peanut gallery, I mean my husband—I kept most of my new purchases under the bed, rotating them through the inventory in the closet when he wasn't looking.

To his eye, from just the shoes I had on the rack in our walk-in closet, I owned less than twenty pairs of shoes. In reality, I owned at least triple that, and kept some under our bed, some under the spare beds in our two guestrooms, and some in a large plastic container in the garage. Eyeing the boxes, I had to resist the urge to grab a favorite pair—or two—and swap them out for the cork-wedge sandals I was currently wearing.

Shoving some of the boxes aside, I found the locked gun case all the way at the back, pressed against the headboard. "There you are, sucker," I said, pushing myself forward with my toes, trying to reach it.

I finally got my fingers on the lid and carefully slid it toward me until I could more easily grab it and take it out from under the bed. Plugging in the code, I opened the box and stared at the revolver. It was a pretty thing when you forgot that it was a lethal weapon that could kill a man faster than he had the opportunity to realize.

I scowled at it, even though it'd actually saved my life before. Having it on my person felt like it was inviting trouble, and trouble was something that I already had. I didn't especially want more.

With a sigh, I took the gun out of the box, checked to make sure it was empty—it was—then shut the case and shoved it back under the bed. Before I left the bedroom, I grabbed a spare notebook from the small desk we kept near the window, and rejoined Oscar in the kitchen.

He was sitting on a barstool at the counter, enjoying his Dr. Pepper and skimming through Elena's missing person's report. Without a word, I laid the gun on the counter next to him, then took the notepad I always have on me out of my purse along with a pen and sat down, and got ready to allow my intuition to do its thing.

Closing my eyes to concentrate, I was a little distracted at first when I heard Oscar get up from his seat, and head out to rummage through our front hall closet, no doubt looking for my holster. He'd find ammo for the gun there too, and he'd probably make me load the gun before we left the house.

Willing myself to focus on Elena, my first impression was of bluebonnets, the Texas state flower, and one that was just starting to blossom this time of year. I simply observed the beautiful flowers, spread out in a field, but then the vision shifted to focus on a large rock, which was oddly shaped like a ball, without any jagged edges. Just smooth and round.

I noted the rock's distinct shape, then waited while the vision painted the green grass immediately surrounding the rock with the outline of a body—very much resembling the chalk outline they used to do in the old days—forming the shape out of more bluebonnets.

My focus shifted again, swiveling to a dirt path—like a trail, that led into a wooded area, and then along a small stream.

The vision shifted yet again, and I found myself facing

away from the trail, back toward the rock, which now had a truck pulling up to it. The truck stopped, and the back doors swung open, revealing a grocery cart, which rolled forward and dumped out onto the field of bluebonnets.

That's when I opened my eyes and saw Oscar coming down the hallway carrying a box of bullets and my gun holster.

"I think I know where Elena is," I said.

His brow rose. "You do?"

I nodded. "She's near the grocery store where she works."

"The H-E-B?" he asked.

"Yep. I know she lives in Cedar Rapids, but the store where she works is in Round Rock, right?" Round Rock and Cedar Rapids are both suburbs of Austin.

Oscar moved to the missing person's report and flipped it open. Scanning the second page he said, "Yep. Store number one-six-six-five off of 620. You think she's alive?"

I sighed sadly. "No."

He grimaced but then said, "Should we go there and see if we can find her?"

"Definitely," I said, taking up the gun.

"Do you think she's Simone?" he asked next, handing me my holster and the box of bullets.

I took the holster but refused the bullets. He frowned and grabbed the gun out of my hand, then began to load it.

With a frustrated sigh I said, "No. I don't think she's Simone. I think Simone's name was her real name, and Elena was murdered outside, in a field of bluebonnets, near a stream and a hiking trail."

Oscar handed me back the gun and pointed at the holster. I sighed again and shoved the gun into the holster, then wiggled my way into the shoulder holster, and adjusting the strap before throwing my hands up in a, *Satisfied?!* gesture.

I made sure my scowl was extra deep.

Oscar smirked and motioned to the front door. "Come on, Coop. Let's go solve a mystery. It'll make you feel better about the day."

I didn't know how discovering the body of yet another murdered woman cut down before her time was going to make me feel better, but I tried to look at it like I was going to help bring closure to the family.

Oscar drove us out to the large grocery store in Round Rock, parking in the massive lot near the entrance. We got out of the car, and he began to make his way toward the sliding glass doors, when I called him back.

"Hold up!"

He looked over his shoulder at me with a curious expression. "What?"

"This isn't right."

Oscar walked back to stand at my side. "Coop, this *is* the H.E.B. where Elena worked."

"I know, but the view is all wrong."

His brow furrowed. "I speak Abby pretty good, but even I don't know what that means."

I pointed to the parking lot and the horizon beyond. The grocery store sat at the corner of highway 620 and a busy two-lane road, and there was nary a bluebonnet in sight. "This isn't right," I said again.

Oscar scratched his head. "Okay," he said, his eyes blinking as he tried to solve the problem of the view not being right. "Tell me your vision again."

I'd told him about it in the car, but I'd skimmed over some of the parts. This time I took it slow and made sure to hit every detail.

Oscar nodded as I spoke, then he too looked up at the horizon, turning in a half circle, scanning for bluebonnets. Turning back to me again, he pointed to the car. "Get in. I think I know how to get us to the right spot."

Oscar drove us around the lot to the rear of the store, and the moment we turned the corner to follow the narrow-paved alley leading to the back of the store, my heart started to thump. To the left of the store was a large, open field and it was absolutely covered in bluebonnets.

"This!" I said, pointing to the field. "Yes, Oscar! This is

49

it!"

"Good," he said. "I was worried my hunch was wrong."

Oscar followed the drive all the way to the loading ramps, where the store's massive inventory was unloaded from the tractor trailers that delivered their goods.

In fact, there was a truck already parked at one of the ramps, and two store employees were pulling out dollies loaded down with shrink wrapped items.

Oscar pulled up next to the truck, and we got out. "You can't park there," a ginger-haired young man in his late teens with an unfortunate intense case of acne told us. By the tag on his shirt, we knew his name was Shea.

"Hi, Shea," I said, waving all friendly like.

"You can't park there," he repeated. His voice quavered, and it held an irritating pitch. It was like a violin being strummed with a sandpaper laden bow.

Oscar approached the dock where Shea was standing. His partner, another young man with greasy blond hair, and a hook nose with a nametag that read, Phoenix, stopped pulling his dolly across the dock, and came to stand next to Shea.

I noted that Phoenix looked nervous and was eyeing Oscar with wide brown eyes. "See, the thing is, Shea," Oscar said, taking out his badge and flipping the leather flap open. "We actually *can* park here."

Shea and Phoenix bent forward together, and their mouths dropped. "You a cop?" Phoenix asked.

"He's a fed!" Shea said before Oscar had a chance to speak.

"Whoa," Phoenix said. And I noticed that he became even more nervous, fidgeting and scratching his arm while shuffling his feet. He caught me staring at him, so he abruptly returned to the dolly and began to haul it into the store just about as fast as he could.

"Should I get my manager?" Shea asked Oscar.

Oscar shrugged, and I knew he'd taken note of Phoenix's nervous body language. "You can if you like, but we're only doing a little sightseeing today."

Shea looked undecided about what to do, so he simply stood there, with his mouth half open. At that moment, another man came sauntering out of the bay and saw Shea just standing there, the empty dolly by his side. "Hey," he called to him. "Buddy, chop, chop! I got another delivery to make today."

Shea jumped at the sound of the man's voice. I observed the guy, who was absolutely massive—he had to be well over six feet tall with bulging biceps and broad well-muscled shoulders. His jeans were tight enough to show the outline of the muscles in his thighs, and I assumed that this guy was probably a body builder in his spare time. His features were handsome, pale skin, light eyes and jet-black hair with a little stubble on his chin. I had a feeling he was probably quite popular with the ladies. Or men. Whichever he preferred.

I also noted that he was wearing a red polo shirt and jeans, but no name tag. I assumed he was the truck driver. "I think I have to get my manager," Shea said to the guy.

It was then that the truck driver took note of us. Pointing to our car, he said, "You can't park there."

I grinned. It just struck me as funny that everyone was *so* concerned with where we parked. Oscar flipped his badge open again and said, "I think we can."

The guy reached the lip of the dock and bent forward to inspect Oscar's badge. "FBI?" he said.

Oscar nodded.

"This about that missing girl?" he said next.

"It is," Oscar said. "Did you know her?"

The driver nodded. "She was a great kid. Worked hard. Was a whole lot faster than this knucklehead." The driver bumped Shea in the arm good-naturedly and Shea jumped about a foot.

The driver then put a hand on the kid's shoulder and said, "Whoa, buddy. Don't be so nervous. They're not here for you." He added a laugh, but Shea was hardly humored. Instead, *he* began to scratch his arm and fidget. "Hey," the driver said. "Go get Alma. Let her know the FBI is here and they've probably got some questions for her."

Shea practically ran off the dock, and I watched him go, then turned to look at the field beyond. It was like it was calling to my intuition, and I couldn't ignore it.

"Let's go," I said softly to Oscar before motioning toward the field.

"Right behind you," he said. He then turned back to the truck driver. "Is Alma the manager on duty?"

"She is," the driver said.

"And you are?" Oscar asked, whipping out his trusty small notebook.

"Tony. Tony Mateo."

Oscar scribbled on his pad, and I didn't feel I could wait anymore, so I began to walk across the pavement to the field. "Where's she going?" I heard the driver say.

Oscar didn't answer him, instead he said, "Tony, tell Alma that we'll come into the store and find her when we're done. It could be five minutes or an hour, so don't have her wait around out here on the dock."

"Got it," Tony said.

I reached the open field and looked down at my shoes which were lost in a swirl of ankle-deep lavender-blue flowers.

"Is your hunch that Elena is somewhere out here?" Oscar asked, catching up to me.

"It is," I said. "We're looking for a hiking trail. I think she's not far from there."

Oscar pulled out his phone, and called up his map app. "We're here," he said, showing me the flashing blue dot on the screen. Then he zoomed the image out a bit and began to search the area for anything that might resemble a trail. "There," he said, tapping the screen.

"It's in that direction, right?" I said, pointing to the southeast.

"Yeah, but, Coop, there's more than one trail here. See all of these offshoots?"

I glanced again at his phone. There were several trails,

some crisscrossing, some having no connection to the others, and they covered what appeared to be a wide area.

"Crap," I said. "I was hoping this was going to be fairly straightforward."

"Which one do you want to try first?" he asked.

I sighed and pulled my gaze away from the screen. "I'm just going to follow my intuition on this one."

Oscar pocketed his phone. "Good a plan as any."

We made our way through the field of flowers, and as I walked, I tried to focus on the tugging sensation in my solar plexus. It was leading me in a direct line southeast, and I worked to not veer off course.

"How far do you think?" Oscar asked me. I glanced at him and saw his eyes scanning the area in front of us, right and left.

"I don't know, bud. But, judging by the strength of the visceral tug I'm experiencing right now, I'd say we're getting close."

We walked another twenty feet in silence . . . when the smell hit us.

CHAPTER 4

The bluebonnets surrounding her were bent, as if in mourning. Some were even splattered with her blood, forever bearing the graffiti of the violence she'd endured.

She was currently surrounded by men and women in uniform, dress shirts and ties, and white hazmat suits, while I was sipping some hot coffee, desperately trying to tamp down the urge to hurl.

Oscar and I had followed the smell of rot and decay until it became too overpowering for me to handle. It'd still put us close enough for me to see the bloated, blackened body of what had once been a beautiful young woman.

"Hey," Oscar said, coming over to stand next to me. "Can I have a sip of that?"

"It's got cream and sugar in it," I told him. All the men at the office drank their coffee black. We only had creamer on hand because I'd insisted on it.

Oscar lifted the cardboard cup with the H-E-B logo on it from my hand. "I'll push through," he said, taking a long sip. Handing it back to me, he added, "God that's awful."

I smirked. "I can head to the store to get you your own cup, if you want."

He shook his head. "Let's both of us go. I gotta get away from that—" he paused long enough to point in the direction of the swarm of police and crime scene techs, "—for a minute."

"Thank the baby Jesus," I whispered. I wanted nothing more than to get away from the scene. It was horrible enough to view from twenty feet away. Oscar had been up close and personal, and I couldn't imagine how he'd ever get that image out of his mind.

Then again, he'd seen dozens and dozens of similar images over the years. I'd been spared such an overload, but there were many nights I couldn't sleep because of what I'd seen.

"How did she die?" I asked softly.

"He cut her throat," Oscar said, his voice hard and his hands clenching into fists. "It looks like he raped her first, the fucker."

"Jesus," I said, feeling the bile rising in my throat. With effort I pushed it back down and took some deep breaths.

We walked toward the loading dock without saying anything more to each other, mostly because I didn't think I could handle any more details about Elena's murder right then.

When the back bay of the store was in sight, Oscar said, "Did you see how nervous Phoenix and Shea got when they saw my badge, and heard what we were there for?"

"I did," I said.

"Curious, ain't it?"

"It is," I replied, however, something else was niggling at me. Something I couldn't quite put my finger on, but I knew I had to keep searching for it—that random thought or memory that would lead to some valuable insight, if only I could put my finger on it.

"You going to interview them?" I asked, Oscar.

"APD is taking over jurisdiction," he said, eyeing the loading dock with squinted eyes.

I couldn't help the small grin that tugged at the corners of my lips. He was looking for Nikki, and she hadn't been one of the detectives at the crime scene, so my guess was—if she was here—she'd be taking witness statements and interviewing the staff.

As if on cue, the detective herself walked out onto the loading dock. The truck was still there, even though it'd been more than an hour since Oscar and I had discovered the body, and I then realized that Oscar's car was blocking the truck's exit.

"Oooo, he's gonna be maaaaad," I whispered.

"Who?" Oscar said, his gaze fixed on Nikki who hadn't seemed to notice us yet.

"The truck driver. You boxed him in."

"Damn," he said. "Well, it'll give Nikki a chance to interview him, if he was the driver who was here the day Elana was murdered."

And in fact, Nikki had stopped in front of the back bay of the truck, and out came Tony, the driver. Nikki flipped open her notebook, and the two began talking.

And then her posture shifted evvvvver so slightly. In fact, it was so subtle that I would've missed it had my radar not been buzzing with energy.

That's about the moment it hit me. "Oscar," I said.

"Yeah, Coop?"

"Didn't Tony say that Elena was a great girl? And that she worked hard?"

"Something like that," he said. "Why?"

I paused, grabbing his arm, my gaze still focused on Nikki and the truck driver. "He said '*was*', Oscar. Like he knew she was dead. I even think he used the past tense twice."

Oscar had been looking at me curiously, but his gaze bulleted over to Nikki, and he immediately reached to his side to unholster his weapon. "Stay here," he said, his tone brokering no argument, not that he'd get one from little old me.

Meanwhile, Nikki continued to nod at the driver, but she'd stopped writing in her notebook, and in fact, she'd casually dropped the hand holding the pen to her side, near her own holstered weapon.

Tony's posture was stiff, but his mannerisms were casual, and he even laughed like he'd just told her a joke.

None of us were buying it.

And he knew it.

Or, at least he knew that she knew it.

And that's when everything changed. Moving way too fast

for her to react, Tony reached up and grabbed Nikki by the throat with one hand while blocking her effort to grab her gun with the other. I gasped, and instinctively began running toward them—Oscar's warning be damned.

For his part, Oscar took off like a shot the second he saw Tony reach for Nikki. The two were in battle with each other, but Nikki was at the disadvantage because Tony was big. Like Dwayne Johnson big. And Nikki was my height and about my build—so, this was about to get very, very ugly.

Still, Nikki managed to score a direct punch to Tony's nose with her left fist, and he backed up a minute before he then rushed forward and slammed her hard into the store's brick wall.

"You son of a bitch!" I yelled, as Nikki's head bobbled on her neck from the blow. "*Leave her alone!*"

Tony looked over his shoulder, and saw both me and Oscar running toward him, and his jaw fell open. He clearly thought he and the detective were the only two there.

Oscar, with his gun drawn, yelled, "Let her go and drop to the ground! DROP TO THE GROUND NOW!!"

But Tony did neither of those things. Instead, he curled Nikki into his chest, folding her into a headlock with one massive arm, while his free hand wrenched her gun from its holster. Oscar had no shot, not with Nikki being used as a human shield.

Tony fired Nikki's weapon at Oscar and missed. I screamed and dove to the ground lest the second shot be aimed at me. Buried in bluebonnets, I rolled to the side, away from where I'd fallen in case Tony shot randomly in my direction, then pulled my own gun out of its holster.

Meanwhile, Oscar hadn't ducked or dropped to the ground, even though Tony was shooting at him. Instead, he continued to run toward Tony, drawing his fire so that Nikki might have a fighting chance if only she could wriggle out of his grip.

But she dangled there, limp in his grasp, her bell rung and no doubt her oxygen supply compromised by the tight headlock he had her in. She'd be dead the moment Tony dispensed with Oscar.

As if on cue, Tony fired her gun again, and the bullet hit Oscar in the upper right shoulder. I heard him grunt and falter, going down to one knee, where he struggled to gain his footing again. Before he could get up, another shot rang out, and it hit Oscar square in the chest. He barked out in pain and flew backward like he'd been punched by the Hulk.

Still, he held his gun out in front of him, but didn't fire. If he missed, Nikki could be killed, and he wouldn't risk it. He was wearing a Kevlar vest, but how many more shots before one found his head or his groin?

With only bad options, I got to my feet, ducking low and ran to my left, trying to get as far as I could to Tony's side. I got about ten feet when I planted my feet, took careful, *careful* aim. "Please, please, my guides and angels," I whispered. "Please don't let this bullet hit Nikki."

Before I could get off a shot, Tony fired again at Oscar. I didn't know if he hit his mark or not because my sole focus was on the shooter. Sweat poured down my brow, and my heart hammered in my chest while I took a small breath, held it, and squeezed the trigger.

Tony dropped like a sack of flour, bringing Nikki down with him. She rolled away from him, clutching at her neck, coughing and sucking in air, but Tony didn't move. He lay completely motionless.

Behind me, I heard a commotion, and knew the cavalry had heard the gunshots and were running toward us, but I stood there, trembling from head to toe, feeling ready to faint.

My arm dropped to my side, still holding the gun, and then I just let it fall out of my hand to the ground. Nikki recovered her gun and pointed it at Tony, but he was either dead or seriously injured, and in no position to fight her anymore.

It suddenly occurred to me that *I'd* done that. And it also occurred to me that I wasn't sorry. I was glad, and I hoped that motherfucker was good and dead.

"Coop!" Oscar called, his voice raspy and pained. I shook myself out of my stunned stupor and turned toward him, trying to get my legs to work as I stumbled toward him. There was a large smear of blood on his hand, and he lay in the flowers, breathing hard and sweating too.

"Oscar!" I cried, rushing forward to drop to his side. "Where? Where're you hurt?"

I looked at the holes in his Kevlar, the tail of the slugs sticking out and felt all over his chest to find the source of the blood.

"My . . . leg, Coop," he gasped.

I looked down and saw a spreading stain of blood on his upper thigh. He had the hand smeared with blood back over the wound, and I pushed it out of the way, yanking off my jacket and wadding it up to press it into Oscar's wound. He hissed and grunted with pain.

At that moment, a uniformed cop reached us and dropped to the opposite side of Oscar. "Dispatch, this is unit 6754! Code 999! Code 52 to my location!"

In the back of my mind, it registered that the cop was issuing the codes for "officer down" and "ambulance needed."

Other people reached us and dropped beside us, and before I knew it, someone had taken over the duty of putting pressure on Oscar's wound, while someone else was helping me to my feet.

"Where's your gun, Ms. Cooper?" the person said.

I gazed dully at a detective I recognized but couldn't place. He worked with Nikki, I thought. What was his name?

"Vargas," he said, pointing to himself, and then I remembered.

I nodded at him, but words were hard to form right now.

"Where's your gun, Abby?" he said gently, commanding me to focus on him with his gaze.

"I . . . it's . . ." I pointed to the area where I'd shot from. I couldn't see the gun from here. There were too many flowers.

"Let's get it," he said, and began to lead me away, but I resisted.

Looking over my shoulder, I saw Oscar being lifted by four uniformed officers. They were going to carry him out of the field.

His face was a mask of pain, and I wanted nothing more than to return to his side, and make sure he didn't bleed to death.

"It's okay," the detective said, still tugging on my arm. "They've got him, and an ambulance is on the way. He'll be okay."

I turned my gaze back to Nikki's partner, blinking dully at him. "My husband," I said, my voice hoarse and no louder than a whisper.

"I'll call him," he said. "First, we need to retrieve your gun. There'll be questions, and paperwork, and we'll need it to document what happened here, okay?"

I nodded feebly and led the way over to where I'd been standing. My gun was resting on the ground, and the detective pulled some black latex gloves out of his back pocket, put them on, then picked up my gun. "That was a helluva shot, missy," he said, and there was something in his eyes akin to respect.

I nodded at his compliment, even though I still felt pretty disconnected from what was happening. "My husband," I repeated.

The detective pulled his cell out of his back pocket and hit a number on the screen. "Dispatch, put me through to the Austin FBI field office."

By now I was trembling so intensely that my teeth were chattering, and even though I'd been sweating my ass off just minutes before, I felt so terribly cold. And a tear or two formed in my eyes, and slid down my cheek, and I didn't really know why I was crying.

The detective waited with the phone pressed to his ear, but then he took one look at me and tucked the phone between his ear and his shoulder and used that arm to pull me into a sideways hug. "It's okay, Abby. It's okay. You did so good out here. You saved my partner. She's alive because of you."

More tears came, and I didn't seem to be able to control them. I didn't feel sad, but it was like so much pressure had built up in my emotional closet, that I had to open it and find some release.

"I need to speak to Special Agent Rivers. Tell him it's Detective Vargas. It's urgent. It's about his wife and Agent Hernandez."

I leaned into the detective, simply trying to brace myself against the internal storm raging its way through me. I listened as he told Dutch the highlights of the afternoon and how Oscar and I were involved, and then he was handing me his phone, saying, "He wants to hear from you. Talk to him, okay?"

I took the phone and put it to my ear, but when I opened my mouth, all that came out was a sob.

"Edgar?" Dutch said, his voice tense and strained. "Are you hurt?"

I swallowed what felt like a boulder stuck in my throat, and managed to stammer out, "N-n-no. No, D-D-Dutch."

"I'm on my way," he said, and I could hear him fumbling around in his office. "Sit tight. Don't talk to *anyone*, do you hear me? If they ask you questions, you tell them you won't answer unless or until I get there, okay?"

I wiped at my cheeks. "Got it," I said. "Just . . . get here."

"Brice!" Dutch yelled, barely covering the microphone on his phone. "We gotta go! *Now!* And you're driving because I'm about to lose it!"

I closed my eyes, focusing on the sound of my husband's voice. Strained and intense as it was, it was still a beacon of light to my battered soul.

"Hey, there, Sundance," Candice said, sauntering up to where I sat on a milk crate, my back against the wall at the far end of the H-E-B. For the last twenty minutes, I'd been watching yet another swarm of police and CSI techs document what'd taken place there. Nikki was speaking to Vargas, and there were many times when her gaze drifted my way, and I took note of her grateful expression.

But there was also worry there too, and, in that, I had the thought that her expression must mirror my own.

Candice sidled up to me and pulled the blanket around my shoulders a little higher. The shivering hadn't fully subsided yet, but at least my teeth weren't rattling against each other.

"Here," Candice said, pushing a large cup of coffee at me. "It's just like you like it. I figured you could use any comfort you can get right now."

"How did you get here so fast?" I asked, gratefully taking the steaming cup and wrapping my fingers around it.

"I was in Leander on that case I told you about earlier. Brice called me, and since he and your hubby are still fifteen minutes out, he asked me to get to you if I could. And I could, so I did."

I nodded. "Thank you." I took a sip of coffee, feeling its warmth and something else. "Mmm," I said because it was really good, but then I connected the dots and asked, "Is there some . . . is there some *Baileys* in here?" The coffee was less just coffee, sugar, and cream, and more coffee and Baileys Irish Cream. And, trust me, I wasn't about to complain, I just wanted to know.

She pointed at me and clicked her tongue. "Who loves you, Sundance?"

I took another sip, feeling the shivers all but subside. "You, Cassidy. Definitely you."

"There's not enough in there to make you tipsy, but just enough to take the edge off, and when APD questions you, *don't* tell them you had alcohol, okay?"

I saluted her. "Noted." Then I asked, "Any word on Oscar?"

The corners of her eyes pinched with worry. "Not yet. I'll let you know the minute I hear something."

"Thanks," I said. We were silent for a minute before I

added, "My intuition says he'll be okay, but still, Candice, there was a *lot* of blood from that leg wound."

She nodded. "The bullet might've nicked the femoral artery. That's serious, but he got help right away, so I'm sure you're right and he'll be okay."

I sighed and rubbed my eyes. "Jesus, what a day."

Candice moved over to grab another milk crate from a small stack nearby, carrying it back to sit down next to me. "I heard you got an A-plus for marksmanship." She wore a slight grin with a hint of pride in her eyes.

"It was the only move I had," I said. "He would've killed us all."

"He would've," she said. "Still, Sundance, that was *a hell* of a shot. You got him square in the temple, and he never saw it coming."

I took another sip of coffee. "It was more luck than skill."

She puffed out some air between her lips. "Hardly. All those Sundays Dutch dragged you to the shooting range have finally paid off. Good on you, and good on him for making you go."

I stared off at the field of bluebonnets. "I guess," I said with a shrug. "I still hate guns."

"I know," she said, wrapping an arm around my shoulders. "But you handled yourself really well, and Oscar and Nikki owe you their lives."

"Maybe I was only returning the favor," I said. And that was a true statement if ever there was one.

"Oh, I think the score is a little more even after today," she said.

"What happens now?" I asked, motioning with my head over to the cluster of police and CSI still gathered around the white sheet that covered the body of Tony the truck driver.

"They'll ask you what happened, and you'll need a lawyer present."

My brow furrowed. "Why would I need a lawyer present?"

"Because you should never, ever, ever talk to the police without one when you take someone's life. And I don't care if it was totally, completely, 100 percent justified, as it was in this case, you still don't talk to them without an attorney."

"Okay, I hear ya. But who?" I knew a few attorneys, but I didn't know any that would want to necessarily represent me in this scenario.

"I've made a call," Candice told me. "She'll be here soon."

Just then someone bolted out from around the corner in front of us, and it was so sudden that I squeaked in fright.

The person stopped at the sound and pivoted on his toes, his eyes searching for the source.

"Dutch!" I cried, handing the coffee cup to Candice before dashing into the arms of my husband. He caught me and swirled me around in a circle, hugging me fiercely. "You are going to be the death of me, woman," he whispered, never loosening his grip as I simply dangled there, my feet off the ground, held tight in his embrace.

"Don't say that," I told him. "Please, don't talk about dying right now, okay? I can't handle it today."

He didn't reply, he simply held on.

Behind us, I heard Brice and Candice talking, and then a third voice that I recognized as Toscano's.

Grateful as I was that they'd all come to my aid, I just wanted to hug my husband for a day or twenty and forget about everything that'd happened since we'd arrived at this place.

"Ms. Cooper?" I heard a woman say. It was a voice I didn't recognize.

Dutch lowered me to the ground but grasped my hand tightly. I straightened my shirt and looked up at a tall, lean, buxom, redhead who looked as much like the cartoon character Jessica Rabbit as any real human I'd ever seen.

And I wasn't the only one taken with her appearance. Every male around us had eyeballs doing a serious, *Barooooooooogah!!!* right about then.

If the woman noticed, she gave no hint of it. She seemed solely focused on me. Extending her hand she said, "Kennedy O'Neil. Criminal defense. Ms. Fusco called me here to talk to you about representation during a police interview."

I took her hand. She had long, elegant fingers, tipped in tapered, and beautifully manicured nails. Everything about her was feminine and gorgeous.

I would've hated her if she weren't about to save me from inadvertently incriminating myself. "Hi," I said, feeling awkward and self-conscious. I have to work at being feminine, and even then, I typically only make it about halfway. I swear like a sailor, I prefer jeans over skirts, sport bras over something lacy, and flats over heels.

All of which I was wearing today, so . . .

"Nice to meet you," I said. "Thank you for coming so quickly. How much do you charge?"

I hadn't meant to ask that immediately upon meeting her, but I earn a modest income, and she looked *expensive.*

"Three hundred an hour," she said. (*Without* flinching!)

"Ah," I said stiffly. I doubted that the PO-PO were only going to question me for an hour, which was about how much Jessica Rabbit I could afford.

"That's not a problem," Dutch said.

I should mention that Dutch earns a modest wage at the FBI, but a BIG, beautiful chunk of change from a side hustle he's got with Dave and Brice. So, Big Spender could definitely afford her. Now, if only he'd pull his eyeballs back in his head.

"Excellent," she said before pointing to me. "Why don't you and I go have a chat, and then we can see about speaking with the police, okay?"

Dammit. She was way too nice for her looks. Someone that gorgeous needed to be mean, snide, cold, or stuck up, and she appeared to be none of those things. "Cool," I said, feeling anything but.

Kennedy and I walked away from our group, and she led me back around to the front of the building where I saw at least a half dozen police cars, several dark-colored sedans, and a CSI truck, not to mention another five news vans with various reporters standing in front of their vehicles giving live updates as the "developing scene" unfolded.

Kennedy continued to walk forward until we reached a sleek, silver jaguar. She opened the passenger side door and made a hand gesture for me to get in. I complied, and she got in on the driver's side. She then pushed her seat back and got out an iPad. Setting it on her lap, she noted the time and began to type. After about a minute, she looked up and said, "Okay, tell me *exactly* what happened here today."

I spent the next half hour with Kennedy, laying out the day from the moment we heard about Elena's disappearance to Tony Mateo, dead on the ground.

As I spoke, I had to give the woman some serious credit. She'd only widened her eyes once when I told her what my job was at the FBI. From that point forward, she'd appeared completely nonplussed about how everything else had unfolded.

She then spoke to me for a good fifteen minutes, cautioning me to *only* answer the question the detective asked me, and to stop speaking the moment I felt her hand on my arm. She said she'd be with me every step of the way, and by the time we exited the car, I felt confident and safe in her care.

Retracing our steps, we found our way back to the dock and Kennedy spoke with Detective Vargas, who was Nikki's partner.

Nikki herself was nowhere in sight which was actually a relief. I didn't think I could talk about what'd happened—how I'd risked shooting her in order to actually save her and Oscar—with her nearby.

"She's ready for her interview," Kennedy said to Vargas.

He nodded and added a wink towards me as a sign of support. "I'll get him," he said to her before saying to me, "You'll be speaking with Lieutenant Walker from IA."

With that, he turned and disappeared into the store.

"Why is APD's internal affairs questioning me?" I asked nervously.

"Standard procedure," Kennedy assured me. "Not to worry. You'll be fine."

I wanted to believe her, but the heavy feeling in the pit of my   stomach   suggested   otherwise.

CHAPTER 5

"How many rounds did you fire?" Lieutenant Walker asked me.

"Just the one."

"That's it?"

I shrugged. "That's all it needed."

"It?"

"The situation."

Walker, a man I'd guess was in his early fifties, was a shrewd, fiercely intelligent, and suspicious character. He'd been grilling me on the details of taking out Mateo for an hour now, and I could tell that Kennedy was getting impatient with him. She'd said, "Asked and answered, Lieutenant," so many times that even I was sick of hearing it.

And yet, here we were, still going round and round.

The hiccup, I think, had started when he'd asked me about my work with the FBI. I'd told him — I mean, I have nothing to hide, but he'd reacted especially hostile to my answer. It was absolutely clear to me that he took me for a criminal; a grifter, a fraud, a liar, and a thief, so he was making the questions personal and uncomfortable, and if I weren't so exhausted from the day, it would've annoyed the shit out of me.

By now, I was answering him dully, almost down to monosyllabic answers, waiting for him to grow tired and move on to another toy.

"That was a hell of a shot," Walker said, and the way he said it made it seem less like a compliment and more like an accusation.

So I just stared at him. After all, that hadn't actually been a question.

"Where'd you learn to shoot like that?" he asked next.

"I took shooting class instead of shop in high school."

Kennedy cleared her throat. It was a subtle warning, and she was probably suggesting that, even in jest, Walker was the kind of guy to note when I might be guilty of lying to the police and press the issue.

I rolled my eyes and said, "I'm joking, of course. My husband, *Special Agent in Charge* Dutch Rivers, takes me regularly to the shooting range." I felt I needed the emphasis, because as big as Walker thought his "swagger" was, my hubby's was bigger.

Walker stared levelly at me. His cop face was as unrevealing as Dutch's. The good news is that I'm so used to Dutch's granite expression that Walker's didn't faze me at all.

"Tell me again how you came to find the body of Elena Navarra," he said next.

I waited for Kennedy to object with an "asked and answered, Lieutenant," but she said nothing, so I took a deep breath and said, "I had a vision that Elena was somewhere near the grocery store, in a field of bluebonnets, near a hiking trail and a river or a creek. Agent Hernandez and I came here to check out my vision, and you know the rest."

Walker scowled. "See, that's the part that I don't understand," he said, when what he meant was, "that's the part I don't believe."

"What's not to understand?" I asked, turning the question back on him. "I'm a professional psychic. Having visions is the entirety of my skill set."

"I don't understand how you could claim to have seen something you couldn't have seen unless you were there."

I glared at him. Goddamn, I'm *sick to death* of closed-minded skeptics like him. "I believe you've just defined my job description, Lieutenant. Knowing things I couldn't have personally experienced is what sets me apart from most people. But to your barely veiled question about whether I was there when Elena was murdered, I was not. And I have a pretty solid alibi in that, during the time of her abduction and murder, I was in D.C."

"We'll need proof of that trip," Walker said to Kennedy.

"No problem," she replied coolly. "We done here?"

Walker shook his head. "I still want more clarification on this other case Ms. Cooper claims to have had a vision on. What makes you think this caller to a national podcast was located here in Austin?"

"Because I have a specific symbol for the city of Austin—"

"What do you mean, you have a specific 'symbol' for Austin?" he interrupted.

I sighed heavily. This man was a serious pain in my ass. I'm sure he was just *super fun* to work for. "My intuition speaks in pictures, Lieutenant. It's its own language, and like any language based in images, certain images always mean that one thing. So, for me, the image of the Frost Bank Tower always means Austin, i.e. when Frost Bank shows up in my mind's eye, I know that the rest of the message will involve or take place in Austin."

"Yet we have no missing persons reports of any other woman besides Elena in the past week, and certainly no murders."

"With all due respect," I said, pushing back my chair, "you don't know that. And you *won't* know that until her body is discovered. And you won't hear about *that* until someone— probably me—finds her."

I got to my feet, and Walker's scowl turned downright scary. "Where do you think you're going?"

"Home. I'm going home."

Kennedy got to her feet as well, and she said, "My client is not under arrest, correct, Lieutenant?"

"I still have questions—"

"About shooting a man in self-defense? Or about the other case I'm trying to solve?"

"Both," he snapped, and pointed to the chair I'd just

stood up from.

I shook my head and offered him a slight smirk. I'd faced down *way* scarier-looking dudes than him in my time. "I've answered every question you've thrown at me for the past hour and a half, which was an hour longer than it should've taken for a simple case of self-defense; especially since I risked my *own* life to *save* one of *your* detectives.

"Further," I continued, "your accusatory tone and line of questioning tells me you don't appreciate any of my *heroic* actions today, so I'm done, Lieutenant. If you have any additional questions for me, send them, *in writing*, to Ms. O'Neil, and I'll *think* about answering them."

With that I flounced out of the small office in the back of the H-E-B that Walker had procured for our interview.

I heard Kennedy's heels clicking behind me, and once we were back in the central portion of the store, she said, "Great job in there, Abby."

I shrugged. "He ain't my first rodeo, Kennedy. I've dealt with suspicious, skeptical, openly condescending LEOs for the entirety of my career. Walker barely registered a four on the scary scale, and I only indulged him to make sure no flak landed on either Oscar or Nikki."

We continued to the front of the store and out through the sliding glass doors, finding Dutch, arms crossed and leaning against his SUV. I quickened my step, wanting only to be wrapped in his arms.

"Hey, you," he said, pulling me into his chest and kissing the top of my head. "How'd it go?"

"So much fun!" I teased. "Let's invite the lieutenant over for Christmas, shall we?"

Dutch chuckled, squeezing me a little tighter. While I nestled against his chest, he said, "Thank you, Kennedy. I've already texted you my contact info. Send your bill to either my email or my home address, and I'll take care of it."

"I will, Agent Rivers. Your wife did very well today. In every circumstance. She's quite impressive."

I grinned and felt my cheeks grow hot, but I continued to

press the side of my face against Dutch's chest. "Thank you, Kennedy," I said.

I felt her lay a hand on my shoulder, and then the clicking of her heels on the pavement told me she'd left our side. "How's Oscar?" I asked after she'd gone.

"He's either still in or just out of surgery," Dutch said. "Brice promised to text me the minute he was out of the OR."

"How bad was it?"

"Not great," Dutch said. "The bullet nicked an artery and broke the bone."

"Will he have to take time off?"

Dutch shrugged. "We'll know more about that soon, I think," he said.

"He was so brave today, Dutch. You should've seen him. He ran straight toward an active shooter, knowing the odds of surviving were not in his favor, but still drawing fire in order to give Nikki a chance to break out of Mateo's grip. It humbles me to think of how much courage that took."

Dutch grunted. "Sounds like Oscar," he said. "That boy is one of the most noble, brave men I know."

I nodded, my cheek rubbing against Dutch's dress shirt. "Did you get a chance to talk to Nikki?" I asked next.

"I did. Briefly. She wanted to get to the hospital, so she only spared me a few minutes to tell me how it all went down. And I think it's a little ironic that you're calling Oscar out for being brave when you were right there with him."

"I wasn't under fire," I said. "Mateo was too busy shooting at Oscar to pay me much attention, so getting into position to take that shot wasn't all that brave."

"Taking the shot sure as hell was, though, Edgar."

My mind went back to the memory of me, standing in that field, feeling all the pressure in the world to try and save all three of us, and I only had the one chance to do it. "I suppose," I said. "But what else was I gonna do?"

"Drop to the ground to not call attention to yourself and hope Mateo didn't shoot you," Dutch said, and the way he said it made me think he was a tiny bit upset I hadn't done that.

"Not my style, cowboy."

"I know," he said with a soft chuckle. "Still, I'm damn proud of you, sweethot."

I loved it when Dutch impersonated Humphrey Bogart's lisp. "Thank you. And, I say this grudgingly, but thank you for dragging me to the shooting range all these weekends and teaching me to shoot."

He chuckled again. "I knew someday it'd pay off."

I sighed into his chest again. "What's next, cowboy?"

Dutch released me from the hug but held onto my arms and said, "Let's grab a quick bite, then head over to the hospital."

"Perfect," I told him.

An hour later we were at the hospital, and I carried in a large to-go order for Candice and Brice, who hadn't yet stepped away from their vigil for Oscar, to get something for themselves.

Also in attendance were Agents Cox, Baldwin, and Williams, which I thought was sweet. And then I noticed Toscano in a chair, speaking to someone on the phone. He caught my eye and waved.

"What's the word?" I asked as soon as I handed off the bag to Candice.

"There's been none," she said.

Even though she tried to hide it from me, there were lines of worry around her eyes. I glanced at my watch. "What the heck is taking so long?"

"Don't know, Sundance," she said simply.

Dutch had moved off to stand in front of Brice, and the two were huddled together, speaking in tones low enough that I couldn't hear them.

I left Candice and walked over to the two men. "Hey," I said to Brice, putting a hand on his arm. "We brought you two a couple of steaks."

"Thanks, Abby," Brice said.

I squinted at him, my radar pinging with info. "You have word on Oscar that you're not sharing," I told him bluntly, tapping my forehead to show him my intuition had tipped me off.

He blanched. "That damn radar of yours." I simply stared at him expectantly, and he sighed, running a hand through his hair. "The bullet severed his artery. He lost a lot of blood, and his organs began to shut down. They had to get him stabilized before they could complete the surgery, which they've done, but they have to go back in because the artery is leaking again."

"Shit," I said as a knot of worry hit my stomach like a gut punch.

"Yeah," he said.

I was quiet for a moment, staring off into space, and then I said, "He'll be okay, Brice. I can sense the wound . . . and his current condition." My intuition allows me to do something like a body scan on people. I can sort of "X-ray" them and sense the imbalances in their system. When I scanned Oscar, I could "see" that his kidneys and liver were struggling to normalize, and I could also "see" the wound on his leg, which was "hot" "angry" and leaking.

Overall, his body felt weak, and battered, but there was also a distinct sense of underlying strength there. I felt confident that, if they could close the wound quickly and return him to a somewhat stable state, he'd surprise us all with how quickly he recovered.

I said as much to Brice and Dutch, and I was glad to note that Brice's shoulders visibly relaxed.

"Thank you," he said, squeezing the back of my neck. "I needed to hear that."

"Tell the others," I said, motioning over my shoulder. "They should know why it's taking so long."

Brice nodded and moved off to his wife and the other agents, and Dutch winked at me and said, "I'm gonna go find Nikki. She's somewhere in the hospital, wandering the halls trying to deal with how worried she is."

"Does she know the full scoop?"

"She does—which is why she's off wandering the halls. Wanna come with me?"

I opened my mouth to say yes but found myself hesitating. My intuition was giving me something of an alert, and I didn't quite know why but knew I needed to stick close by. "I think I'll stay and try to reassure everybody that I feel Oscar's gonna be okay. You go ahead, though."

He kissed me on the forehead and walked toward the central corridor. I watched him go, but my mind was still attempting to process what my radar was trying to hint at.

It took a minute, but finally, I felt a little tug in my solar plexus and the sense that I needed to move off to the central corridor too.

I glanced at the others gathered around Brice, listening intently, each holding a worried expression. Knowing they'd be reassured in just a minute, I obeyed the suggestion from my radar and moved off into the hallway.

Once there, I had the option to turn right or left. Dutch had gone right. My radar told me to go left.

Walking along the hallway, I passed a number of people, some pedestrians, some patients, and some staff, but nothing really jumped out at me. And then I arrived at the nurse's station, behind which four nurse's and two doctors were focused on charts and files.

My radar told me to stop and stand there, and I had no idea why. One of the doctors, sitting at the counter, writing in a chart looked up, probably because she sensed someone standing there. "You lost?" she asked.

I bit my lip. How was I going to explain that I wasn't lost, and that my intuition was demanding that I just stand there. "No, thanks. I'm . . . waiting for my husband. We're looking for another friend, and we'd agreed to meet here when we were done with our search."

"I could have them both paged," she said, helpfully.

I studied her for a moment and felt a strong tug of something akin to recognition, even though I was positive we'd never met.

She was a tall, slim woman, with dark skin, gorgeous almond eyes, and bright white teeth. Her hair was braided into long coils, tied back in a ponytail that fell down to her waist. I liked her immediately. "That's okay," I said. "I'm sure he'll be here any minute, but if I'm bothering you, I can go stand someplace else."

A buzzing sound came from her pocket, and she reached for her cell while telling me, "You're fine. You're not bothering me."

I smiled, and she eyed the display on her phone, and then I saw her brow rise. Answering the call she said, "Hi, Mama. I'm on shift. Can I call you ba—"

Her voice cut off, and I watched her expression shift from, one of surprise, to instant concern. "No, I haven't heard from Simone. When was the last time you spoke to her?"

My jaw dropped, and I thought, *Holy shit!*

"How many messages have you left her?" the doctor asked. I waited tensely and tried not to stare, only to listen. "Since Monday?" she continued. "Did you go over to her apartment?" The doctor waited a moment, then said, "Have you tried any of her friends?"

The note of concern had risen, and I could hear the fear in her tone. I wanted nothing more than to ask her to get off the phone and talk to me about who I assumed was her sister, but even that conversation was going to be very tricky, and my mind raced with ideas about how to broach the topic with her in a way that didn't come off as batshit crazy.

"Well call Latisha and Creed," the doctor said. I glanced at her long enough to find her name, pinned to her lab coat. She was Dr. Tonya Shaw.

Taking out my own cell I sent out a quick text message to Brice, Candice, Toscano, and Dutch. *I'm at the central nurse's station on the first floor, and I need the four of you immediately. Come here now!*

Dr. Shaw lifted her wrist to look at the time. "Mama, I've

got another two hours on this shift. I can come over afterward to help you make some calls. I'm sure she's fine; she probably just went off with a new boyfriend for a couple of days and forgot to check in. Or maybe she lost her phone. We'll find her, okay?"

Dr. Shaw nodded and reiterated the assurance that, what I assumed was her sister, Simone, was okay, and then she clicked off the phone and put it back in her pocket. My heart was hammering in my chest when she went back to writing in the chart, while her mouth was set in a thin line of worry.

I turned my head and looked anxiously at the hallway where I'd come from and let go of the breath I'd been holding when I saw Brice, Candice, and Toscano round the corner, hurrying toward me. As they reached me, Dutch also came into view. He was practically running and only slowed down when he saw that I was okay.

Brice stopped in front of me. "What's the emergency?"

I pointed toward my approaching husband, then to the far wall a bit away from the nurse's station. "I need to tell you guys something."

Dutch got to us as we were forming a huddle. "What?" he said, a little out of breath.

I motioned with my chin toward the bent head of Dr. Shaw. "I just overheard that doctor take a call from her mother who was reaching out because she hadn't heard from her other daughter, the doctor's sister, whose name is Simone."

Every set of eyes widened, and almost as one, their heads pivoted to look at Dr. Shaw. "You're kidding," Toscano said.

"I'm not," I assured him.

"How in the hell . . .?" he said, shaking his head in wonder.

"My intuition told me to come this way and stand right there at the nurse's station, and that's when the phone call came in."

"What do you want us to do, Edgar?" Dutch asked.

"We have to tell Dr. Shaw that we need to speak with

her—in private—about a case we're working." Focusing on Toscano again, I added, "Mike, do you have access from your phone to the recording of Simone's call to us at the podcast?"

"I do," he said.

"We can play it for her up to just before the shot rings out and ask Dr. Shaw if that's the voice of her sister. If she identifies her, we know we've got the right girl," I said, even though the thought of watching Dr. Shaw go through that experience was quite likely more than I could emotionally bear. In fact, my eyes got misty just thinking about it.

"Who wants to be the one to ask her for a moment in private?" Brice asked.

"I'll do it," Candice said. I looked at her so gratefully that the misting got a little more intense.

Dutch, however, laid a hand on Candice's shoulder. "Thank you, my friend, but I think it should be someone with a badge, so she'll know the gravity of the situation right off the bat."

Candice frowned, but she nodded in agreement too.

Dutch took a deep breath. "Which means, I'm up." We all looked over at Dr. Shaw, who happened to look up at us in the same moment, and I saw her brow arch in surprise. Dutch held her gaze and walked to her while we waited.

I could see her confusion as he spoke—and her nervousness when he flipped out his badge. They spoke for a few moments, then she looked at her watch again, turned to the other doctor behind the desk and nodded to Dutch, coming out from around the counter to follow him toward us. "There's a staffing break room down this hall. It's close to shift change, so it's probably empty."

"Good," Brice said. Extending his hand to her he added, "Dr. Shaw, I'm Special Agent Brice Harrison. I lead the Austin bureau office. Thank you for agreeing to meet with us."

"Is this about a patient?" she asked him.

"No," he told her. "This will be a personal matter, and I would like to take the opportunity to caution you that what we have to tell you will be difficult. I want you to brace yourself before we get to the break room."

Dr. Shaw blinked at him, and I knew that her mind was swirling with both fear and confusion.

She was probably wondering if she'd broken some federal law, so I said, "You've done nothing wrong, Dr. Shaw. This is simply to confirm something you might know, but it will still be difficult to hear, and I'm so sorry for that."

"Okay," she said, but I could tell she felt anything but.

We allowed her to lead the way to the break room, which was empty of personnel, and that was lucky because no way did we want any more witnesses to overhear what we were about to play for Dr. Shaw.

After filing into the break room, we all took a seat around a large table that sat the six of us comfortably. "So, what's this about?" she asked.

She'd set her shoulders squarely, and her expression was calm and measured. I guess we in the crime fighting community had our granite expressions and those in the saving lives community had their own version of a flat expression to keep their emotions in check.

Toscano got out his cell phone and set it on the table. "Dr. Shaw, my name is Mike Toscano. I'm a former FBI bureau chief out of D.C.; retired now, and in my spare time, I host a podcast called the Toscano Files. Have you ever heard of it?"

She shook her head, her eyes darting between Toscano and his phone.

"This is Abigail Cooper—" he paused to point to me, and the good doctor's gaze flickered to me, then back to Toscano. "Abby is a civilian consultant with the Austin bureau. She has a *very* unique talent for solving difficult cases, and her track record is exemplary. Her specific skill set is one I didn't believe in until I worked my coldest, hardest case with her from fifteen years ago, and she solved it within two weeks."

Again, her gaze traveled to me, and I chose that moment to say, "I'm a professional psychic, Dr. Shaw. I've worked with the bureau for nearly a decade now, and I've proven my abilities to them dozens and dozens of times. I don't know what your viewpoint is on someone like me, but I assure you, I'm the real deal, and these men can back me on that."

Every male head at the table nodded.

Dr. Shaw's brow was deeply furrowed, and I knew right away she didn't believe in the paranormal. It didn't really matter at this moment, but the moment had still needed a thorough explanation, so I left it at that.

Toscano took up the conversation again. "A few days ago, Abby and I were in D.C., recording a new episode for my podcast, updating my followers on that cold case I mentioned. After we talked about the case, we took a few calls from our live listeners, and that's when this call came in . . ."

Mike tapped at his phone, and we heard Toscano's producer, Ray, introduce Simone. And then we heard her quavering voice and immediately, I knew that Simone *was* Dr. Shaw's sister. All semblance of the calm, detached demeanor was gone. Her eyes had instantly widened, and she'd leaned in toward the phone, as if she were anticipating the opportunity to talk to her sister.

Toscano let the recording play on, right up until Simone stammered out the word "murder", and then he quickly hit the pause button.

Dr. Shaw stared at the phone, then back at Toscano, then at me, and her eyes brimmed with tears. "That's my sister," she said. "What's happened to her?"

No one spoke for a long moment. No one wanted to be the one that told her Simone had been murdered.

Live. On air.

Finally, Dutch said, "The recording ends with a gunshot and no further sound from your sister, Dr. Shaw. This morning, we received a grainy photograph of a murdered woman, lying on the ground, and the source of the email that sent it to leads us to believe that the photograph is your sister's body."

Dr. Shaw gasped and put a hand to her mouth. Tears formed and slid down her cheeks while she shook her head vigorously. "No," she whispered before a sob overtook her. "No. No, no, no, no, no!" Then she looked pleadingly at Dutch. "Let me see the picture."

He held her gaze. "She's lying face down, Dr. Shaw, and the image is grainy. Are you sure you want to see it?"

She nodded. Dutch pulled out his own phone and scrolled through some things before he held the screen out to her. She leaned forward, the tears continuing to flow, and stared at the image. Her lip quivered, and she said, "I don't know. I can't tell. Oh my God, what am I gonna tell my mother?"

Once more a sob overtook her, and Candice, who was seated next to Dr. Shaw, reached over and wrapped her arms around the woman.

I found myself crying too, and one look around the table told me that everyone else there was pretty moved too. I swallowed hard several times, taking deep breaths and finally got myself under control. It wouldn't help Dr. Shaw to see me this way, and I didn't want to distract from any information we might get about Simone from her sister.

Candice released Dr. Shaw, but held onto her shoulder with one hand, letting her know she wasn't alone in her grief.

"How can you be sure she's dead?" the doctor asked. "I mean, even if I could identify her from that photo, you don't know that she's dead, right? What if all this is just some elaborate joke?"

"We don't know for certain that your sister is dead," Brice conceded. And then he glanced pointedly at me, and I knew what he was asking.

"Dr. Shaw," I said. "Do you have a recent photo of your sister that I can look at?"

She blinked at me, and she was slow to respond, so I simply waited for her to decide if she wanted to show me a photo of Simone. Finally, she took out her phone and said, "We took one together just a few weeks ago," she said. Scrolling through her photos, she stopped at one and turned her screen toward me.

My talent for being able to look at a photo and determine if someone is dead or alive came into play. The way it works is that, when I look at a photo, if someone is deceased, there's a subtle shift in the way I see them. They take on a flat, one-dimensional appearance, while anyone else in the photo has a more two-dimensional and "livelier" look about them.

As I observed the photo of Dr. Shaw and her sister, each leaning into the other and smiling brightly for the camera, this was exactly what I saw. Simone, who looked similar enough to her sister as to almost be her twin, was flat and one dimensional, and Dr. Shaw's image had depth and energy.

I nodded to her and said, "Thank you," then waited until she pulled her phone back to stare at the screen before I glanced at Brice and gave a subtle nod.

"If you could text me that image, Dr. Shaw," Brice said. "It might help in our search for your sister."

"Of course," she said hoarsely.

Brice slid a business card to her, and we all waited while she plugged in his number and texted him the image.

"According to my mom, my sister's been missing since Monday."

"Does she have a roommate we can talk to?" Candice asked.

"No," Dr. Shaw said. "She lives in a tiny apartment near school."

"Which school?" Candice pressed.

"UT."

There was almost the sound of a "bing!" in my head when she named the University of Texas.

"What year is she?" Candice asked.

"She's a senior. She's studying hydrogeology."

"What's that?" I asked, something else *binging* in my mind.

"It's the study of water below the earth's surface. Simone identifies very strongly with the African American community at school. She wants to find ways to bring water to remote African villages. She spent all last summer in Sudan, studying the need."

My mind recalled the pail of water that had materialized on the desk in my vision, and I knew my radar had been pointing me to that clue about Simone.

"Did your sister ever talk about having any issues with other classmates? Boyfriends? Or anyone else?" I asked next.

Dr. Shaw shook her head, wiping her cheeks and looking pleadingly at us, as if she wanted us to believe her when she said, "Simone's such a nice person. She'd give you the shirt off her back. Her whole life's purpose is about helping people."

I nodded sadly. "Sometimes, it's the nicest people among us that become targets. Did you ever hear her talk about someone scaring her, or speaking inappropriately to her?"

Simone's sister leveled a look at me. "She's a Black woman living in *Texas*. That's almost an everyday occurrence with us. Shit, in the last month alone, I've been spit on, called the N word, and told my patient wants to see a *White* doctor at least five times."

I blanched. "Yes. Of course. That was an obtuse question. Please allow me to rephrase and ask, did she ever talk about someone harassing her more than once. Especially in recent weeks?"

Dr. Shaw rubbed her eyes. She looked exhausted and heartbroken. "No," she said. "At least not to me. I've been so busy here that I haven't had much time to spare for her. My mother would know more than me."

"Would you like for us to tell your mother about Simone? Or would you like to do it, Dr. Shaw?" Brice asked as gently as he could.

She stopped rubbing her eyes to look at him. "You probably want to talk to her as soon as possible, right?"

We all nodded.

"Can we do it together?" she asked.

"Of course," he said.

Dr. Shaw looked at her watch again and got to her feet. "I have a few patients that I have to check on before I can skip out on the rest of my shift. Give me an hour to do that and clear it with my attending."

"We'll be waiting," Brice said. "Text me when you're done, and we'll follow you to your mother's house."

She left the room, and we sat there for a minute or two in silence until Candice said, "We should head back. Cox, Baldwin, and Nikki are bound to start wondering where we are."

We all got up and tucked in our chairs, then filed out of the room. As we left, I thought about what a quiet, sad bunch we were. Of course, it didn't help to also know that the rest of the night and following days to come, chasing after this monster, weren't going to be any better than today.

In fact, as I noted with a bit of alarm, my radar was suggesting that the days ahead were about to get so much worse . . .

CHAPTER 6

They sat together, huddled in sorrow, the sound of their broken hearts pouring out into the room like a somber song.

Meanwhile, we were gathered there too, seated or standing, forming a half circle of empathy and support, waiting out their tears, hoping to help connect the dots and bring the body of their loved one home to them soon.

Mrs. Shaw sat clutching her daughter, shaking and sobbing, her breath ragged and strained, tearing into and out of her like a cruel, cold wind.

Candice sat with them on the couch, rubbing Mrs. Shaw's back, helping her feel our kindred heartbreak. "It's a mistake," she kept repeating. "It's not her, Tonya! Say it's not her!"

"Mama," Dr. Shaw whispered. "I'm so sorry. I'm so sorry. It's her, Mama. I heard the recording. It's her."

Mrs. Shaw cried into her daughter's chest, and I kept having to wipe my own cheeks. This part of the job was so, fucking hard. Long days, early mornings, dangerous encounters, and low pay were *nothing* compared to witnessing the heartbreak of the families leveled by the news that their loved one was gone. And when that heartbreak was compounded by the knowledge that their beloved had been taken on purpose, by some evil, malevolent piece of shit who had *intentionally* caused that loved one pain and terror in their final moments . . . well, it made me not want to do this job anymore.

It was all so painful to witness without any balm to make it better. Not even serving some justice on these motherfuckers took much of that gutted feeling away.

Watching Dr. Shaw and her mother destroyed over the news we'd brought them made me wish—like sincerely wish, that I didn't have to be there to witness it. But, of course, I did. I was the only one that could put some of this together, and it was better to get the information we needed to find Simone from the source, rather than hearing it secondhand. My radar would ping on anything Mrs. Shaw or Dr. Shaw might say that could be the clue to finding out where she was murdered and where her body might still be.

So, we waited patiently for nearly forty minutes while Dr. Shaw comforted her mother. At last, the poor woman sat up, wiped her eyes with a tissue that Candice offered her, and said "Can you find her?"

"We can," I said quickly. I knew we would. I just knew it. "But we need a place to start, Mrs. Shaw. That's why we need to ask you a few questions about your daughter, and I know this is so difficult and painful for you, but the sooner we can get our questions answered, the sooner we can get started on finding her."

She nodded and took another deep breath. "What do you need to know?"

I took up the questioning from this point, allowing my intuition to be the guide. "Did Simone speak to you about being afraid of anyone? Or hint that someone might've been harassing her?"

Mrs. Shaw shook her head. "No," she said. "She's been so happy lately. She just learned that that singer, you know from that eighties' Irish rock band? He wants to give her money to help bring water to Sudan."

I blinked and my jaw dropped. "You mean Bono? From U2?"

She pointed at me. "Yes, that's the man. She submitted a schematic of a drill and pump system she invented to help bring up enough water for an entire village. Enough even to grow crops with. He was so impressed that he offered her a grant to build a bunch of them and distribute them to about a dozen villages to start with. He's going to support her fully once she graduates." Mrs. Shaw's lip quivered as the realization that her daughter would never graduate seemed to hit her.

"That's incredible," I said. "What an admirable accomplishment. Simone sounds absolutely amazing."

Mrs. Shaw nodded and dabbed again at her cheeks.

I plugged on. "Was anyone helping her with this project? Or did she design this system all on her own?"

"It was all hers," Mrs. Shaw said. "My girl didn't need anyone else to come up with it."

I nodded, trying a different angle. "Can you tell me about Simone's routine? She went missing on a day when she might've had classes, correct?"

Mrs. Shaw nodded. "She has class every Monday, Wednesday, and Friday. She gets to campus around noon, and she's there sometimes until late at night, studying."

"Where does she like to study when she's not in class? The library?"

Mrs. Shaw shook her head. "She's called me a couple of times from some empty classroom in Burdine hall. She has a few classes in that building, and she said she found a way to sneak up to the top floor, which is supposed to be blocked off because there's some big issue with the plumbing, and none of the bathrooms work. The university plans to replace the plumbing in the whole building this summer, but for now they've closed the top floor."

My radar pinged loudly in my mind. *The abandoned classroom,* I mouthed to Dutch and Brice. They both nodded.

"I told her not to go up there," Mrs. Shaw continued, "but she said that no one ever checked to make sure the floor was empty, and she likes to study without other students coming and going."

"Do you know if she was there on Monday afternoon? Right around one o'clock?" Brice asked.

Mrs. Shaw shook her head. "She was already in class at one," she said.

"How do you know she was in class?" I pressed. My radar was going off like fireworks, and I just wanted to confirm my hunch.

"I talked to Efram—he's lived on our street since he was a little baby. He and Simone grew up together. I called him when Simone wasn't answering my texts or calls, and he said he saw her walking to her first class at just before one. She wouldn't have gotten out of class until two o'clock, which is why that recording you say you have of my girl just doesn't make sense!"

Fresh tears streaked down Mrs. Shaw's cheeks, and I knew she was desperate to cling to any hope that her daughter was still alive and that we'd been mistaken to assume the poor girl had been murdered on our podcast. But my radar wasn't dissuaded from the notion that we'd identified the right person.

I stood up and walked to Mrs. Shaw offering her my hand. She took it, and I said, "Thank you for answering our questions in this most difficult moment. I promise you that we'll find your daughter, and if any harm has come to her, I also promise that we'll bring the person responsible to justice."

She mouthed the words *Thank you*, and I motioned to the boys and Candice that we needed to go.

After filing out of the house, I turned to the group and said, "She's up on that abandoned top floor of Burdine Hall. That's where she was shot."

"What about what her friend, Efram, said?" Toscano asked. "He saw her at one o'clock walking to class."

I shook my head. "He was mistaken, or he wanted to falsely reassure Simone's mother that she was okay."

"Let's go," Brice said, pointing to the line of cars we'd rode over in.

"I'll call campus police and have them meet us at the building," Dutch said. "They can get us in and up to that top floor to do our search."

"If they give you any guff about the late hour, send them

my way," Brice said.

I glanced at my watch. It was close to ten p.m. This was a long day that'd turn into a long night at the end of a long couple of weeks. Sighing, I followed Dutch to his car, and I thought about how nice it'd be to take a week or two off from all the emotional chaos and gut-wrenching tragedies we continually found ourselves in the middle of.

He looked over his shoulder at me. "How're you holding up, Edgar?"

"I'm holding," I told him. "By a thread."

He reached back and grabbed my hand leading me to the passenger side door, which he opened for me. I got in, and he leaned forward, offering me a soft kiss, then he said, "Soon, dollface. We'll get away the moment this case is solved."

I smiled and stroked his cheek. "I love it when you read my mind."

He kissed me again, then shut my door, and a few moments later, we were off to the university.

On the way, Dutch called the campus police, who actually did give him a little guff. I could see the frustration etched onto his features as he asked to speak to the sergeant or lieutenant on duty. He made more headway when he spoke with her, and she agreed to have two campus police officers meet us at Burdine hall with the instructions to help us conduct a search for a missing student.

We arrived at the University of Texas, and, because our car was the lead in the convoy of black SUVs carrying federal agents, Dutch kept a close eye on his phone's navigation as we wound through the maze of buildings.

Very few students were out and about at this hour, but enough young people carrying overloaded backpacks dotted the sidewalks to let us know we were on campus grounds.

Dutch's navigation app declared that our destination was six hundred feet ahead on the right, and even if it hadn't told us, the spinning blue strobe light atop a campus police car would've given us a clue.

Dutch parked just behind the CPD car, and we got out as

the line of SUVs behind us also pulled in at the curb.

There was an officer with a bald head, bull neck, and thick arms standing by the car. He greeted us as we approached by extending his hand.

Dutch took it as the cop introduced himself. "Brady Mitchell, sir."

"Special Agent in Charge, Dutch Rivers," my husband said. Then, pointing to me, he said, "This is my wife, Abby. She works as a consultant with our Austin bureau."

As the others in our group joined us, Dutch briefly introduced each of them, and then he pointed to the building and said, "Can you get us in there?"

"I can, sir," the cop said. "Follow me."

We followed behind Mitchell as he took us over to a side entrance. Using a key fob hanging from a lanyard around his neck, he swiped it against a black panel to the side of the door, and it clicked open. We filed into the building, which was lit, but dimly.

"You're searching for a missing student?" he asked as we gathered in the hallway and looked around at our options.

"Yes," Brice said. "We have reason to believe she's on the top floor."

Mitchell eyed Brice curiously and scratched at his bald head. "Sir, that floor's blocked off. She can't be up there."

"She's there," I said. I could feel it in my bones. Simone Shaw was here in this building, four floors up.

The CPD looked at me like he wanted to argue the point, so Dutch said, "Please indulge us, Officer Mitchell. If we're wrong, then it'll be a quick look around, and we'll be on our way."

Mitchell frowned, but with a sigh he said, "Okay. The elevator's this way. It's programed to stop on three, but we can get to the stairwell from there and head up."

Once we'd all crowded into the elevator, Mitchell pressed the three button, and the elevator jolted into action, beeping as the floors were ticked off. My attention went to the control panel, and I saw the sign taped there that read: *Elevator stops on three. No access to the fourth floor.*

I squinted at the sign. There was something off about it. At that moment, the elevator gave a loud double ping, and it stopped moving up. A moment later, the doors parted, and we began to file out, but my radar told me to hold back for a moment.

Dutch waited for everyone else to get off, holding down the open-door button while Officer Mitchell led the way down the hallway. "After you, babe," Dutch said softly.

My brow furrowed, and I eyed the control panel. I had the strongest desire to push the button for floor number four.

"What?" he asked.

Instead of answering him, I reached around him and hit the button for the fourth floor—which didn't light up—and then moved his finger away from the open-door button. He eyed me quizzically as the doors closed, and I knew he expected us to just sit there, firmly rooted to the third floor, but after the doors had fully closed, the elevator gave another jolt, and we headed up.

"Whoa," he said, looking at me with approval. "Now we know how Simone accessed the fourth floor."

"Whoever programed the elevator didn't have very good follow-through," I said.

The elevator binged, and the doors parted. Meanwhile, Dutch's cell vibrated loudly, and he glanced at the display. "Brice wants to know where we went."

"Tell him to take the elevator to the fourth floor," I said, stepping out into the dark hallway. There were no lights on up here, so I used the flashlight on my phone to illuminate the area, and Dutch did too.

Right or left were our only two options. "Which way, Edgar?" he asked.

I weighed the choice against my radar and felt the urge to lean to the left. "That way," I said, pointing the light from my phone to the left corridor leading away from the elevator.

Dutch walked next to me, which I was quite relieved about because this darkened, still floor was super creepy at night.

I allowed my intuition to tug at my solar plexus, leading us forward all the way to the very end of the hallway, which dead-ended at a classroom door with packing paper over the small window within the door.

Not particularly unusual, given that all the windows on the doors down this corridor had similar window-covered panes to keep out prying eyes, and I wondered if it wasn't an effort to further section this area off as much as it was an effort to deter an active shooter.

They don't build classroom doors with windows anymore. The thought gave me a shudder.

"Do you think it'll open?" Dutch asked as I reached for the handle.

I turned the knob, and the door came open. "Yeah, babe. I think it'll open."

Dutch reached his arm across my torso to prevent me from going into the room first. "Stay behind me," he whispered. He then drew his gun, and I actually did take a large step back. No way did I want to get in the middle of another shootout.

Dutch pulled the door open and aimed his flashlight inside, first to the right then to the left. I watched him from behind and noticed the little hitch in his movements when he pointed the light left.

Then he reached over to something on the wall, and on came the lights. Clicking off the flashlight on his phone, he lowered his hand, took another step inside and stood there, staring to the left with sagging shoulders.

"Dammit," I whispered. I knew exactly what he was looking at. And even though I knew in my gut that Simone was dead, there had still been this tiny part of me that was hoping that I'd been mistaken, and that we'd be able to reunite Simone with her family.

Once I stepped into that room and looked at what was there, that shred of hope would be extinguished. Taking a deep breath, I gathered myself and walked into the room, turning to look in the same direction as Dutch.

She lay there on the floor in the fetal position, her wrists tied behind her back and a dark, almost black stain along her head. The photo of her hadn't done the macabre scene justice. It was *much* worse in person.

Her body was already starting to bloat, and the smell was nauseating, but not overwhelming. Yet.

Next to her was a chair, it faced away from the other chairs in the room, tucked underneath desks set in orderly rows. He'd made her stare at a wall while he also forced her to plead with us to find some way to prevent the inevitable end to her short, but promising life.

She wore a green and white plaid shirt, black joggers and hiking boots, and her hair was long and braided like her sister's. I couldn't see her facial features, and I definitely didn't want to get closer to her body than I already was, so when Dutch began to walk toward her, I said, "I'm going to wait out in the hallway."

He grunted in acknowledgement while stepping carefully around Simone's body to look down at her from the front side.

As granite as his expression normally became during moments like this, I wasn't prepared to see the hard expression soften into sorrow.

It was more than I could handle today.

Once back out in the hallway, I sat on the floor with my back against the wall. Down at the far end I saw bouncing beams of light and knew the calvary had arrived. Candice spotted me first, and she trotted ahead of the others to reach me. "You okay?" she asked, her eyes darting back and forth between me and the open door to the lit classroom.

"Been better," I told her. "But I'll manage."

The others were arriving and paused in front of me. Thumbing over my shoulder I said, "She's in there."

Brice and Toscano stepped forward past me into the classroom, while Officer Mitchell asked, "How'd you two get up here?"

"The sign on the elevator is a lie. If you press the button for the fourth floor, it won't light up, but it will take you up. That's how Simone—the girl we've been looking for—got up here. And it's also where she was murdered."

Officer Mitchell's eyes widened, and he immediately pulled up the microphone to his radio, which was clipped to his waist, and began speaking. "Dispatch I need a detective and CSI crew at Burdine Hall. Fourth floor. Room 429. Possible homicide victim here. Tell them to ignore the sign and use the elevator to access the fourth floor."

And then he stepped past me into the classroom.

I knew that, as soon as the detective from the campus police arrived, there'd be a fight over jurisdiction between the CPD and our agents. Brice would want jurisdiction, but he knew he wouldn't get it, so he'd demand it, and when they refused—as they almost always did—he'd "compromise" by insisting on a joint investigation.

During all of that and the couple of hours it took to process the scene, I'd be stuck here, tired, emotionally drained, and wishing only to go home, take a quick shower and climb into bed.

My back still against the wall, I pulled my knees to my chest and laid my forehead on top of them. "Hey," I heard Candice say at the same time I felt a nudge on my upper arm.

Opening my eyes, I looked up. "Yeah?"

"I asked Dutch if I could take you home, and he said he was about to ask me that very question, so come on, Sundance. It's been an insane day for you. Let's get you home for some shut-eye."

I sighed with relief then scrambled to my feet and fell in step with her. "Thanks, Cassidy."

"Of course," she said. "This day has been hell for you. I'm surprised to see you can still stand."

I sighed again, but this time it was an exhausted sound. "I feel kind of guilty leaving the scene."

"Why?"

I shrugged. "I guess because it feels like I failed her."

Candice slung an arm across my shoulders. "There was absolutely nothing you could've done for her when she was still alive, Abs. And now that she's gone, *you're* the one that's made sure we found her and can get her back to her mom and her sister."

As we walked down the hallway, our footfalls echoed off the walls and it was unsettling in a way I don't think I could explain.

"Did you want to stop somewhere to pick up a midnight snack?" Candice asked,

I leaned over to nudge her with my shoulder. "That'd be great, sistah. Thanks."

We were silent as we continued the dozen more steps to the elevator, but as the doors closed on us to carry us down the four floors, I asked my bestie if she'd seen Simone's face and could identify that it was 100 percent the young woman we'd been looking for.

"I did, Abs. It's her."

"That poor girl," I said.

"At least her family and friends can get some closure, and that's all thanks to you."

"Wasn't all me," I said. "I'm pretty sure the spirit of Simone Shaw pointed me in the right direction."

"Yeah, but how insane is it that, because Oscar got shot, we're all at the hospital where Simone's sister works, and you just *happen* to overhear her conversation with her mother about Simone going missing."

I shook my head. "There're times even I can't really believe how interconnected we all are. Once we start listening with our minds instead of our ears, that interconnectivity can bring all the discordant parts together to form a much larger, interlaced picture."

Candice leaned against me. "Let's just hope that interconnectivity leads us to the son of a bitch who murdered Simone before he has a chance to do it to someone else."

I told Candice that I couldn't agree more, but I also couldn't escape the unmistakable feeling in the pit of my stomach that we were already too late for some other poor woman.

CHAPTER 7

Her desperate cry for help came the next day, directly to my phone. It was a call I'll never forget. A call that still haunts the worst of my nightmares.

Maybe, if I hadn't been surprised by the sound of the ringing desk phone, taking up space and gathering dust at the far right of my desk, I could've avoided hearing the scene unfold. The phone with my extension at the bureau office never rings. Like, *never*.

In fact, I've complained about it taking up legit space on my desk more than a few times to Brice, but he's always pushed back saying that if I work for the bureau—even as a consultant—I need a landline number with an extension so that, should someone need to leave a message with sensitive content, they could do so without fear of my cell being hacked.

I'd rolled my eyes at him when he'd explained that to me, because A) I didn't even know my extension, and B) I told everyone to contact me on my cell because, C) who the hell would leave a lowly consultant like *me* a message with sensitive content?

I shouldn't have been so quick to dismiss Brice's point, and maybe if I hadn't, I would've finished telling Cox, Baldwin, Toscano, and Williams my funny story about Eggy and Tuttle fighting over the right to chew the same leather loafer matching another loafer in Dutch's closet.

But the sound of the phone startled me, and purely out of reflex, I grabbed the receiver off the cradle and said, "Hi. Abby here . . . uh, I mean Abigail Cooper speaking. Abigail

Cooper, consultant to the FBI speaking. How may I help you?"

Baldwin, Cox, Toscano, and Williams were all looking at me like they couldn't believe I didn't know how to professionally answer my own phone, so I scowled at them and made a shooing gesture.

They stayed put, and thank God for that because the very next moment a woman's sob filled my ear with a heartbreaking plea. "Abby? Abby Cooper? Please, please help me!"

My eyes went wide, and intuitively, I knew exactly what this call was all about. Punching the speaker button I said, "I want to help you! What's your name?"

"Zhee. I'm Zhee," she said, and I noted a heavy foreign accent.

My heart was pounding in my chest, and next to me, Baldwin placed his phone, which was running a recording app, on my desk. Meanwhile, Williams ran to alert Brice and Dutch who were both in Brice's office, and Cox had run to his computer, probably to try and trace the call. "Zhee," I said. "Where are you?"

"I'm—" there was a loud *slap!* sound on the other end of the line, and the woman gasped in pain.

My hands curled into fists. After a moment of silence, I said, "Zhee, are you okay?"

Zhee was crying in earnest now. "He says he's going to kill me," she whispered. "I don't want to die."

I looked up at Dutch, who was now hovered over me. I mouthed, *What should I do?*

He made a rolling motion with his hand. He wanted me to try to extend the call. "Zhee," I said, my brain racing to find a way to stay her execution. "If you can tell me what he wants, then I can try to get it for him, and then we can find you and bring you home."

Zhee gave a startled cry, like she'd been poked with something sharp, and I heard her whisper, *"Please!"* followed by another sharp cry.

"Zhee!" I said. "Tell me what he wants. I promise you that I'll get whatever it is and bring it to him, personally. Then we can bring you home."

"He . . . he . . ." she stammered through her sobs. "He wants you . . . to . . . to solve . . . my murder."

Before we could even react, there was a loud *Bang!* And the sound of another body hitting the floor. And then the line disconnected.

I slapped a hand over my mouth as a dial tone echoed out from the speaker on the phone. I looked at Dutch who was definitely shaken but also as angry as I'd ever seen him. The rest of the agents gathered around my desk all wore similar expressions of shock and fury.

And then my stomach roiled, and I jumped out of my chair and bolted to the ladies' room.

I barely made it in time.

Several minutes later when I was sitting against the stall door, sobbing my eyes out, I heard the door to the ladies' room open.

"Edgar?" Dutch said.

"It's my fault," I sobbed. "It's all my fault."

He jiggled the stall door. "Hey. Let me in, dollface."

I glanced up at the knob to unlock the door. It seemed like a mile away, and my arm felt so, so heavy. I wanted to melt into the floor; to disappear. To become as irrelevant as a few tiles, outlined in grout.

"Abby," Dutch said, his voice gentle. "Please."

I took a deep, ragged breath and reached up to turn the knob, letting him in. He opened the door, and I fell against his shins, my hands covering my face in shame and guilt.

I heard Dutch's knees creak as he squatted down next to me and took hold of my wrists, gently pulling my hands away from my face.

"Hey," he said, close enough to kiss me.

I stared into his midnight blue eyes and waited for him to say something that would take all the pain away.

"This guy would've found an audience even without you

in the equation. He probably would've called Toscano's podcast anyway, which would've sent HQ into a tailspin, searching D.C. for a serial killer who was actually based here in Austin.

"It's because of *you*, my beautiful wife, that we were able to find Simone, and I know it'll also be because of you that we'll eventually catch this motherfucker."

Tears continued to leak out of my eyes. "We need to make sure he doesn't do this again, Dutch. We have to catch him before he has a chance to torture and murder his next vic."

"We'll all do our best, babe. You know we will."

I reached my arms out and wrapped them around his neck. He wrapped his own arms around my torso and lifted me up to dangle eight inches off the ground, pressed tightly against his chest.

"You ready to go back and get to work?" he asked after a good long hug.

I released my arms and slid down to the ground. With a heavy sigh I said, "Yeah. I think so. Thanks."

When we walked back into the office, I wasn't surprised to see the place abuzz with energy. Someone had gotten out the big whiteboard, and several photos and notes had been jotted down on it. Every clue we'd discovered along the way would make its way onto that whiteboard.

Looking at it, I felt reassured. Solving crime is a process, and it takes hard work and lots of rearranging of clues to find out how the puzzle comes together. Having a visual aid in the process really helps us—especially me, because I'm a visual gal living in a clairvoyant world.

"We've tried to trace the call," Dutch said. "It keeps going to a D.C. number. He might not have heard that we found Simone, so he's still routing us through the wrong place."

"Yep," I said. "If we can keep him in the dark about how much we know, that might play in our favor."

"We won't be able to keep the discovery of Simone's body a secret for long," he said. "Maybe another couple of hours."

"See if campus police would be willing to keep a tight lid

on it," I suggested.

"Will do."

I left Dutch's side and walked over to the whiteboard to stare at it with crossed arms. Everything we knew about Simone was up on the board. And it was a bit frustrating to see that we actually had very little information on her.

One line simply read, *UT senior.*

I moved my gaze to the driver's license photo of Simone, studying her features, hoping for another clue to her murderer.

My gaze traveled back to that UT senior line, then to her photo, and down again to the UT line.

I stepped forward until I was maybe six inches away from the whiteboard, staring at the line and allowing my mind to go blank, which allowed my intuition to take over.

In my mind's eye, I saw the class schedule from my senior year of college. I remembered it well because that was the hardest semester I'd had in my four years there. I'd taken stats, an advanced economics class, an advanced calculous class, and an accounting class. It'd been math, math, and more math, and it'd nearly killed me.

I wrote down the words *class schedule* putting a question mark at the end. I felt like Simone's class schedule was important because someone would've had to have known her daily routine on campus to know that she liked to study in that abandoned room on the fourth floor of Burdine Hall.

And then, another thought occurred to me; what if the man who murdered her was a student? In fact, wasn't it *likely* that he was a student? I wrote *student suspect* under the class schedule line.

I moved over one step to the line written at the top of the whiteboard. It simply read, *Zhee.* Thinking back to the sound of her voice, she'd sounded on the young side. I guessed that she was probably in her early twenties, and that made me think that perhaps this psycho was targeting college students, and if he'd had personal knowledge of Simone's schedule, and he was likely a student himself, then it was logical that

Zhee was also a student at UT.

Still, something about that name was throwing me, but I couldn't figure out what. And then I had it; what if whomever had written her name on the whiteboard had written it out phonetically instead of how it should be spelled.

I thought back to my very brief conversation with the poor girl. She'd had an accent . . . Had it been Asian?

I thought it might've been. What if her name was spelled with a soft g or a soft j?

Going to my computer, I sat down and searched for Asian girl names that sounded like Zhee.

I had it in two minutes.

Going back to the whiteboard, I erased Zhee and replaced it with Ji. Her name had been Ji, but Ji what? What was her last name?

"Scott?" I called, without taking my eyes from the whiteboard.

"Yeah?"

"Can you get me a roster of all the students at UT?"

Agent Baldwin didn't immediately answer me, so I turned to look at him. His eyes were wide.

"What?" I asked.

"Cooper, there're, like, forty or fifty *thousand* students at UT."

It was my turn to widen my eyes.

"Okay," I said, tapping my lip with the dry-erase marker. "Then can you do some kind of specific search for a UT student named Ji?" I pointed to the way I'd spelled her name to emphasize what I was specifically looking for.

"I can try," he said.

"Great," I told him. "Thank you."

Baldwin picked up his phone and began to dial. I turned back to the whiteboard and stared at Ji's name, hoping for another clue. Into my mind popped the lit flashlight on the desk from my vision about where we could find Simone.

I reached for the dry-erase marker again and wrote under Ji's name, *lit flashlight*.

I figured everyone would know what I was referencing because everyone had a copy of my vision.

And then I happened to glance again at Simone's photo, and there was something niggling at me. Something about what I'd heard that could fit another piece of the puzzle into place.

I glanced back at what I'd just written under Ji's name, then back to Simone. "If the flashlight represents Ji, then what represents Simone?" I asked myself softly.

In my mind's eye I saw the pail of water and immediately that same niggling feeling came back to me, telling me to connect the dots.

My gaze traveled to the *class schedule* line, and like a lightbulb being lit, I figured it out. It was something Dr. Shaw had said . . . or was it her mother? Someone had mentioned that Simone had wanted to work in Sudan to help get water to remote villages. "Dutch?" I called out..

"Yeah?"

"What was the name of Simone's major? It was water something, right?"

"Hydrogeology," he said.

I nodded vigorously and looked over my shoulder at him. "Thank you!" I said, scribbling *pail of water* underneath Simone's name and photo.

And then I felt like I might be on the verge of connecting one or two more dots and tapped again at my lip with the marker.

"You okay?" I heard someone next to me say.

I jumped at the sound. I'd been deep in thought and hadn't realized Toscano had sidled up next to me. "I'm still shaky," I admitted. "But I'm trying to work through it."

Toscano grunted and stared at the whiteboard too.

"What's with the flashlight and pail of water?"

"They were in my vision," I reminded him.

"Yeah," he said, "but what do they mean?"

"Not sure." Off to the side of Ji's name I wrote down, *rock,* and *stuffed bunny,* the other two items on the list. Stepping back from the whiteboard, I stared at it, willing to see a possible connection. "Whoa," I said, thinking I had it right. "What if each of these objects represent an original element?"

Toscano cocked his head to one side. "Original element," he repeated before pointing to the pail of water. "You mean earth, water, air, fire?"

"Yes," I said. "Simone's major was hydrogeology, which connects to the pail of water." For emphasis I wrote down *hydrogeology* next to the pail of water, underlining *water*. Then I moved over to Ji's name and the lit flashlight. Another set of dots connected, and I wrote down, *fire* with an arrow pointing to the flashlight.

"Fire?" Toscano said. "Couldn't the flashlight be something like energy? Or light?"

I shook my head. "The British term for flashlight is literally *torch*, Mike."

He scratched his head. "You have the better mind for metaphors, Abby."

I offered him a sideways smile. "I've had a lot of practice at it."

"Okay, I believe you, but what does it *mean*?"

"It's a clue about where to look for the next victim," I said, then wrote down under Ji's name, *majoring in the study of fire.*

"You think Ji was a student?" Mike asked, looking at what I'd just written.

"She sounded young enough to be," I said.

"Why did you give her fire and not air or earth?"

"I don't know," I told him honestly. "My intuition just pushed me to write that up there."

"So, if Ji's a student at UT, then she'd be studying . . . actual fire?" he asked.

"Maybe not directly," I said. "But I'd bet dollars to doughnuts that her field of study involves something to do with fire."

Toscano's brow furrowed as he thought about it. "What about chemistry?" he said. "There're lots of chemical reactions going on that involve heat and fire."

I nodded and stepped forward to write down, *chemistry major?*

"What else could represent fire?"

Toscano chewed on his lip. "How about the weather? Something like meteorology?"

I offered him a quizzical expression. "Not seeing the link there, my friend. Try again?"

"Lightning strikes can cause fire," he said simply.

I brightened. "Ah! Yes! That's very true." I wrote *meteorology* under *chemistry.*

"Anything else?" I asked. My intuition was telling me that we hadn't yet determined what field of study Ji was majoring in.

"I can't think of anything, Abby, but I'll keep trying. I'll do a little research on the fields of study offered at UT and see if anything jumps out at me."

I patted his shoulder. "Good, Mike, thank you."

Toscano ambled off to the empty cubicle he'd claimed for his own, and I went back to eyeing the whiteboard, but no other clues were illuminating themselves in my mind's eye.

Walking over to where Dutch was hovering above Agent Baldwin's desk, I peeked over his shoulder and saw a long, and I do me looooong list of names on the screen.

"Whoa," I said. "What's going on there?"

Baldwin glanced up at me and scowled. "It's just one of the student rosters from one of the major fields of study at UT. This one alone has four thousand names on it, Cooper. Each department keeps a separate roster, which—when combined—forms the entire population of undergrad and post grad students. I've been calling around to each individual department and having them send over a copy of their roster. I've only gotten through a third of the departments, and I'm already up to twenty thousand students."

"Yikes," I said. "Can't each department sort through their lists and send over only those with a first name Ji?"

Baldwin actually laughed. "I ask that every time I call, and each time I get shot down because none of the department assistants has time for that. They tell me they can either send the whole list or nothing at all. They don't have the manpower to go through each class roster which means *I* have to upload each list and then manually download it into a spreadsheet."

I winced. "Maybe I can whittle that process down for you," I offered.

"How?"

"Stick to the science majors. I just have a hunch that Ji was studying something to do with the sciences."

Baldwin sighed heavily. "That's still gonna be about ten to twenty thousand names, Cooper. But I'll do it. I have to download them into a spreadsheet before I can sort them and there's not an easy way to do that right now."

"Can I help?" I offered, knowing that it wasn't likely that there was anything I could do.

"Yeah," Baldwin said, surprising me. "I'll send you a couple lists, and you can help input them into my spreadsheet."

"Oh, okay. Great," I said. *Dammit!* I thought. *Why did I have to ask?*

Heading back to my desk, I noticed Dutch following after me, and he whispered, "You walked right into that one, Edgar."

"Don't I know it," I told him.

He squeezed my shoulder. "I'll take you out for a prickly pear margarita later."

I plopped down in my seat and opened up my laptop, already seeing a large file that Baldwin had sent over. "Better make it two prickly pears, cowboy."

Hours later I was back at Baldwin's desk, once again looking over his shoulder. We'd uploaded all of the names from just the BS undergrad and MS graduate rosters into the master spreadsheet that Baldwin had created, and he was now sorting them alphabetically by first name.

"There!" I said, pointing to his screen when he scrolled

down to the Js.

"I got it, I got it," he replied a bit irritably, slowing his scrolling past the Jacks, Jaysons, Jaydens, and Johns, etc., et cetera. "Okay, here we go," he said, finally getting to the Jis.

"There're sixty Jis," he said, isolating and highlighting them.

"*Sixty*?"

"Yep. Must be a pretty common first name."

I scowled. Earlier, Dutch had reached out to APD to see if there were any reports of a missing woman, first name Ji, or if there were any reports of a dead body fitting the description of a young Asian woman. None had come in.

"What do we do with all those Jis?" I asked Baldwin.

"We start calling and see who answers. If they answer, they're alive and they can be removed from the list."

I looked at my watch. It was nearly six, and I was so hungry I couldn't concentrate. I'd thrown up breakfast, skipped lunch because I was too busy with this needle in a haystack project, and now I was feeling decidedly hangry with a side of splitting headache. No way could I spend one more minute on this damned list without eating first.

"I need food," I told Baldwin.

"Me too," he agreed. "Pizza?"

I sighed. He was planning to work through dinner. The bastard. "Scott, I can't. I really need a break from this, so I'm going to grab my husband, go out to dinner, and not think about any of this for an hour."

Baldwin grinned at me. "Investigation work ain't the barrel of laughs you thought it'd be, huh?"

"Nope."

He chuckled. "Go on and get your dinner, Cooper. I'll order pizza and start making calls. If I get anything that stands out, I'll let you know."

I wrapped an arm around his neck from behind and squeezed him across his collarbone. "Bless you, good sir."

"Ready to roll?" Dutch said, looking as tired and stressed out as I felt.

"I was born ready, Freddy."

We left the office and headed out to Dutch's SUV. I climbed in and bounced a little because we were going to one of my favorite Mexican restaurants where the tortilla chip basket and the salsa bowls were never allowed to reach empty and the prickly pear margaritas were to die for.

"Man! Do I need a break from today," I told Dutch, rubbing my eyes which had been in a state of squint for hours on end.

"Me too," Dutch said. "We all worked our assess off and got nowhere."

"I feel like we made progress though," I reassured him. "At least we know where this guy is and who he's targeting."

"If we confirm that Ji was a student at UT, we'll have to alert the university," Dutch said. "I'm debating if we should give them a heads-up even before we confirm it."

Dutch took a left, and I sat up a little. "Hey, you're going the wrong way, cowboy."

"I thought we'd stop in and say hi to Oscar before we head to dinner, dollface. Visiting hours are over at eight o'clock, and I doubt we'd be able to have time to eat dinner and make it to the hospital in time to see him before then."

My stomach gurgled, but no way was I gonna turn down a chance to see Oscar. "Great," I said, trying to appear enthusiastic.

Dutch smiled and pointed to the glove box. "There's some trail mix in there. It'll tide you over until we eat."

By the time we made it to the hospital, I'd eaten all of the trail mix and was looking for any other goodies in Dutch's glove box, but none were to be found.

"We won't stay long," he assured me when I came up empty-handed.

I sighed, feeling guilty about making a show of foraging for food. "I'm just reeeeally hungry, Dutch."

He parked in a slot in the visitor's parking lot and said, "I know, dollface. We'll be quick."

We made our way inside and inquired about which room

Oscar was in at the information desk, then wound our way up to the third floor to room 316.

The door was partially open, but Dutch knocked anyway. "Come in," a woman's voice called.

Dutch and I exchanged confused looks. Had we been sent to the wrong room? Still, Dutch pushed the door open to reveal Nikki sitting in a chair next to an empty hospital bed. "Hey, guys!" she said brightly.

"Hi, Nikki," I replied. "Where's Oscar?"

"He's getting an MRI. His surgeon wants to make sure that artery isn't leaking."

"Didn't he patch it up so it wouldn't leak?" Dutch asked.

"He did, but he also said that the artery was damaged so severely that he's not sure it can take the pressure of blood flow through the vein. He had to shrink the circumference of the artery in order to close it."

"What will they do if the artery is leaking?" I asked.

"Oscar will have to go back into surgery and have the artery replaced with a pig artery."

I made a face, and Nikki laughed. "I know, but the surgeon assured us that it would work and that it was something they do all the time."

"As long as he recovers," Dutch said. "That's all we're worried about."

Nikki stood up and stretched. "Tell me about it." And then she eyed me keenly and said, "Hell of a shot yesterday, Abby."

I grinned. "Thank you. I was almost too nervous to pull the trigger."

"If you hadn't, Oscar and I would both be dead. Maybe even you too."

"That thought occurred to me right before I pulled the trigger."

"Thank you," she said, and her eyes welled. She swallowed hard and pointed to the empty bed. "I saw him get hit, and it was my worst nightmare. Thank God he was wearing Kevlar."

"They all wear it everywhere they go," I said, and for emphasis, I turned slightly and punched Dutch hard in the stomach.

My fist hit nothing harder than his abs, and he immediately doubled over and made an *oomph* sound.

"Maybe not *everywhere* they go," Nikki said, giggling.

"Ohmigod, Dutch!" I cried, bending over and mimicking his posture. "I'm so sorry! I thought you were wearing your vest!"

He coughed, his face red, and those midnight blues looked angrily at me. Slowly, clutching his stomach, he stood tall again, but not without a few extra coughs. "Give a guy some warning next time, Edgar," he said gruffly.

I felt really bad, and sometimes when I feel bad about something I did, I get defensive. "Well, why *aren't* you wearing your vest? I mean, how was I supposed to know?"

Dutch coughed one last time. "Ah, so it's my fault?"

"In part!" I insisted, even though there is *no way* my argument would ever hold up in court.

"Really?" He growled. "That's the hill you want to die on?"

"Whoa, whoa, whoa!" we heard from behind us. Turning we saw Oscar being wheeled into the room. "Who's dying on what hill?"

"Abby punched Dutch," Nikki said, sooooo unhelpfully.

Oscar eyed me quizzically, and I was glad to see his color had returned to normal. "Why'd you do that, Coop?"

I was starting to feel less defensive and more and more guilty as I watched my husband still holding his stomach. "I thought he was wearing his Kevlar," I said meekly.

Oscar grinned. "Coop, as a standard practice, you should ask a guy about that before you deliver a right hook."

"Thank you Captain Obvious," I muttered, then turned to Dutch and mouthed, *I'm really sorry.*

He stood up tall again and nodded, then he rolled his eyes and grinned to let me know we were okay again.

The orderly pushing Oscar into the room gave us all an

odd look, but he got on with the business of helping his patient back into bed.

We waited for Oscar to get settled before Nikki asked, "How'd the MRI go?"

Oscar grinned again. "No leakage. The patch is holding like a champ. Surgeon said I can be discharged tonight, and he'll sign off once the paperwork is finished."

I sighed with relief. "That's great news, Oscar." And then my stomach gave another rumble.

Oscar pointed at my belly. "Sounds hangry."

"Maybe a little," I admitted.

Oscar looked at Dutch and said, "Better get her something to eat. But not here. They only serve one-star meals here."

"Can we bring you anything, buddy? A to-go order? If you're discharged by the time we finish dinner, we can drop it off at your house."

"Where're you guys going for dinner?"

Dutch pointed to me. "Her favorite place. El Naranjo."

"Ooo," Oscar said. "I could go for something from there."

"Great," Dutch said, taking my hand. "Look up their menu and pick out enough food for you and Nikki, and we'll drop it off downstairs if it's past visiting hours, or at your place if you get discharged in the next two hours."

We left Oscar and Nikki and headed to the lot. "I'm really sorry, Dutch," I said. Still feeling bad about the sucker punch.

"It's okay, Edgar," he said. "I normally wear a vest all day, but tonight, for dinner, I wanted to hang with my lady and not be reminded of the day's ugliness every time I moved and felt the vest rub against my ribcage."

"That's my excuse too," I mocked.

I paused at the passenger side door to Dutch's SUV, and he sweetly reached over and opened it for me. As I was getting in, he said, "You need to drag that thing out of your closet and put it on if you're going to work with us in the field," he said. "The fact that you weren't wearing it yesterday when you were in a shootout with Mateo really, really bothers me, babe."

"Technically, he never shot at *me*."

Dutch waited to pull out of the parking slot before he turned to eye me sternly. "Again, finding out that you weren't wearing one yesterday when you were in a shoot—"

"Okay, okay! Jeesh! I'll put it on tomorrow."

"I only want you to be safe. It's not too much to ask, especially when we're on the hunt for a serial killer who likes to taunt you. I worry that this psycho might switch from taunting you to hunting you."

I was quiet for a long moment, thinking about that.

"I get it," I said at last. "Dutch, I'll wear the vest from now on. Pinkie swear."

"*And* wear your gun," he insisted.

"The APD took mine, remember?"

"I'll get you a loaner until they give it back to you."

We drove in silence for several minutes before Dutch reached over and held my hand, something that always felt so intimate. His palm easily covers my whole hand, and it always makes me feel like he's shielding me from harm. Tonight, that thought had a more poignant and urgent energy about it, and that bothered me the whole rest of the way to the restaurant.

CHAPTER 8

The email arrived at eight a.m., but, by then, we already knew she'd been discovered in the bowels of a damp and dirty basement. No dignity had been granted to her; she lay exactly as her predecessor had—on her side, her hands tied behind her back with a halo of blood and a bullet wound in her temple that'd allowed her soul to leak out, leaving her body cold, empty, and still.

We'd been called to the scene by campus police, and we were grateful that they hadn't tried to completely take over the investigation and cut us out. They actually seemed relieved when we showed up, and I understood what they might be thinking.

It was one thing to deal with drunk and disorderly students. It was a whole other thing to discover what appeared to be a serial killer on campus, executing young women indiscriminately.

I waited on the outskirts of the crime scene, my back pressed hard against the back wall of the lowest level in the campus's Buildings and Ground Maintenance Center, and if I could've disappeared into that wall, I would've.

Dutch was standing near Ji, speaking with a campus officer who kept eyeing her nervously, as if he expected her to come to life like a zombie ready for a brain snack.

Meanwhile, Dutch kept eyeing *me* like he was regretting not dropping me off at the office before he headed here. We'd driven in together that morning, and we were on the edge of entering downtown when Brice had called us to let us know Ji's body had been discovered.

Dutch had only to continue to point his SUV toward downtown to reach the campus, and we were the first on scene besides the campus police.

Brice and Baldwin had arrived together. Scott looked like he'd been up all night—and he probably had, but at least now we might get a positive ID on Ji, if she had any ID on her.

"Cooper," Baldwin said after leaving the ME who'd responded to the scene and was currently inspecting the young woman, looking for clues.

"Scott," I replied softly.

"How you doin'?"

"Not great," I admitted. I then lifted my phone to show him the screen, which had the email from another Guerrilla account and an attached image of Ji's lifeless body. The angle in the photo was different from where I stood, but the scene was still just as horrifying, no matter which way you looked at it.

"Have you shown that to your husband yet?"

"No. It just came in, and he's busy gathering what he can from the responding officer. I'll show him when he's got time to look at it."

Baldwin nodded. "If it just came in, he doesn't know we've found the body."

"That was my take as well, which means he's not on campus right now or he would've seen all the cop cars and sedans parked out front."

Scott grunted his agreement, then held up a small evidence bag containing a student ID. "Ji-Hye Jeong," he said.

I closed my eyes; so sick of this random violence against women. "I hate this case, Scott."

"I know, Coop," he said. "I hate them all."

I opened my eyes and looked up at him and saw that he was dead serious.

Baldwin had been with the FBI for nearly thirty years, which was a whole lot of cases to hate.

"The only thing that ever makes me feel better is when we catch these fuckers," he said. "And that's what I live for. I want to hunt these guys down like the animals they are and serve them up some cold hard justice."

I studied him for a moment. The way he'd said that last sentence made me think that when we caught this asshole, Scott was hoping he'd have a chance to deliver some "justice" by way of his gun.

I'd known Baldwin for as long as I'd known Oscar. Both of them had given me a really hard time when Brice brought me onto the team, and I'd had a hell of a time wining them over, but eventually they'd come around.

Oscar, of course, is now more friend to me than he is a teammate, and our platonic affection for each other was something I didn't share with Scott or any of the other agents in the office.

In Baldwin's case, I thought that was mostly because he was older than me by about eighteen years and we'd never hung out much together. So I didn't know him as well as I knew Oscar, and his statement caught me by surprise. I hadn't ever pegged him for the vengeful type, but in that moment with Ji, lying dead across the room, executed for simply being a vulnerable woman, I couldn't help but wish that Baldwin actually got the chance to put a bullet in the brain of this killer.

At that moment, Toscano arrived, and after surveying the scene—his gaze lingering on the lifeless body of Ji-Hye Jeong—he spotted us and headed our way. "What's the word?" he asked.

"Bleak," I said miserably. "I don't know how to catch this guy."

"It's not all up to you, Abby," Toscano replied.

"I know, but I can't shake the feeling that time's against us, and there's something bigger that I think I'm missing here. I mean, I know this asshole has more executions lined up, but if we don't find a clue to point us in his direction soon, I'm convinced we'll lose out on the chance to stop him from the next execution. And the next. And the next."

Baldwin pointed to where the CSI techs were combing

over the area to the right of Ji's body. It was easy to tell why. The blood splatter dotting the walls and the floor suggested he'd shot her from that angle. "Let's see if they find anything that might give us a direction."

I frowned. My gut told me there was nothing there that would help very much. And then I looked at Baldwin's hand and Ji's student ID. "Are you going to start interviewing people?"

He nodded. Holding up the baggie again he said, "She lived in Kinsolving. One of the dorms on campus."

"Let's go," I said.

"I'd like to go too," Toscano said.

"Sure, Mike," Baldwin said. "Let me just tell the boss where we're going."

I let Scott head over to Dutch to speak to him without tagging along. I didn't want to get any closer to Ji's body than I had to, and I definitely didn't want to risk seeing her expression frozen in death. I had enough trauma haunting my nightmares.

Dutch eyed me a few times as he spoke to Baldwin, and then I saw him point to Scott's holster, and I knew he was telling him that, if I went with the agent to interview some people, he'd be responsible for my safety.

He'd given me one of his guns that morning, and refused to leave the house until I strapped into my shoulder holster and settled the gun against my ribcage, and hid the ensemble under a light windbreaker.

Given that I was already packing, I didn't like the feeling of being babysat, but I liked being shot at, kidnapped, or otherwise physically harmed even less, so I didn't offer my husband my usual scowl or roll of the eyes.

Baldwin came back to us and made a swirling motion with his finger. "Let's roll."

We ended up walking to Ji's dorm. It was only a few blocks away, and it looked like your typical boring brick student housing; namely six floors of ho-hum with a side of yawn and maybe a soupçon of zzzz.

"Charming," I said flatly as we walked to the front door.

"Student housing isn't supposed to be pretty," Toscano said. "It's supposed to be functional."

I scoffed at him. "There's no reason it can't be attractive *and* functional, Mike. For what students and their parents are paying in tuition, books, and housing, the *least* UT could do would be to offer them something nice to live in."

"We don't know what the inside looks like yet," he cautioned. "Maybe it's spectacular."

Baldwin got us in the door by flashing his badge at a student manning a desk in the lobby. After being buzzed in, we stepped through the entrance into an area that was clean, but that was about all it had to aesthetically offer. A chair rail divided boring white and rust brown walls, and an ugly yellow and rust brown tile flooring. There were a couple of bulletin boards decorated with a few attempts at cheer, but otherwise, I gave the interior an even lower grade than the exterior.

I turned smugly to Toscano. "You were saying?"

"Yeah, yeah," he said rolling his eyes, then he focused on Baldwin. "What floor is she on, Scott?"

"Five," he said, studying the student ID through the plastic baggie.

I pointed to one of two elevators across the room. "Shall we?"

We rode the elevator up to the fifth floor and got out, looking right and left. Scott pointed us right, and then he led the way down the corridor, glancing at the room numbers while we walked along. A few students passed us, and they gave our trio curious looks, but there wasn't a whole lot going on this early in the morning.

"Here," Scott said, stopping abruptly about midway down the hall. "Room 522."

Baldwin knocked on the door, and to our surprise it was opened by a young woman of Asian descent. She started at the sight of us, and I saw the fear creep into her eyes immediately. "Yeah?" she asked.

Scott flashed his badge. "Agent Baldwin with the Austin

FBI, ma'am. Is this the residence of Ji-Hye Jeong?"

The young woman paled. "Yes," she said. "Is she okay? She didn't come home last night."

"May we come in and speak to you?" Baldwin asked.

The poor girl began to tremble. It was clear that she was intimidated and afraid of the fact that the FBI had just shown up at her dorm room door.

"Hi," I said, getting her attention. "I know you're probably wondering why we're here, and we'll tell you as much as we know, but doing it out here in the hallway isn't private enough for this conversation. Is it all right if we come in?"

The girl hesitated a little, but at last she said, "Sure. Come in."

We filed in through the door and found ourselves in a tiny space, even by dorm room standards.

The beds were bunk beds and there was room for them and two desks with chairs and not a lot else.

"May I ask your name?" I said to her as we settled ourselves in the small space.

"I'm Hae. Hae Hak."

"That's a beautiful name," I said, trying my best to put her at ease. "We'd like to ask you some questions about Ji. Some of them are quite personal, but I want to assure you that we have specific reasons for asking them."

"What's happened to Ji?" Hae demanded, finally finding her voice.

I looked at Baldwin, and he looked at me. Normally, we don't reveal anything about the victim of a murder until we've notified next of kin, but I was wondering if it might be okay in this one instance.

Before Baldwin could even say something to Hae, however, Toscano said, "She's been murdered."

Baldwin and I turned our heads toward Toscano in shock, but he was staring steadily at Hae. For her part, the poor girl went paler still, her eyes filling with tears, and her head shaking back and forth. "No," she said. "No. No that's not . . ." Her voice trailed off, and we all waited for her to process the shock of the news before speaking any further.

"How?" she asked.

"She was shot," Toscano told her. I wanted to wag a finger at him. It wasn't his place to reveal these details. Baldwin was in charge right now, and Toscano should've deferred to him.

For his part, Baldwin looked like he wanted to punch Toscano, and I knew he was regretting his decision to have Toscano come along with us.

But Toscano wasn't budging his position. He didn't even seem to regret it.

"How could she have been shot?" Hae asked, as if the idea that her roommate died from a gunshot wound was too far-fetched to even comprehend.

"We believe she was kidnapped and taken to another location," I said. "She was murdered there."

"Why?" Hae asked, her eyes still wide and her expression incredulous. "Why would anybody want to shoot Ji?"

"We don't know," I told her. "Which is why we've come to talk to you."

Hae was sitting in a chair behind her desk. She continued to stare at us as tears formed and began rolling down her cheeks. "I still don't understand."

"Do you know how to get in touch with her parents?" I asked, trying to avoid repeating the information.

Hae nodded. "Her parents and my parents are best friends."

"Do they live here in the states?" I asked next.

She nodded. "They live in Hawaii. On the big island, in Nanawale." She reached forward on the desk and picked up her cell phone. "Are you going to call them?"

"We are," I assured her.

She rattled off the number to Ji's parents, and Scott plugged it into his phone. "Thank you," he said. "Are you okay to answer some questions?"

She nodded reluctantly.

"Good," he said. "I know this is coming as a shock to you,

Ms. Hak, but we're trying to establish a timeline of Ms. Jeong's whereabouts yesterday. We hope that we might be able to pinpoint when she was abducted and from where."

"Ji was in school most of the day," Hae said. "She's got a really full schedule this term."

Something pinged against my radar. "What was she studying?" I asked.

"Environmental science. She's really interested in volcanology. She wants . . ." Hae's voice trailed off for a moment. I knew it was starting to hit her that Ji wouldn't be wanting anything more. Ever.

"She wanted what?" I asked gently.

Hae laced her fingers together. "She wanted to be a volcanologist. She wanted to travel the world and study volcanoes."

Toscano looked sharply at me, and I could tell he'd connected the dots to the symbol for fire I'd drawn on the whiteboard.

"Wow," Baldwin said, genuinely impressed. "That's a dangerous profession to go into."

Hae nodded. "It is, but Ji and I lived next to Mount Kilauea for years, so we're more desensitized to the danger of being near an active volcano. When it was really active, Ji and I could see it from our houses. She was obsessed with Kilauea. She wanted to study it and other volcanoes like it to help predict when a volcano might be ready to erupt. She had planned to go to Naples to study Mount Vesuvius when she graduated."

As I listened to Hae, my radar was pinging so loud it was hard to focus on anything else. Ji was quite literally studying fire, and this fed into my thinking that the ancient elements had some sort of ritualistic role to play in this psychopath's plan.

"When was the last time you spoke to your roommate?" Baldwin asked next.

"Yesterday. I saw her right before she left the dorm for her first class."

"Did you ever hear her speak about someone who might've been following her? Or hassling her?"

Hae shrugged and shook her head. "Ji didn't mention anything like that to me."

"Did she ever appear frightened or concerned after returning here from class?" I asked next.

Again, Hae shook her head. "No."

"Where did your roommate like to hangout?" Baldwin asked her.

"She didn't," Hae said.

"What does that mean?" he pressed.

"She was either in class, or she was here studying. She didn't go out or hangout anywhere else. She was totally focused on her grades."

"What about other friends?" Toscano offered. "Is there anybody else who knew Ji that might be able to tell us if she ever mentioned something strange to them?"

Hae tugged at a tendril of hair, twisting and pulling on it. Something she probably did every time she was stressed or worried. "Yuze," she said almost absently.

"Yuze?" I repeated. "Yuze who?"

Hae shook her head. "I don't know the surname, but Ji used to talk about him a lot. He was competing with her for the top grade in their major. They both wanted to be valedictorians. I thought Ji might have a crush on him, but they never went out or anything like that."

"So, he was in her classes?" Baldwin asked.

"At least a few of them," she said.

Baldwin was jotting everything down that Hae was saying, and I gave him credit for being able to think up so many relevant questions without any preparation. "Do you know her class schedule?" he asked.

"It's up there," she said, pointing to a place right over Baldwin's shoulder.

He turned, and we could then clearly see that Ji-Hye Jeong's schedule was tacked to the door.

Reaching up, he lifted one corner and looked back at Hae.

"May I?"

She nodded, her eyes welling with tears again.

I looked at Hae with sympathy. "I'm so sorry for your loss, Hae. I know this must be incredibly hard. If you could keep news of Ji's death to yourself until we've had a chance to notify her parents, we'd appreciate it."

Hae dropped her gaze to her folded hands. "She was such a sweet person. I never heard anyone say one mean thing about her. I can't believe she's gone."

As if trying to take in the totality of that statement, Hae then lifted her gaze to look up at the shelves above Ji's desk which were lined with simple framed photographs of Ji with friends and family. And then her gaze drifted over to Ji's bed, which was neatly made, then she looked over to the closet where I assumed Ji's clothes were. "Why would anyone want to kill her?" she all but whispered.

"We don't know," Toscano said. "But I promise you, we're going to find out."

I plucked a business card from my wallet and set it down on the desk in front of Hae. "If you think of anything, or anyone who might be responsible, please let us know."

She took the card, studying it for a moment before she said. "I will."

We then took our leave of her, heading back out into the hallway.

Having gotten relatively nothing useful from the interview, I could feel myself growing increasingly frustrated that I couldn't tether us to any one clue that would help break the case wide open.

"I need to see Oscar," I said once we were back at the elevator.

Baldwin shot me a look. "What am I? Chopped liver?"

I smiled. "No, Scott. I only want to sit down with him and see if he and I can work our magic and tug out some more details from the ether."

"Is your car here?" Baldwin asked next.

"No. It's at home. Dutch and I rode in together."

"I'll take you to your house so you can get your car and then you can go see Oscar," he said.

"What're you going to do?" I asked.

"I'm gonna call Ji's parents and deliver some really hard news."

"I don't envy you," I told him when the elevator doors parted, and we entered it.

"Me either," Toscano said. "Thank God those days are over for me. Worst part of the job."

Baldwin nodded.

"What about Yuze?" I asked.

Scott said, "When I get back to the office, I'll do a search on his name. We'll track him down today."

"Cool. Text me when you do and, when I get done with Oscar, I'll meet you, and we can talk to him together."

"Perfect," Baldwin said.

"Which one of you two wants me to come with you?" Toscano said.

Poor guy. I could tell he was feeling pretty left out of this investigation. Apparently, you can take the boy out of the FBI, but you can't take the FBI outta the boy.

"Come with me, Mike," I told him, just to throw him a bone. "Three heads are better than two after all."

Toscano brightened and smiled gratefully at me while Baldwin snuck me a subtle *thank you* look. I understood him completely. Toscano had a hard time keeping his investigative instincts in check, and I knew that Baldwin was probably still irritated with Toscano for spilling the beans to Hae about Ji's murder.

Still, if it led to another good clue, maybe it was worth it in the end.

About an hour later, I was with Toscano at Oscar's front door.

Oscar lives in a cute little ranch house that he sweated purchasing. It's his first home, and you can see the pride he has for the place in a perfectly tended yard, two well groomed, white crepe myrtle trees set at an angle to the house, and a hedge that lined the front facade that was perfectly edged and trimmed.

I also knew that the house itself had undergone a few updates with a new front door with frosted glass pane, new shutters, new garage door and inside, a brand-new kitchen done in soft gray-green cabinets with gleaming silver pulls, a white marble countertop, and new wood floors in an ash brown throughout the house.

The place was warm and welcoming and reflected Oscar in every way.

Through the glass door, we heard Oscar call out, "Who's there?" in answer to the ring of the doorbell.

"It's Abby and Toscano!" I called back, raising my voice above the excited yapping of Amigo, Oscar's small brown and white mutt with terrier ears.

"Go around to the back!" Oscar said, raising his own voice. "The rear door's open!"

Toscano and I left the front door and headed to the right of the house where the gate to the fenced-in backyard was. I unhitched the latch and had to close it quickly because out of a doggie door at the back entrance bounded Amigo. "Hey, pup!" I said, bending down to pick him up. Amigo covered my face in kisses and I laughed and carried him with me as we headed to the back door.

Through the kitchen window, I could see Oscar sitting in the living room on the couch, his leg propped up and an assortment of snacks and drinks at his side, along with various prescription bottles too.

I opened the back door, and Toscano and I walked forward through the kitchen to the living room where I set Amigo down and he promptly trotted over to Oscar, leaping up on the couch and snuggling next to his owner.

"Hey guys!" Oscar said jovially. "What's up?"

I took a seat on the couch and immediately trained my radar on Oscar, looking for any sign of infection or trouble with his wound. "That looks like it's healing well," I said, pointing to his thigh. "No sign of infection or leaking of the artery."

He squinted at me before picking Amigo up and placed him in his lap in an obvious effort to cover his private parts. "Careful where you aim that thing, Coop."

I blushed fifty shades of red, and Toscano chuckled heartily.

"I was *not* doing that!" I said. Oscar and I had a great friendship. Occasionally, he likes to tease me that I like him more than just a friend, which always makes me blush. The truth is, I think he's a great-looking guy, but my husband is *the* most beautiful thing I've ever, ever laid eyes on, and that's how I've felt from the beginning. *No* man can compare.

And yet, here I was blushing. Meh . . . *boys!*

I rolled my eyes as both Oscar and Toscano laughed at my discomfort. Levelling my gaze at Toscano I said, "Traitor."

He feigned a gasp, and reached for a throw pillow to cover himself. "Whoa!" he said. "Don't go aiming that thing at me now!"

This sent both Oscar and Toscano into gales of laughter.

I shook my head, rolled my eyes again and stood up. "I'm leaving."

Toscano tossed the throw pillow aside. "Okay, okay, we'll stop."

Oscar shook his head. "Not me. You're freaky with that X-ray vision, lady."

I smirked at him. "It's cute that you think that little bundle of fur would block my radar, honey." And for emphasis I focused on Amigo and smirked like I knew exactly what the puppy was covering.

It was Oscar's turn to blush. "Cut it out, Coop!"

I giggled and curtseyed before sitting down again. "Don't dip your toe in the water if you're afraid of the shark, buddy."

"I got it, I got it," he said, still laughing. "I promise I'll be good." There was a bit of an awkward pause before Oscar added, "So what brings you by?"

"We found Ji," I told him.

Oscar knew that another call had come in with an execution, but I didn't know if he knew we'd discovered the body.

"Where?" he asked.

"On campus. In the Building Works Center. She was in the basement."

"I hate this asshole," Oscar said with a snarl.

"Preachin' to the choir," I told him. "And we've interviewed her roommate. Ji was studying environmental science. She wanted to be a volcanologist."

"Why is that relevant?" Oscar asked.

"Remember the objects on the desk in my vision?" I asked him.

"I do."

"It's my theory that the four objects reflect the ancient elements. The pail of water is obviously water, the flashlight is fire—"

"How'd you get that?"

"We call it a flashlight, but in other English-speaking countries it's called a torch," Toscano said.

"Ahh," Oscar said, then pointed at me. "That's clever. What about the other two objects?"

"The rock is obviously earth, and for some reason, the stuffed bunny must represent air, but I haven't figured out how yet. Still, I'm going with my theory that the four objects represent the ancient elements, and I think this psycho uses them like he's following a ritual when he's selecting his victims."

"Why do you think that?" he asked.

"Simone was studying hydrogeology—a science involving water, and Ji was studying volcanology—a study of fire."

"Wow," Oscar said. "That's an impressive detail, Coop."

I shrugged. "Thanks, but I don't know that it's helped us so far, which is why I wanted to stop by and ping my radar off of you to see if I can't get a little more detail. We need a solid clue, Oscar, and so far, I haven't been able to land on anything that can point us in a clear direction."

"Gotcha," he said before setting Amigo off to his side again then leaning forward. "Okay, so this guy is selecting his victims because they're part of a larger ritual. If it's obvious that he's gathering the four elements by way of executions, then that also means he's got at least two more planned."

I nodded. "That'd be my take as well, which scares the shit out of me."

"I bet," he said. "Can we narrow it down to a field of study he'll target for earth and air? It might allow us to pull together a list of students he could be thinking about targeting."

"I'm hoping that earth is something obvious like geology, but air is going to be tricker. I mean, what field of study could be air?"

"Maybe there's a department of study at UT for renewable energy," Toscano suggested.

Oscar pointed to him. "Yes," he said. "Wind energy, Coop!"

"Hmmm," I said. "That could be it."

Oscar lifted his iPad from the table next to him and began to tap at the screen. I knew he was looking for a field of study at UT that matched our theory, so I waited in silence.

"In the College of Natural Sciences there's the general study of environmental science," he said. "That includes courses in renewable energy."

"Does it say how many students are in that field of study?" I asked, dreading another long list to comb through when we didn't even have a name to go by.

"It doesn't, but it does say that the College of Natural Sciences has over twelve thousand students."

"Ugh," I groaned. And then I thought back to the symbol for air that lay on the desk in my vision. The stuffed bunny just didn't fit the narrative of the study of wind power. And I wasn't even sure that the College of Natural Sciences held a student that the killer would target next.

"There has to be another way to narrow things down," I complained. "We're thinking too broadly."

Oscar and Toscano nodded. "We should look at the two vics we already know about," Oscar said. "What do *they* have in common?"

I pointed at him. "Yes! Yes, that's where we should start! There has to be some connection between the girls for them to have been selected by our unsub."

"What do we know about Simone and Ji?" Oscar asked.

"Both are women," Toscano said, leading with the most obvious.

Oscar nodded and looked at me. "Is this guy focusing only on women, Coop?"

"Yeah. I think so. And another thing Simone and Ji have in common is that they're both smart. And accomplished. Simone was working on a project with Bono—"

"Hold on," Oscar interrupted, his eyes wide. "You mean *the* Bono?"

I nodded. "From U2. Yes, *that* Bono."

"Wow," he said. "What's the project?"

"Simone wanted to bring water to villagers in Sudan, and I know from reading about him that Bono has been funding water projects all over Africa for years."

"Amazing," he said. "And you're right. That's an incredible accomplishment for a woman still in college."

"Agreed. Ji was also quite accomplished. She was battling it out for the valedictorian spot in her major with another student."

"Got it," Oscar said. "So, this guy hates women, especially smart and accomplished women."

"They're also both women of color," Toscano said.

My intuition binged, bigtime. "Yes," I said. "There's something with that, Mike."

"What do you mean?" Oscar asked.

A swastika bloomed in my mind's eye. "This guy's a racist," I said, curling my lip in disgust.

"Not really surprising," Toscano said.

I frowned. "For sure," I acknowledged. "But I think he's specifically targeting these women *because* they're women of color."

"You mean he's not looking at any White women as possible targets."

I weighed that question against my intuition for a moment, just to make sure. "No," I said, staring off into space while I sorted through the messages lighting up my mind's eye. "He's looking to make a statement. A big statement. This guy feels like he's writing or has written a manifesto. I get the distinct sense that he's talked himself into a warped view of the world, and these murders feel like the proof he's trying to provide to the community to show that he's right."

My vision focused again on Oscar, and his expression was grim. "Shit," he said. "Coop, if we don't catch him in time, will he stop at two more victims?"

I bit my lip. The answer was clear, but I didn't want to give voice to it. Finally, I said, "No. No he won't, Oscar. My gut says that he'll keep on going until he's caught or killed."

The room was silent for a long couple of moments.

Oscar was the first to speak. "We still need to dig into Simone and Ji's lives. Maybe they knew each other."

I smirked at him. "We?"

"Yeah, *we*, Coop. I'm not totally sidelined. I can start digging from here."

"You should be totally sidelined," I said. "Jesus, bud, you almost *died* yesterday."

He grinned at me. "Nah, Coop. It ain't like that. I'm like a cat. I got nine lives."

I shook my head but couldn't help grinning at him. "What life are you on, anyway, assuming you're keeping count?"

"Five," he said without hesitation.

Toscano and I laughed. Then I got to my feet and pointed at Toscano. "Come on. Let's head back to the bureau and see if we can't hone in on the next victim . . ."

My voice trailed off as an image burst into my mind's eye. It was so sharp and clear that it startled me.

"Coop?" Oscar said.

"Abby?" Toscano said.

I blinked and shook my head a little to clear it. "I know this is gonna sound weird, guys, but the next victim has something to do with a bobcat."

It was their turn to blink at me.

"Explain," Oscar said.

"When I spoke about the next victim, the original vision I'd gotten about this unsub came into my mind, but this time, the scary looking lion was attacking a bobcat."

"Yikes," Oscar said. "What does it mean?"

I recalled the image in my mind again. "I don't know. I want to say that the bobcat might be a mascot, but so far this asshole has chosen women from UT. Their mascot is the longhorn, so maybe she's not from UT."

Oscar snapped his fingers and pointed at me. Then he focused on his iPad which was still next to him and he began to quickly type something on it. "Whoa," he said, his eyes still focused on the screen.

"What?" Toscano and I said at the same time.

Oscar swiveled the screen toward me. I squinted at the tablet and saw Toscano lean in to look as well. Oscar had pulled up a webpage which featured the rough outline of a snarling bobcat in gold and red and below it was the address for Texas State University in San Marcos, thirty miles away.

"Whoa!" I said, taking the iPad out of his hands to study it. "Great job, Oscar!"

"Don't congratulate me yet," he said. "The only thing we can speculate is that this guy is gonna target a girl from TSU."

"We should call their campus police and give them a heads up," Toscano said. "Maybe they can even offer up some information."

Again, Oscar frowned. "How do we convince them that they might have a problem?"

"What do you mean?" I asked.

"Coop, the only thing we have to offer them as proof is your vision, and I doubt they'll take it seriously."

"We still need to call them," I insisted. "I mean, we don't have to tell them about me. We could simply do it as a courtesy call, you know, letting them know there've been two murders on the UT campus, and we have a suspicion that the killer is getting ready to move to another campus, so we're reaching out to all the major colleges and universities in the area, blah, blah, blah."

Oscar nodded, waved at me to hand him back my tablet, then reached for his phone. Glancing at the tablet's screen while dialing the number for TSU, he said, "I'll tell them just like you said. Only, I'll probably leave out one or two blah, blahs."

I smiled. "Good compromise."

CHAPTER 9

We got back to the office in time to meet Baldwin before he scuttled out the door to go interview Yuze Tian—the young man competing with Ji for the top spot in their class.

"Mike!" Brice called from his glass enclosed office when he spotted us. He then waved his hand in a come here motion and Toscano left my side to go speak with Brice.

Meanwhile, Baldwin placed two fingers on my elbow and whispered, "Let's go."

I walked along with him toward the door. "We're going without Mike?" I asked.

Baldwin nodded. "Hae made a call to her mother about Ji, and in turn, her mother, Mrs. Hak, told Ji's mother, Mrs. Jeong, that her daughter had been murdered before I had the chance to tell her. She was an absolute wreck when she answered the call and hung up on me the minute I tried to question her about her daughter."

"And you blame Mike," I said. "He told Hae that Ji was dead before we'd had the chance to tell her parents."

"Yep," Baldwin said. "I don't want the same thing to happen when we interview Yuze."

I glanced over my shoulder as we exited out the front door to see Toscano with his back to us, standing in front of Brice's desk while the two chatted. "He's gonna be bummed when he finds out we left without him," I said.

Baldwin was unmoved. "Don't care," he said. "Toscano isn't an active agent anymore, and he's only here and inside this investigation as a courtesy. If you want my opinion, he should've been kept out from the get-go."

"Why don't you like him?" I asked.

"Because he's still acting like an SAIC," he said, using the acronym for Special Agent in Charge. "It's inappropriate. He needs to butt out."

I was reminded that, while I genuinely liked Scott Baldwin, sometimes it was hard to investigate cases with him because he was so by the book that it often made things more difficult.

And I realized that was the reason I liked Oscar so much. He was willing to bend a few rules now and again as long as doing so didn't actively break the law and we got the results we were after.

Baldwin and I made small talk on the way to the address that he'd pulled for Yuze. When we arrived, Baldwin turned to me and said, "Remember, don't let him know that Ji is dead unless I tell him first, okay?"

I saluted him. "Yes, captain."

He rolled his eyes. "Don't make me regret bringing you along, Cooper."

I offered him a winning smile. "And miss out on all this charm? Perish the thought, Scott!"

He shook his head, but I could see the slight grin before he turned away and got out of the car. I followed suit and looked up at the apartment building where Yuze lived.

"Yikes," I said, taking it in. It was a grimy, dingy place, covered in weather-worn clapboard and a roof that had definitely seen better days.

"At least we know the rent is cheap," he said. "Come on. He's on the second floor in apartment 12B."

I followed Baldwin inside the building and over to the stairs, noting there was no elevator even though the building was four stories high.

Once we arrived at Yuze's door, Baldwin knocked three times firmly, and I marveled at the way all LEOs seemed to knock in the same manner. Three hard booms to let everyone inside know they'd best come open the door. Quick.

And quick it was, opened by a gaunt-looking young man

with a round face, square chin, and an enormous Adam's apple, dressed in a white T-shirt and gray sweatpants. He looked back and forth between us, then focused on Baldwin who was considerably taller and far more intimidating than me.

"Hello," he said, then immediately followed that with, "Yes?"

"Yuze Tian?" Baldwin asked.

The young man trembled. He could smell trouble on us. "Yes?" he repeated.

Baldwin flipped out his badge. "Agent Baldwin with the FBI." Motioning to me with his thumb he added, "This is my associate, Abigail Cooper. We're here to ask you some questions."

Yuze's trembling intensified. His face became ashen, and it was obvious that he thought he was in deep trouble. "No," he said softly, shaking his head. "I have visa! I have student visa!"

Baldwin's brow furrowed. "We're not here about your immigration status—" he tried to explain, but Yuze had already scuttled back into his apartment, leaving the door open. We watched as he began to riffle through papers stacked high on a lopsided desk.

"It's here!" he said. "You'll see. I have student visa!"

I looked pointedly at Baldwin. He'd scared this poor kid to death! "Mr. Tian," I said taking a step into the apartment. "Please, we're not here to question you about your visa. We need to talk to you about Ji-Hye."

Yuze triumphantly pulled out his multicolored card and held it up to us. I think it was then that he realized what I'd said. "Ji?" he said. "She was born here."

"Yes, we know," I said. "I hate to be the one to tell you this, Mr. Tian . . ."

Baldwin cleared his throat loudly, giving me a warning to tread carefully.

I ignored him and continued by saying, "I'm afraid that your friend Ji was kidnapped the day before yesterday, and we're looking for information that might lead us to her kidnapper."

Yuze blinked a dozen times, as if I'd said something that his mind couldn't translate. "I don't understand," he said. "How could she be kidnapped?"

"That's what we'd like to try to find out," Baldwin said, tucking his badge into his pocket and waving a hand at the threshold. "May I come in?"

Agents always had to ask for permission to come inside a witness's house, unless he or she had probable cause. As a civilian, however, I could head right in through any open door I liked.

Yuze nodded at Baldwin, and he came in to stand next to me. Meanwhile, Yuze continued to tremble. "I didn't kidnap Ji," he said, grabbing his right forearm with his left hand.

I nodded. "We're not saying you did. We just want to ask you a few questions about who she might've been associating with, or if she ever mentioned to you that someone was bothering or harassing her."

Yuze took two steps back to press himself against the wall. He continued to hug himself and stare at us with big, frightened eyes. "I don't know about her," he said. "We only took some classes together."

"You never spoke to her?" I asked.

Yuze thought about that for a moment. "Yes, I talked with her, but I never heard her say bad things about any person."

"Do you know any person that might've had it out for Ji?"

"Out for?" he asked. English was obviously his second language, and he was quite fluent in it, which impressed me.

"Yes," I said. "You know, someone who might be jealous of her or wish for her to be frightened or in pain."

"In pain?" he asked, and his trembling inched up one more notch. "You didn't say she's in pain!"

"We don't know that she is," I said gently. "But someone abducted her, Mr. Tian. Someone who probably knew her schedule and her routine."

Yuze shook his head vigorously. "No," he said. "She's a

good girl. Maybe she is just with a friend, and you only think she's been kidnapped."

"What friend would she be with?" I asked carefully. Hae had told us that Ji hadn't had any friends besides her.

Yuze shrugged. "I don't know. You should ask Hae Hak. That's her roommate. She would know."

I nodded, and Baldwin scowled. We weren't getting anywhere with this guy. "When was the last time you saw, Ji, Mr. Tian?" he asked next.

Yuze shrugged again. "The day before yesterday. We had a chemistry midterm together. She finished first." He frowned at this statement, as if it brought him shame.

"Ji is very smart, I hear," I said.

Yuze nodded. "We're the top students in our class. We have the same GPA. We both want to be valedictorian."

"So, you saw her leave the classroom after turning in her test?"

"Yes, but she waited for me outside the classroom so we could compare answers."

"How long did you guys talk?" I asked.

"Maybe . . . five or ten minutes. We stopped talking when some of the other top students began coming out."

"Did you and Ji part ways then?" I asked.

He nodded.

"Did Ji say where she was going next?"

"Lunch," he said. "She asked me to come, but I had to get a new tire for my bike." He pointed to the corner of his tiny apartment where a bicycle leaned up against the wall. The front tire looked new.

"Do you know where she might've gone to have lunch?"

Yuze nodded again. "She always goes to the same place. Oseyo on Cesar Chavez."

I didn't know the place, but I was very interested in seeing if Ji had ever made it there. Something told me she hadn't.

"Thank you, Mr. Tian," Baldwin said. He seemed satisfied Yuze had nothing to do with Ji's disappearance, which I also believed.

136

Still, I had one more question for him. "Mr. Tian, do you think Ji knew another student by the name of Simone Shaw?"

The young man blinked at me again. "No," he said simply.

"No, she didn't know Simone? Or you don't know if she knew her?"

"I don't know who Ji knows," he said. "I just know her from the same classes we take. That's all."

I nodded. I believed him. "Thank you," I said, then I offered him my card. "If anything comes to you that you think might be important about Ji's kidnapper, please call me at the bottom number on this card."

He took it and nodded, adding a slight bow.

We left Yuze's place and headed down the stairs to the parking lot without speaking. Once we were in the car, Baldwin turned to me and said, "Oseyo?"

"Yep. Hopefully, the restaurant has a surveillance camera, and we can see if she made it there and if she was with anyone."

"My thoughts exactly," Baldwin said.

He plugged the address for the Korean restaurant into his phone, and we were off.

The little restaurant was fairly close to campus, and just up the street from a bus stop, so Ji wouldn't have had a problem getting there.

Baldwin found a place to park, and we headed inside. We were greeted at the door by a small Asian woman with dark circles under her eyes and the faraway stare of someone perpetually tired.

"Two for lunch today?" she asked, grabbing two menus.

Baldwin shook his head and out came the badge. The woman's detached gaze got focused real quick. "Agent Scott Baldwin with the F.B.I., ma'am. We're here to ask you and your staff if you saw this woman . . ." Baldwin paused while he rooted around in his inside pocket and came up with a photo of Ji's student ID.

Holding it out for her, the hostess leaned forward to look, and she immediately recognized Ji because she began to nod her head. "That's Ji-Hye," she said. "Is she in trouble?"

Her worried expression told me that the woman knew and had liked Ji.

"She might be," Baldwin said. "We have a report that she's gone missing, and we're retracing her steps. The last place she's known to have been is here. Do you remember seeing her the day before yesterday?"

The woman put a protective hand across her heart. "No," she said. "And I remember because Ji always comes for lunch on Wednesday, but this week she didn't. I thought maybe she was sick or something and she'd be back soon."

I glanced at Baldwin knowingly. I knew she hadn't made it to the restaurant, which meant Ji had been abducted somewhere between her last class before lunch and catching the bus to Oseyo.

And then my radar binged, and I got a hunch that I knew I needed to follow through on, because when I thought about it, abducting Ji on campus seemed super risky to me. The place was a beehive of activity, especially around lunchtime, so my thinking was that someone had to have either followed her here or had been lying in wait.

"Do you by any chance have a security camera out in front of your restaurant?" I asked.

The woman blinked at me, but then she nodded. "Yes," she said. "We had some trouble last year, someone broke in and tried to steal the cash register, so my husband put up the video camera."

"Do you think you still have the footage from Wednesday?" I asked next.

The woman nodded. "It saves to the computer for thirty days, then gets erased."

"May we see it?" Baldwin said, taking his cue from me.

Behind us, the door opened and in came a group of four people, all chatting in Korean. Our hostess eyed them, then us, then back to them again. "Wait here and let me seat these customers, then I will take you to the computer," she said.

We stepped to the side, and the hostess hurried to get the

four seated with menus and glasses of water. Once they were settled, she motioned us to follow her into the back and through a door that opened to the kitchen which was bustling with activity and awash in delicious smells.

My stomach rumbled, but I ignored it for the moment and focused on the task at hand.

Our hostess barked out something in Korean to one of the servers, who jumped at the sound and then hustled out the door, no doubt to take over the care of the foursome that'd just entered.

At last, we arrived at a closed door, and the woman unlocked and opened it, waving us inside. We stood next to her in the cramped office while she took a seat and lifted the lid of a laptop sitting on a desk. "Here," she said, after she'd pulled up the footage from Wednesday. "You can look. I have to go back to the front."

Baldwin nodded. "Thank you, ma'am," he said. "We won't be long."

She nodded and bustled past us out the door. Baldwin sat down and scrolled his finger across the mouse pad, moving the footage forward from early in the morning to eleven a.m. And then we allowed the recording to play out in real time.

Several pedestrians walked past the restaurant, and a few more came inside, but there was no sign of Ji until right around eleven forty-five a.m. And it was such a quick glance of her, that I almost missed it, and Baldwin didn't see it at all until I pointed it out.

"There!" I said, pointing to the far right of the screen. "Scott, go back a few seconds."

Baldwin tapped at the timeline and brought us back too far, so we had to wait in a tense silence until Ji showed up again. "There!" I repeated.

Baldwin hit pause, and we both squinted at the screen. "That's her, all right," he said.

The quality of the video was terrific, probably because the camera was only a year old. There was no grainy quality like we'd seen in many older camera footage.

"So, she did make it here," I said.

Baldwin tapped and untapped the pause button to slow down Ji's movements frame by frame. She seemed happy as she came into view, a smile on her face, no doubt still feeling good about her efforts on the chemistry test. She took three or four steps into the video's circumference, and then she stopped abruptly, and looked over her shoulder.

She then turned around to face the way she'd come from and cocked her head to one side. And then she walked back out of the frame again.

"She knew him," I whispered.

"You think that was our guy?" Baldwin asked.

I nodded. "Definitely. He called out to her to get her attention, and then he coaxed her to come to him."

Baldwin grunted, then tapped the footage forward frame by frame while we looked to see if Ji ever came into camera view again, but she didn't, and we probably scrolled forward twenty minutes or so.

"She was taken from out front," I said, looking toward my left in the direction of the front of the restaurant.

Baldwin got up from the chair and said, "Wait here a sec." And with that he headed out the office door while I was left to wonder what he was up to.

A few moments later he returned with the owner who quickly sat down in the chair and began to fiddle with the computer. From over her shoulder, I watched as she saved a copy of the footage and sent it to the email address on Baldwin's business card.

"There," she said. "You're good."

"Thank you, Mrs. Gwan," he said.

"You find, Ji, okay?" she said, getting up and looking at us with worry in her eyes.

I cast my gaze to the ground so that she wouldn't see the sadness in my eyes that was still so acute from hearing Ji's terrified voice, right before she was murdered.

"We'll do our best," Baldwin said softly. There was a note of compassion in his tone that I think I'd only heard a half dozen times before when he was speaking to a witness, and it surprised me that he allowed himself to voice it to her when he'd been so, "Just the facts, ma'am," earlier.

We left the restaurant by retracing our steps through the kitchen and into the now bustling restaurant that was nearly full of patrons. If it'd been less busy, I would've asked Scott to let me order something to go, but with the lunch rush, it'd likely take too long.

Once we were back out on the street, Scott and I walked to the spot where Ji had come into view of the camera, and we stood where she had, looking back toward the bus stop.

The view wasn't much to look at; the bus stop was fifty yards away in front of a parking garage that took up a huge section of the block.

I pointed to it. "He was there," I said.

"The parking garage?" Baldwin asked.

"Yeah. He came by car, probably surveilling Ji on campus until she made it onto the bus, then he beat the bus here, parked in that garage, and got out to wait. Once she was off the bus and headed to Oseyo, he called out to her and got her to come to him. And that's when he kidnapped her."

Baldwin inhaled deeply and released it in a tired sigh. "Come on," he said. "Let's check it out."

We headed down the street to the parking garage, which was typical for the structure—brown brick with gray mortar and a damp, cavelike interior. "There," I said, pointing to a small square section of the garage to the left and just past the ticket gate where the stairs to the upper floors were. Walking forward to prove my point, I went right up to the door of the stairs and stepped to the side of the door. "He could've stood here, completely unnoticed," I said to Baldwin, who'd followed me.

Scott sidled up next to me and looked around. From this vantage point we could clearly see the bus stop. He then moved from my side over to the entrance of the ramp leading to the first level and he began scanning the ceiling.

I knew he must be looking for security cameras, and if we

could only find this guy on tape, we might get lucky and track his ass down before he had a chance to hurt anyone else.

Abruptly, Baldwin pointed to the section of ceiling to the right of the ramp. "There," he said.

I looked over and saw the camera. "Awesome," I said. "How do we get the footage?"

"I'll call the management company," he said, taking out his phone to take a picture of the signage posted to the front of the wall at the top of the first ramp.

He then pivoted and moved back out to the sidewalk again, and I followed. "Bingo," he said, pointing across the street to an ATM machine.

"You need some cash?" I asked.

"No, Cooper. All ATMs come equipped with cameras that run constantly. I can call the bank and have them send me the footage from the timestamp on the video from Oseyo. With any luck, we'll get Ji's abduction on film."

I could feel a little of the tension I'd carried since the beginning of this case ease from my shoulders. We were on to something. I could tell.

A bit later, Baldwin and I got back to the office. Toscano was the first to greet us. "You two left without me," he complained.

"Sorry," Baldwin said, and everyone knew his tone was in the "not sorry" zone.

And that sort of got Toscano's dander up. "You got a problem with me, Agent Baldwin?"

"Yep," he said.

My eyes widened. The tension between these two was palpable.

"Uh-huh, and what might that be?" Toscano shot back.

"With all due respect," Baldwin began, and again, everybody within earshot new Baldwin wasn't about to lend Toscano *any* respect. "You have no business sticking your nose into an active investigation. You're *retired*, sir. And today you got in our way and made my job harder."

Toscano blushed a deep red hue.

"Hey guys," I said, trying to insert myself in the middle before this escalated. "How about we focus on the present rather than the past?"

Both Toscano and Baldwin seemed to ignore me while they locked eyes and wore matching scowls.

"You're talking about Hae Hak?" Toscano said.

"Damn right I'm talking about her," Baldwin snapped. "You had no business telling her that Ji was dead, and when I tried to make the notification to the family, you made it harder because Miss Hak had already called her parents who then called Ji's parents. When I reached her, Ji's mother was inconsolable, and that's on you!"

"Boys, boys—!" I tried.

"Well, *you* weren't getting anywhere pussyfootin' around the roommate," Toscano said, and while his tone was considerably quieter, it was no less threatening.

Baldwin's eyes narrowed, and I could tell this was going to continue to escalate unless someone intervened, so I stepped right between the two men—a tight fit—and put a hand on each of their chests. "We found the location where Ji was abducted," I said loudly. "We think we got the killer on film!"

Gazes that were already pointed in our direction became even more curious, and Agent Cox and Williams got up from their desks and walked over to us.

A quick glance toward the back of the room told me that Dutch was busy with someone on the phone, and likely hadn't heard the commotion, and Brice wasn't in the office.

Toscano was the first to blink. "You did?" he asked me.

I nodded. "Scott has to make a call or two, but we're pretty confident we'll have the actual abduction on film. And if we have that, then we're one step closer to nailing this asshole."

All eyes turned expectantly to Baldwin. He glared at me for a moment, then said, "Guess I have some calls to make."

It took a while, but Scott was finally able to obtain the footage from both the bank and the parking garage. The footage from the garage came in first, and, frustratingly, there was no sign of a single male driving up the ramp, and no sign of our culprit lurking in the shadows of the parking garage around the time that Ji was abducted.

I figured I must've been wrong about how the whole thing went down until we got the footage from the ATM machine across the street.

"Whoa," I said, as we watched the video from the bank. "He's right there!"

On the screen was a man, probably in the five-ten range, wearing a hoody, baggy jeans, and a pair of checkered Vans. The hoody completely obscured the features of his face, which it seemed he was careful not to point toward the ATM machine.

There was no doubt that he was our guy because of the way he walked; hunched forward with the hood of his sweatshirt pulled down low to cover his face. He strolled forward with his hands in his pockets, then headed toward the corner of the parking garage where he could lie in wait for Ji.

He'd come at the parking garage to wait in the exact spot I'd said he did, on foot. "He must've parked somewhere else, to avoid the garage's camera," I said.

"If he even came by car," Cox replied.

We fell silent again as we waited through the next several minutes until the bus came into frame. Our view of the garage was blocked by the bus for several moments, and when it finally moved, allowing us to watch what happened next, Ji was already turning toward the man in the hoody.

She began to walk toward him and he toward her. There was no doubt she knew him because there was nothing tense in her stance or her walk. When she reached him, however, he pulled his hand out of the hoody's pocket and revealed a gun.

Ji stiffened, and her fear was palpable. He leaned toward her and seemed to speak covertly to her; she nodded, and the pair moved off down the street with him wrapping an arm around her while he pressed the muzzle of the gun up against her ribcage.

The pair was out of view within moments, and there were no other clues that could point us toward his identity or even any further sighting of Ji.

"He knew where all the cameras were hidden," Cox said.

Baldwin grunted. "Clever little rat, I'll give him that."

"The Vans could be something," Toscano pointed out.

"How so?" Williams asked.

"My team and I developed some software back in the day that could use the background to pinpoint an unsub's height, weight, and shoe size. If we can figure out what size shoe he wore, we can start to sift through the sale of checkered Vans that fit that size."

Williams blew out a breath. "That'd be a lot of sales."

"Not if he got them in Austin," Toscano insisted. "There might be a couple dozen at most."

Baldwin considered Toscano for a long moment, and I could see he seemed to regret his earlier grumpy response to the veteran agent. "Could you get your hands on that software?" he asked.

"Sure," Toscano said, without any hint that he might be holding a grudge. "Get me a couple stills from that footage, and I'll send it to my guy in D.C. We should have a rough description of height, weight, and shoe size by tomorrow morning."

"What if he bought the Vans online?" I asked. Practically nobody under twenty-five went to a retail outlet anymore. The kids these days all order most of their stuff online.

"We can look at shipping addresses, giving shipments to UT special priority."

"Good," I said. "That's good, Mike. Let's make that happen."

CHAPTER 10

Dutch and I drove home that evening without a single mention of the day's events. I liked that about many of our drives heading home together. Sometimes there was just this unspoken agreement between us that we didn't talk about work. We talked about us.

Most of those conversations tended toward the distant future—where we'd live when we retired, the places we'd travel when we had the time, who would age more gracefully, (him, like, duh) and who would be the first to shake their fist at a group of kids in the neighborhood and shout, "*Get off my lawn!*" (me, like, double duh).

Tonight, Dutch kept it light and humorous, by asking, between the two of us, who would be the first to let themselves go. "Totally unfair," I told him when he posed the question.

"Why is that unfair?"

"Because you're naturally breathtaking, and I have to work at it, which means I'll be the first to abandon the effort."

He chuckled. "Edgar," he said. "It's cute you think you traded up, but I *promise* you, I'm the envy of all my friends, and hands down I win the *Trophy Wife* award at my regular poker games."

"You play poker with Brice and Oscar," I countered. "And as Candice is a whole lot hotter than me, and Nikki also brings an A game to the table, I doubt that's true."

"First of all," he began, navigating *that* mine field carefully, "Candice is—at best—your equal, but personally, I don't think anyone can hold a candle to you.

"Second, I wasn't talking about my poker games with those two, and yes, you're right, they're biased, but that's beside the point. I was referring to the guys in the hood."

Recently, Dutch had made an effort to get to know our neighbors a little better, and he'd gotten chummy with a couple of guys on our street.

I perked up a little. "You boys talk about how hot your wives are?"

He glanced at me with an *Are you kidding?* look. "We're men, Edgar. Of course we talk about how hot our wives are. We talk about how hot any of the women in the neighborhood are."

I blinked at him. "You think some of the women in our neighborhood are hot?"

He leveled another look at me, but then he softened. "I think some of the women in our neighborhood are attractive, sure, but no one, Abigail, and I mean, *no one* compares to you. You take my breath away. You make me feel whole. You're my world. My rock. My day and my night. I love you down to my DNA and even now, ten years on, I still can't believe how much you turn me the fuck on."

His eyes were smoldering, and his voice had thickened, hinting at his deep, deep desire for me.

So, in response, I crossed my arms and said, "*Which* of these women, *exactly*, do you find *attractive*, Dutch?"

He sighed and pulled his smoldering gaze away to stare dully out the windshield. "You're a lot of work sometimes, cupcake."

"And sometimes, pushing your buttons is just too irresistible, cowboy," I said, giggling. Then I caressed his cheek with my hand and added, "Now get us home so you can push a few of mine, if you get my drift."

Dutch growled low and seductively, before stomping on the accelerator to rocket us forward.

A bit later, he proved that he definitely got my drift.

Very early the next morning, Dutch and I were both just waking up, our limbs tangled around each other, each needing the warmth and closeness to push back against the horrors of the past few weeks when a pounding knock exploded into the silence of our intimate world.

"Who the hell is that?" I gasped, when Dutch and I both let go of each other to sit bolt upright.

He glanced at the clock. It was five-twenty a.m. "Someone with bad news."

Dutch clicked on a light and threw off the covers, grabbing the pajama bottoms that lay on the floor next to the bed. I did the same with my own pajama bottoms, but added a top, and we both headed out of the master bedroom, which fed directly into the kitchen, then out to the short hallway leading to the front of the house. Eggy and Tuttle were at the door, barking away—ever the protective duo.

I whistled to them, and they stopped the racket and came running over to me while Dutch continued forward to answer the door.

Even before he got there, the pounding started again.

Bam! Bam! Bam! Bam!

Only cops knock like that.

"Hold your horses!" Dutch said, reaching for the knob. He opened the door to reveal Toscano standing there impatiently.

"What's happened?" I asked, because something definitely had happened, and by the look on Toscano's face, it was nothing good.

Without even speaking, he crossed the threshold and held his phone out toward us. Tapping the play icon on his phone he said, "Listen."

"Hey, Mike," came a male voice. He sounded friendly enough. "Hopefully this'll wake you up, 'cause I'm really enjoying your podcast, bro, and I'd love to see it back on the air. Super bummed you took it down. Simone would've liked it that she was so popular.

"But I've got another caller for you, Mike, and this one, you should really think about putting on the air. Sydney wants to be famous too. And I'm thinking that it'd be a shame not to grant her a last wish. So, here's my proposal; you go back on the air this morning and take her call. If not, I'm gonna take a video of her being slowly taken apart, piece by piece, an inch at a time. I've got the pruning shears, knife, and saw all sharpened and ready to go. Oh, and I sent you a little gift to show you how serious I am."

I could feel the color drain from my face, and I stared at Toscano with wide, horrified eyes. He paused the recording and began to lift an evidence bag out of his pocket. I turned my head away before I could see what it contained, but I heard Dutch say, "Jesus . . ."

"Found it on my windshield right before I headed here," Toscano said. "I've already taken a print and woke Baldwin up to check if she's in the system. Maybe we'll get lucky."

"We won't," I said, feeling the heaviness in the pit of my stomach. "Can you please put it away?" I added, referring to whatever finger was in the evidence bag.

I heard some crinkling, and then Toscano said, "It's back in my pocket, Abby. There's more to the voice mail. You ready to listen?"

I brought my chin back to center and nodded.

Mike hit the play button on his phone again, and the sick fuck's tinny voice echoed out from the speaker. "If you're not back on the air by six-thirty a.m., I'm gonna move on to her ring finger and every ten minutes after that, I'll cut off another piece of her. Oh, and Abby Cooper, the super psychic, better be on with you. I'm loving proving to your listeners that she's a total fraud, Mike. She's getting what she deserves too."

Mike clicked off the voicemail and stared at us, and if the call wasn't enough of a horror show, his pained expression only intensified the emotion of the moment.

"Fuck!" Dutch whispered. Then he turned his gaze to me.

I was already crying. I knew it'd be my call whether or not to put us back on the air. Hell, this bastard knew it'd be my decision to make too, which is why he'd left Toscano the voice message. He wanted me to know that the other adults in the room weren't going to weigh in. That it'd be my decision how Sydney died.

And die she would, there was no doubt in my mind or in the ether that her life would end today, and there wasn't a goddamn thing I could do about it except either listen to her suffering mentally for a short period of time while she asked me to solve her murder, or physically suffer horribly for a long, long time. This guy could keep her alive, while cutting off small body parts for *days* if he wanted to. And I knew he wanted to.

I also knew that he understood that if I chose to spare Sydney the torture he intended for her, I'd be eliminating the opportunity to find her. If I allowed him to cut off pieces of her to give us time to find her, then we theoretically might be able to do that, but how long would that take and how much of Sydney would even be left by the time we got to her.

But my gut said we wouldn't get to her in time to spare her hours and hours of unbearable torture and even then, my gut insisted that Sydney was already as good as dead.

"If he wants you two back on the air by six-thirty, that means he wants to avoid any possible witnesses or passersby. He's gotta be someplace where he could be discovered."

Toscano nodded. "Yeah, but where?"

Dutch turned to me and I could only stare at him while my heart began to thud hard against my ribcage.

"Can your intuition give us any clue about where she might be?" Toscano asked, and his tone hinted that he didn't expect me to perform a miracle, but he knew I should at least try.

I bit my lip and wiped away a tear. Goddamn this son of a bitch! Taking a shuddering breath, I tried to settle my frantic thoughts and calm myself so that I could then reach out and see if I could feel Sydney.

It took a minute, but I finally got there and extended my radar, searching for her in the ether. What I connected with was an individual who was so panicked that I couldn't get past the emotion. There was also pain there, and my radar was drawn to her right hand and a sense of heat, which is how I sense pain, radiating off that hand in such a powerful manner that I winced.

I tried to expand my radar out a bit to get a feel for her location, but all that came back to me was a sense of decomposition, and I didn't know what to make of that, other than to feel a sense of revulsion.

I opened my eyes and found Dutch and Toscano staring at me intently. "She's in a lot of pain," I whispered, the tears once again sliding down my cheeks. "I can't see where she is, but there's this sense of . . ."

"Sense of what?" Dutch asked gently.

I shook my head. "I don't know how to describe it, Dutch. There's something like decay around her."

"Other bodies?" Toscano asked.

My gaze settled on him. "I don't know, Mike. Honestly. I just don't know."

"Do you think she's on campus?" he pressed.

I stared up at the ceiling. He was putting a lot of pressure on me and my intuition doesn't work well under duress. "Maybe," I said. It was so odd, because I felt like Sydney was on campus but not anywhere obvious, and I couldn't connect the sense of decay around her with anything that felt recognizable on a university's campus.

"Okay," Toscano said, and I could tell he intended to continue to pressure me. "If she is on campus, can you tell if she's in a building and what floor she's on?"

I lifted my gaze to Dutch, silently pleading with him for help.

"If her radar came up with that kind of detail, Mike, she would've led with it. She's not a substitute for Google. You can't just plug in a query to her brain and expect a Google map's location."

Toscano looked like he wanted to continue to press the point, and irritated as I was that he seemed undeterred from pressuring me, I still understood it. What I do sometimes looks like magic, and the idea that my intuition can at times come up with astonishing detail and at other times come up with bubkes, but that's simply how it works.

"The more pressure you put on me, Mike, the more it'll make my radar shut down. And I'm sorry for that, but I've been continually traumatized for several weeks *straight* and I can feel myself shutting down as a result. It's a natural mechanism born out of self-preservation."

To his credit, Toscano appeared chagrined. "I'm sorry, Abby. I know this has been harder on you than anyone else on the team. I'll back off."

I sighed in relief, but still felt guilty for not being able to come up with an answer that would save Sydney. "I'll keep my radar open," I promised. "If I get anything that seems like it could pinpoint her location, I'll call it out."

Toscano nodded then looked at Dutch who then looked to me. "How do you want to handle this, Edgar?" he asked gently.

I wanted to scream, because I knew that whatever happened next to Sydney would be my call. And that broke me. I shook my head and leaned in to bury my face against Dutch's chest, and I couldn't tamp down the sob that escaped my throat.

He wrapped his arms around me and held me. Kissing the top of my head he said, "I know, dollface. This is so unfair and it must feel like the weight of the world is on your shoulders." I nodded and then Dutch pulled me away from his chest to grip my shoulders, dip his chin, and look me in the eye. "Whatever you want to do is the right decision, Abby. Know that. *Know* that."

I swallowed hard, trying to get past the guilt of deciding Sydney's fate. There was no option that felt like the right option. But I finally choked out, "We go back on the air."

He didn't say a word. He merely nodded.

Turning his attention back to Toscano, he said, "How long ago did that voice mail come in?"

"A little after four a.m. I heard my phone buzz, but I was pretty out of it, and I didn't check to see who'd called until about thirty minutes ago. I got here as quick as I could."

"Does the rest of the team know?"

Toscano nodded. "I called Baldwin first to send him a scan of the fingerprint, and he said he'd let everyone else know to get to the office asap."

Wiping my cheeks I asked, "Can we even get back on the air in time?" And by that I meant, in time to hasten Sydney's execution so that she didn't suffer the additional trauma of having her ring finger removed and possibly another digit depending on how long we took.

"If we hurry," Toscano said. "I can cobble together some equipment at the bureau office, and I have my laptop with all the needed software."

I nodded. "I'm gonna change. It'll take me three minutes. Tops."

"If we have an hour," Dutch said before I could rush away, "then we should send an alert out to CPD to do a grid search of UT's campus. Maybe they can find this guy in time to save Sydney."

I nodded again, but I knew that, even if CPD found Sydney and her abductor in some abandoned room somewhere on campus, if this unsub saw or heard even a hint that the cavalry was closing in, he'd shoot Sydney dead before any LEO had a chance to break the door in.

Still, I didn't want any chance, no matter how slim, to escape our effort, so I said, "We should also call over to Texas State and have their CPD look for her."

"The bobcat," Toscano said, referring to the school's mascot.

I nodded.

Toscano turned his attention to his phone. "I'm on it. You two get dressed, and we'll be ready to roll."

He didn't have to tell me twice. I turned and rushed back to the bedroom—Dutch close on my heels. With trembling fingers, I zipped myself into a pair of jeans, and reached in my closet for a sweater, mindless of its color or style. I simply needed to get dressed as quickly as possible because every second we delayed was more time for this guy to mentally and physically torture Sydney.

We got to the office, and Toscano had clearly called ahead because the place was abuzz with activity. To my surprise, Oscar was there, wearing a large brace that completely encapsulated his leg but also allowed him to walk.

"Hey," he said, the first to greet us.

"What're you doing here?" Dutch barked.

I knew he wasn't angry at Oscar. It was the tension of the moment that was being exhaled out of him like a bad virus.

"The doc cleared me," he said. "As long as I wear this thing . . ." He paused to tap the brace, "I'm fine to return to desk duty, sir."

Dutch pressed his lips together and nodded. I knew he didn't like the idea of Oscar returning to work so soon after being so severely injured, but I also knew he was relieved to have such a valuable member of our team back on the mission.

"We've got you set up in the conference room," Oscar said, swiveling his gaze between me and Toscano. "I stopped at a Walmart on the way here and got you a set of microphones and headphones, so all you'll have to do is plug and play."

"Good thinking," Toscano said.

"Hey," Brice called to us as he approached. He looked the least tense of all of us, and it actually helped to see some calm reassurance in the moments before I'd be forced to listen to a woman being executed and know that not only wasn't there anything I could do to help her, but also that I'd chosen the manner in which she died. By making it quick and sparing her the torture that her abductor and murderer intended to inflict on her, I'd also made it impossible to find her given the short window we had between now and then.

"Let's go in the conference room and talk this through," Brice said.

We followed him into the conference room and took seats around the table with Toscano and I sitting toward the head where the microphones and headphones had been placed.

Dutch, Brice, and Oscar also took their seats, and then

Cox, Baldwin, and Williams filed in, all of them catching my eye and giving me a nod of support and understanding. They knew what a softie I was, and how traumatizing this would be for me.

And then Candice stepped into the room and walked right up to me to wrap an arm around my shoulders and squeeze. "I'm here," she whispered in my ear, and tears welled in my eyes again.

Candice then stood behind me, her back against the wall, just allowing her presence to lend me courage.

I thought Brice was going to start talking right away, but instead he seemed to be waiting. I glanced at my watch. We had forty minutes before Sydney began losing more fingers.

About thirty seconds ticked by, and then Gaston stepped into the room, his jaw set and his eyes calculating. "Where do we stand?" he asked us.

"We're going on the air in thirty-five minutes, sir," Toscano said.

Gaston's eyes narrowed. I could tell he didn't like that decision. "Have you thought this through?" he seemed to be asking all of us.

"Yes," I said, before anyone else could.

Gaston's gaze shot sharply to me and it was damn hard to look him in the eye because I knew on a level, I was not just failing Sydney, I was also failing Gaston and the entire squad "If we wait, Abigail, it gives us time to find her."

I swallowed hard, dropping my gaze to my lap and I said the words I knew in my heart were true. "We won't find her in time, sir. And even if we did, he'd shoot her the second he sensed us coming through the door." I paused for a moment to draw in a deep breath, because the next few words felt impossible to say out loud. "She's already as good as dead, Director."

"Can we identify her?" Gaston pressed, addressing the room again, and it was one of the very few times I can remember him not immediately taking me and my intuitive word. "Her name is Sydney which is somewhat unique. Have we combed through the student roster to see if we can figure out who she might be?"

"I've been looking," Baldwin said, his eyes squinting at his laptop computer screen. "I found thirty-four Sydney's, sir. So far. And nothing came back on the print of her pinkie finger."

Gaston's eyes found mine again. "If we gave it two or three hours, we could figure out which Sydney out of the thirty-four she is and that might lead us to her whereabouts," he said.

I did a quick calculation. Every hour was six pieces of Sydney horrifically removed from her person. Six unimaginable, excruciatingly painful amputations. Gaston was talking about allowing twelve to eighteen of them. That was all ten fingers and maybe eight or nine toes if he stuck to the smallest bits first. And that was likely the *best-case* scenario.

I closed my eyes, trying to do the unthinkable, and put myself in Sydney's shoes. How would I feel knowing that I had only nine minutes and fifty-nine seconds between each amputation. And how would I feel not knowing when the torture would end?

I think I'd go out of my mind, if not from the pain, then from the expectation.

So, I set my imagination aside and used my radar to ask if it would make a difference. How many hours would we need to find Sydney?

The answer came back shockingly fast. Twenty-six, my radar said. We'd find her in twenty-six hours.

Which was a hundred and fifty amputations.

She'd be long dead by then. She'd bleed out at probably the fifth or sixth hour. Maybe sooner.

Opening my eyes to look at Gaston with firm resolve I said, "We won't find Sydney until around this time tomorrow, Director. No matter how fast we move now, my radar says she won't be discovered until then."

"You've trained your radar at her and tried to find her location?" he asked, and I understood that he was asking me to do the impossible. He wanted me to do for Sydney what I'd managed to partially do for Simone. But he was perhaps forgetting that Simone's mother had provided the missing link with the admission that Simone had a habit of studying on an abandoned floor of a specific building, which matched my vision that she'd been murdered in a classroom. We had no such detail about where Sydney could be.

Still, I knew that Gaston expected me to try, so I allowed my gaze to go unfocussed and aimed my radar once again at Sydney.

Just like before, the only thing that came back to me was how much pain she was in. Her terror and physical pain were completely overriding any hint of even the smallest detail of where she might be. Even the decay around her that I'd detected earlier seemed muted.

I pushed again at her energy, demanding that my radar find her and give us a damn clue, but it was like throwing a rubber ball at a brick wall. My effort to locate her simply bounced off of her unbearable psychological and physical distress.

With a trembling lip I focused on Gaston again and said, "I'm sorry, sir. I can't see where she is. She's in too much pain. She's too terrified. The only detail I can make out is her emotional and physical agony. It's too loud for me to get around."

He tapped his index finger against his leg, thinking through the decision. "Twenty-six hours?" he asked.

I swallowed hard again and nodded.

He shook his head like he wanted to reject my prediction, but he didn't and I knew that, as angry as he was at this unsub for this particular ultimatum, he was starting to accept that there just wasn't enough time to find her and spare her the torture to come.

We all waited on him to say something and after he inhaled deeply, letting it out in a measured sigh, he turned to Brice and Toscano. "This isn't going to go over well at HQ," he said. "They won't want this to air publicly."

"It's the only way to prevent the girl being tortured to death," Toscano said. "Plus, this is several hours earlier in the day than my regularly scheduled time for the podcast, and I've turned off the auto alert to my subscribers so, unless they're specifically trying to find my podcast at this exact moment, we should be able to avoid more than a couple dozen from tuning in. And, Bill, you have my word that I'll shut it down the second . . ."

Toscano's voice trailed off. We all knew what he was talking about. He'd cut the live feed the moment Sydney began to say "solve my murder".

Gaston continued to look conflicted. To put on the live stream meant Sydney would most certainly die, but even setting aside my prediction of twenty-six hours till we found her, Gaston knew that I could be wrong and there was perhaps at least a small chance that if we didn't cooperate, if we stalled, we might be able to find her before she lost too many body parts.

The section of the voice mail left from the killer that bothered me the most, however, was what this fucker had said about his saw being sharpened. If he had a saw, he meant to cut through bone, and he could easily hack off a foot or a hand without Sydney bleeding out.

I didn't know this girl, so it was a very difficult decision to make on her behalf, and I could only put myself in her position and ask myself how I'd want this all to end.

If I were her, I'd have to face and accept the fact that I was going to die. That no one would get to me in time, and I could either go out in a prolonged excruciating manner or end it all quickly. I'd want to be spared the torture and opt for the bullet to the head, so I stuck by my decision to spare Sydney as much pain as I could.

"If we give in to this unsub, what's to prevent him from abducting another woman and demanding you live stream her execution too?" Gaston asked, his gaze once again settling on me.

"Nothing," I told him bluntly. "But between now and

then we'll have some time to continue to hunt for him. He won't get away, sir. Eventually we'll track him down."

Gaston lifted his watch and stared at the dial. I knew we were cutting it close by continuing to discuss how to proceed, and I felt physically ill when I thought about Sydney losing another digit only to get shot a few minutes later.

"Sir," I said, my voice hitching. "We have to do this. We have to spare her the torture."

Gaston's gaze locked on me a final time, and he stared at me for a long silent moment before he finally offered me a subtle nod, then he lifted his cell to make a call and exited the room.

Toscano got to work opening up the live stream option on his computer, and I donned the headphones and pulled my microphone close. With the noise-cancelling headphones on I couldn't hear any bits of conversation from the others, and it made me feel cocooned.

I closed my eyes and tried to think about what I would say to Sydney in those final moments. I didn't know if I'd even get the chance, but I hoped I'd be able to make a connection and offer her something in the way of comfort before that bullet took her out.

As I sat there thinking about what was going to happen in the next few minutes, my heart began to pound so hard that I thought I might slip into a panic attack. There was nothing on earth I wanted to do less than be involved in this nightmare, but I couldn't see a way out that wouldn't haunt me forever.

Someone laid a hand on my shoulder, and I jumped. Opening my eyes I saw Dutch squatting down next to me, his gaze filled with concern and sadness. I took off my headphones and said, "Can you sit with me?"

Dutch got up, grabbed the nearest empty chair and rolled it over to park it right next to me. He then took up my hand and squeezed it reassuringly.

"Thank you," I told him.

"I've got you, love. I'm right here."

I cleared my throat and blinked back the tears, squeezing his hand in return.

Looking over at Toscano and Baldwin, I saw that they were working out how to connect his laptop to the projector. Baldwin got it to work, and in the next moment I could see myself projected onto the screen on the far wall. It was a hard thing to witness, if I'm honest, me sitting there at the conference table, holding my husband's hand, while looking gutted and agonized. I averted my gaze and focused back on Toscano who was already motioning to me before putting on his headphones.

It was go time.

I put the headphones back on and listened to the opening strands of the Toscano Files podcast, and then his rich baritone voice filled the silent void I'd been immersed in earlier.

"We're here to record a new addition of the Toscano Files, but today's live stream will be very disturbing, and I want to urge as many of you who might be listening to avoid this particular show."

I stared at Mike as he spoke, his voice sounding calm and rational while his expression told a completely different story. It was clear he was as upset about what was about to go down as I was.

"Joining me again is Abigail Cooper from Austin, Texas. Abby is an accomplished professional psychic who's been working with the Austin bureau for the past several years.

"This morning, we'll be taking a call from the same unsub who murdered Simone Shaw on air as I was live streaming our most recent episode of the Toscano Files earlier this week.

"The last thing I want to do is give this guy more airtime, but he's contacted me personally to let me know he's abducted another young woman, and he's demanded that we go back on the air. If we refuse, he'll start torturing this poor girl in an unspeakable way. To spare her from that, we've agreed to his conditions, but please know that this was an agonizing decision to make. In the end, we wanted to do for Sydney anything we could to spare her from further torture. And to the unsub who's abducted her and plans to murder her, know that we'll be hunting you with every available avenue we have at our disposal. We *will* find you, and we *will* bring you to justice, and none of us will rest until you're brought in to answer for your crimes."

Toscano's gaze suddenly flickered to something on his computer screen, and I looked up at the image being projected on the far wall.

A call was coming in from a source named Sydney. Toscano hesitated only a moment to lock eyes with me before he admitted the call into the virtual room.

I was expecting that we'd only hear Sydney, so I was very surprised to see her, seated in a chair with a camera pointed at her.

Her hands were bound to the arms of the chair, and the pinkie on her right hand was gone, an open wound weeping blood that'd dripped down to coat the chair rail.

I swallowed back the bile at the base of my throat as I continued to take her all in.

Her face was a mask of pain and absolute terror. Wide brown eyes stared into the camera, and her chest was heaving with panic. Her feet and torso were also bound to the chair with rope.

She wore running shoes, jeans, and a simple gray sweatshirt which was dirty and stained with her blood. Her skin was dark and shiny from perspiration, and her black hair fell mostly loosely about her face, except for the several tendrils stuck to the sweat against her temple and forehead.

She was trembling so badly that the chair was tapping against the concrete floor. "He—hello?" she called out.

"I'm here, Sydney," I said.

"Are you Abby?"

"I am. I see you, and I'm going to stay with you all the way, okay? I promise you that."

Sydney dissolved into tears; her sobs so heartbreaking that

I didn't think I could stand it. Dutch squeezed my hand, and behind me, I felt Candice lay a hand on my shoulder.

"He . . . he . . . he wants me to ask you if—"

I cut her off. "I know what he wants you to ask me, Sydney, and I promise you I will find you, and I'll bring you home to your family. No matter what, okay?"

Sydney nodded, and her sobs consumed her ability to say anything else for a long moment.

And then my intuition kicked in, and I saw the image from my vision where the lion carried the bunny to the dead bobcat. Out of my mouth—completely unbidden—came the words, "Sydney, who's bunny?"

The poor girl's breath caught, and her chin lifted while she stared into the camera, her expression surprised and something resembling recognition glinted in her eyes.

I got to my feet, the urgency of needing that answer driving me out of the chair. "Sydney! *Who's bunny?*"

Sydney's mouth opened and closed, and then she whispered, "Me."

BAM!

The noise was so loud it hurt my ears, but my gaze and my focus were on the projection at the far wall where Sydney's head whipped so sharply to the left that she fell over, slamming onto the ground with a sickening thud.

Toscano immediately cut the feed, but he hadn't been quick enough. I screamed, yanked my headphones off and threw them against the far wall, where they crashed and broke apart, pieces flying everywhere, but I began to gag so I didn't care.

Pushing past Dutch, I sprinted out of the room to once again heave my guts out in the ladies' room.

CHAPTER 11

Candice found me sitting against the wall near the sinks, hugging my knees with my head buried and the sounds of my sobs reverberating off the walls.

"Abs," she said gently.

I didn't lift my head or even acknowledge her presence. All I could see in my mind was Sydney's head whipping to the left and an explosion of blood spraying out from her head as her body jerked violently, carrying her to the floor.

It replayed like a terrible nightmare over and over in my mind, and no matter how hard I squeezed my eyes shut, I couldn't stop seeing the scene.

"Abby," Candice said again. I felt her hands wrap themselves around my wrists, trying to lift me out of my pose. "Sundance, come here."

I shook my head. I didn't want comfort. I didn't want anything except to go back to that time when I'd made the call to go live on the podcast and seal Sydney's fate.

Had I made the right call?

Is that what she would've wanted?

Her eyes had been so haunted and filled with agony and heartbreak. Maybe she could've endured the torture. Maybe I was wrong, and we could've found her in time to save her.

"You didn't kill her," Candice said firmly, her hands tightening around my wrists. "Abby, you *didn't* kill her."

I shook my head again. It was too much. It was all just too much.

Candice began to stand up, taking me with her. For the record, Candice is shockingly strong for a woman with a slight, athletic frame.

"Leave me," I whimpered. I didn't want to stand up. I didn't want to do anything except melt into the floor and disappear.

"Not a chance," Candice said, tugging on me even harder.

"Abs," she said again as I tried to pull away. "Stop, okay? Just stop for a minute."

I gave in. I was too traumatized to fight her anyway, and as she got me to my feet and wrapped her arms around me, I found myself glad for her presence and support.

"Did I make the right call?" I asked her pitifully.

"Yes," she said without pause, and I was so grateful to her for that.

"Why are you so sure?" I pressed, still unconvinced.

Candice released our tight embrace to hold me at arm's length. "Because it's what every single person in that room would've chosen, Sundance. Not a one of us would've opted for the longer version, holding out the very slim chance that we'd be found before the torture really began. And what would Sydney have looked like and what kind of a life would she have had if we'd somehow performed a miracle and found her in an hour or two. That fucker could've taken off her nose, both arms, her legs, and left just her torso. None of that would've killed her outright if he'd applied tourniquets. Would she have *wanted* to live like that? I sure as hell wouldn't."

I stared at her and allowed her calm, measured reassurance to seep into my soul. These had been my thoughts too.

"You can't be sure of the depravity he would've stooped to, Abs. We already know what he's capable of. He enjoys inflicting pain, both mental and physical. He's the sickest bastard we've ever had to chase. And when we find him, between you and me, before we turn him over to the warden, we'll make sure he gets a little of his own medicine."

I'm a little ashamed to admit that I wanted that too. I wanted this son of a bitch to suffer. I definitely wanted him dead, but even more than that I wanted him to feel some physical torture. I wanted him to squirm, beg for mercy, and be denied it. I wanted him to scream in agony. I wanted his pain to be long, all consuming, enough to drive him insane. I wanted his pain to be drawn out and for his suffering to go on, and on, and on.

I've never had such dark, depraved thoughts about an unsub before. Not even the last motherfucker we'd brought in—who'd also tortured women in the hollows of an underground tunnel. I'd had the chance to take him out and hadn't. I'd wanted him to face justice. Alive.

But this guy? I really, really wanted him to die. In some horrible fashion. Preferably in excruciating agony.

And I wondered at the difference in perspective between these two serial killers. Why was I suddenly willing to exact a final vengeance with one but not the other?

The difference, I decided, was that I'd made a connection to the women this mother fucker had murdered. I'd been the one, desperate hope they'd been given to spare them from being murdered, and even as they'd made that connection, they'd known it wouldn't make a difference.

So, it was torturous for both them and me, and I didn't know if I could emerge from all this with my soul intact, and *that* pissed me the fuck off and made me think murderous thoughts and not feel an ounce of guilt over it.

Looking at Candice, I could tell she understood, and that she was as pissed off as I was. "We'll get him, Sundance," she assured me. "He'll pay. I promise you."

There was a lightness in my solar plexus. My radar was saying she was right. We would get him.

And we'd make him pay.

After I'd had a chance to run a little cold water over my face and clean myself up, I nodded to her, and we walked out of the ladies' room together.

The minute I pulled open the restroom door, I saw Dutch, leaning against the opposite wall, his face a mask of concern. No doubt he and Candice had debated who should go into the ladies' room and tend to me. I don't know what Candice had told him to convince him it should be her, but I was glad for it. She'd said all the right things. All the things I needed to hear, and she was willing to join my wishful conspiracy that this unsub die rather than be brought to justice.

I knew that my husband would never choose capital

punishment over doing the right thing and bringing him in to face justice, which was something I loved about him, and I couldn't risk him knowing that the same wasn't true about my character. If he ever looked at me differently, it'd kill me.

"You okay?" he said so softly, it was almost as if he'd mouthed the words.

"No," I told him. "But I'm gonna pull it together and keep going until we find this goddamn piece of shit!"

Dutch reached out a hand to me, and I grabbed it. He then pulled me to him and squeezed me tight. "If it's too much for you, I can pull you off the case, Edgar."

"It's too much for me, Dutch, but no way in hell are you pulling me off this case. Not until he's caught. Not until this is over."

He sighed into my ear and kissed me on the head. "Got it. But I'm not going to let him or anyone else put you in that position ever again, dollface. We're done doing snuff films. And I don't care what he threatens."

My stomach muscles clenched. I knew he could threaten even worse things, and that meant that I also didn't know how to avoid turning down the invitation to put him on the air. He had power over all of us at the moment. Again, murderous thoughts swirled in my mind, and they gave me a bit of relief against the backdrop of the terrible scene I'd witnessed twenty minutes before.

"Let's get back to it," I said, pulling out of his embrace.

He let go but immediately took up my hand, and I welcomed it. Together, the three of us walked back to the office and into the conference room.

Toscano still sat in the same seat, and he looked terrible. Soaked in sweat, his face flushed and a brimming anger that was downright scary. I sat down in the seat I'd taken when we'd gone on air and waited for him to fill me in.

"We've alerted campus police," he said. "They're combing every basement and abandoned classroom on the campus, but so far, there's no sign of Sydney."

"Have we ID'd her yet?" I asked.

"Baldwin and Cox are on that, and they've looped in UT's president. He's assigned a few of his staff to help the effort to track her down."

"He should think about sending the kids home," Brice said.

"It's the middle of midterms," Cox said, coming into the room. "I already suggested that, and he balked hard. It'd create an administrative nightmare."

"As opposed to the nightmare of having a serial killer target some of his female students, huh?" Candice said, her voice hard.

"Hey, I'm on your side, Fusco. I tried to tell him that by keeping the university open he'd be risking more deaths, but he—" Baldwin paused to lift his fingers up in air quotes, "'doesn't see the need at this time to take it to take it to that level.'"

Candice grunted her distaste and shook her head. I felt her pain.

"The bunny clue is significant," I said, trying to get us back on task.

"What do you think she meant when she said, 'Me'?" Brice asked.

I glanced at him, and he looked just as upset as the rest of us, which was unusual for Brice. He was Mr. Calm, Cool, and Collected in times like these. "I think 'Bunny' was her nickname."

He nodded. "My guess as well. How do you think that'll help us identify her?"

"Social media," I said. "We need to do a search on all the usual platforms cross-referencing the name Sydney with bunny and UT."

"On it," Dutch said, getting up from the table and heading out of the conference room.

Candice took up the chair that he'd just vacated. "Abs," she said. "Now that Sydney is . . . out of pain, can you point that radar of yours toward where he might've taken her to murder her?"

I sighed tiredly, but nodded. "I can try."

I closed my eyes, but the truth is I really, *really* didn't want to point my radar anywhere near that crime scene. It still felt too raw. Too fresh. Too traumatic.

And yet, something did immediately come back to me. "So odd," I said, reviewing the image swirling in my mind's eye.

"What?" she asked.

I opened my eyes. "I feel like she's in the jungle."

Candice studied me curiously. "The jungle? You mean like, he took her to South America?"

I frowned. "No," I said. "At least I don't think so."

Doubt began to leak into my thoughts. "It might be because I'm still so thrown off by what we all witnessed earlier, but I when I reach out to where she might be, Candice, I see tropical plants and it feels humid and hot, like a scene out of a jungle movie."

"Is it outside?"

I sighed and closed my eyes again. Goddamn this was hard. "Yes? No? I can't tell. It feels like both."

"But you think it's somewhere here in Austin, right?"

I opened my eyes to look at her. "Maybe?"

I sounded so unsure, and I hated that I wasn't more confident in what I was seeing.

Candice got up and began to pace the room, tapping her lip. Then she took her phone out of her blazer pocket and dialed a number. She left the room when someone on the other end answered. I wondered what she was up to.

"Can I get you anything, Coop?" Oscar said softly.

I turned my chin in his direction. He was seated at the far end of the table, looking at me like I was a fragile egg, ready to crack.

I rubbed my temple. A headache was really starting to set in. "Do you have any aspirin?"

Oscar fished around in the messenger bag he'd brought with him. "No, but I've got these," he said, holding up a prescription bottle. "They'll take all your worries away if you want a break from feeling too much today."

I narrowed my eyes suspiciously. "I'm not taking an opioid, Oscar."

Oscar sighed heavily and rolled his eyes. "Jesus, Coop, what do you take me for? I wouldn't push an opioid on you. These are tranquilizers to help me sleep. The pain was keeping me up at night, so the doc prescribed these."

"How strong are they?"

"Wicked strong."

I got up and walked over to him, holding out my outstretched palm. "Gimme."

Oscar tapped out one small pill into my hand.

"That's it?" I said. "One pill?"

"Trust me, that's all you'll need."

I opened my mouth and threw the pill to the back of my throat, swallowing it without water.

"Hey, whoa!" Oscar said in alarm. "I didn't mean pop it *now*, Coop! I meant, like, take it at lunch or later this afternoon."

"How fast do they work?" I asked. There was no going back now.

"Twenty minutes or so."

"Good. I could use a break from all this, Oscar. A good, solid nap is just what I need."

"It won't be a nap, Coop. You'll be down for eight to ten. Maybe longer."

Before I could answer, Candice came back into the room. "Hey," she said, flushed with excitement. "I have a contact over at the Austin Studios. They're filming a remake of George of the Jungle there. The film crew hasn't arrived yet, but the set designers are done, and there're real vines and plants and stuff to give it an authentic look, so they also had to set up a humidifying system to keep the plants alive through the filming."

"Wow," Oscar said, getting to his feet. "Great job, Coop!"

"What's going on?" Dutch said, coming back into the room.

"Abby focused on the crime scene and got a jungle

atmosphere. They're filming a remake of George of the Jungle over at the Austin Studios Production Company," Candice told him.

Dutch's eyes widened in surprise. "Wow. That's a great hit, Edgar."

"Want to come with us to check it out?" Candice said, pointing to Oscar and me as if it was already a forgone conclusion that we'd be the ones to go with her to the studios.

"Can't," I said, dully. My eyes blinked heavily, and I stared at Dutch with a foggy mind. Turning to Oscar, I said, "Wow, these tranquilizers really work fast."

"Tranquilizers?" Dutch said, now eyeing me in alarm. "What's she talking about?"

Oscar's face flushed. "I'm sorry, sir. I offered her one of my tranquilizers, thinking she could at least get some sleep tonight in spite of the tough morning. She knocked one of the pills back before I could stop her."

My lids drooped over my eyes, slightly obscuring the view of my husband. "Time for bed," I sang, wobbling a bit on my way to the closest chair where I sat down heavily.

"Jesus, Hernandez," Dutch said crossly. He then came over to me and looked at me closely. "She'll be out before I get her home."

"I'm very sorry, sir," Oscar repeated.

"It's not his fault," I told Dutch as he pulled me up out of the chair. "He was just looking out for me."

"Yeah, yeah," Dutch said. "Come on, Edgar. Let's get you home."

I don't remember a thing after that. I don't even have any memories of being loaded into (or unloaded out of) the car. All I know is that when I woke up, it was dark out, and the clock on the nightstand read 12:13 a.m.

Sitting bolt upright, I was immediately aware of two things; first, my husband was softly snoring next to me, and second, I had to go to the restroom *bad*.

Once I'd taken care of the call from mother nature, I opened the bathroom door to find the light on and Dutch sitting up in bed, looking sleepy and trying to fight off the urge to close his eyes again to go back to sleep. "Hey," he said as I walked toward the bed. "You're finally awake."

"*Seventeen* hours?" I asked him. "I've really been asleep for that long?"

Dutch glanced at the clock. "Sounds about right. That tranq hit you *hard*, cupcake."

"I'm starving," I told him. I hadn't eaten a thing the day before, which was probably why the tranquilizer hit me so hard.

Dutch wiped his face and threw off the covers. "Come on, Edgar," he said. "I made butternut squash gnocchi for dinner hoping the smell would wake you up. There's plenty of leftovers."

He didn't have to tell me twice. I beat him to the kitchen.

My husband is an absolutely fabulous cook. Which is a good thing, because if it were left to me, we would've starved to death long ago.

Most of the stuff I cook is over a flame. Or *in* a flame if you ask the fire department. Whatever. Well-done is underrated.

Anyway, Dutch heated up the gnocchi, and I cuddled with Tuttle who'd woken up and demanded my attention. Eggy was out like a light in his doggy bed, the white hairs now dominating his chin, standing out in stark relief against the blue bed he lay in.

"Catch me up to speed on the day," I said.

Dutch scratched the back of his head. A habit he had when something was bothering him. "We didn't find her," he said.

"She wasn't at the studios?"

"No. Oscar, Candice, and Williams combed the entire twenty-acre lot and couldn't find any sign of her."

"Dammit," I muttered. "I hate that I sent them on a wild goose chase."

Dutch placed the steaming plate of pasta in front of me. "You didn't," he said. "Thanks to you that's one less place we have to look."

I smirked at him. "Thank you for trying to make me feel better about it."

"That's rule number six in the husband handbook, babe."

My smile was more genuine this time. "I love you like crazy, you know that, right?"

"I do," he said. "And the feeling is mutual."

Dutch leaned in and gave me a sweet kiss, and then I got to work on the gnocchi, which tasted almost as good as that kiss.

After I was finished, I said, "Did you guys have any luck identifying her, Dutch?"

He shook his head, taking my plate to the kitchen sink. On a big yawn, he said, "No. Baldwin and Cox called all the Sydneys on the list, and there're five we still have to track down, but nothing came back leading to out vic."

"What about the social media angle for the nickname Bunny?" I asked next.

He took a glass out of the cupboard and reached for the filtered water pitcher in the fridge. "Also a bust. I couldn't find anything about a Sydney that went by 'Bunny' related to UT."

I frowned again. I was missing something. Something big. Maybe I just needed some time to suss it out.

After taking a long sip of water, Dutch said, "You coming back to bed?"

I got up and put a sleepy Tuttle back in her own bed. "No. I'm not tired, so I'm going to give the case a little more thought and see if I can't pull a few more clues out of the ether."

"Do you want me to stay up with you?" he asked next, and I was so touched that he actually meant it.

"Definitely not. You go on to sleep, cowboy. I'll be back in bed to cuddle with you in a few hours."

Dutch shuffled over to me, gave me a warm hug, another

of those sweet kisses and turned toward the bedroom. "Wake me if you get a breakthrough."

"Will do," I told him.

Once he was back in bed, I moved myself out to the living room where the light wouldn't disturb him and sat in my favorite spot on the couch to think. For about a half hour, I allowed my mind to wander wherever it wanted without specifically focusing on any one thing, and my thoughts were all over the place. They floated from memories of the previous morning, which caused me to physically flinch, to a grocery list, some items I'd need to order online, a dentist appointment I needed to make, and a dozen other things in between.

Finally, once I felt the "monkey mind" was out of the way, I closed my eyes and tried to pull in anything I could about Sydney's murder.

Again, my mind went to the jungle atmosphere, and I couldn't shake the feeling that I hadn't been wrong. Wherever Sydney was, she was in the center of a space that was overgrowing with plants and high humidity, and again that scent of decay lingered in the background as well.

But where would a space like that exist if not on some movie set? That was a puzzle I just couldn't seem to work out.

Setting that puzzle aside for the time being, I moved on to how to find out which Sydney was the one we were looking for. Was she one of the five remaining on Baldwin's list?

And then I was reminded of the bobcat from my earlier vision. The bobcat that was the same mascot as the one from Texas State University.

What if Sydney weren't a student at UT? What if she were a student at Texas State? And what if that bobcat had another significance? What if it represented an actual athlete?

Was Sydney an athlete at TSU?

I got up to head into the study and retrieve my iPad. Bringing it back to the couch I began searching TSU's website, looking for anything that felt like I was heading in the right direction. I even hopped over to the records from the student paper, again searching for a Sydney on any team roster I could find.

The search netted me bubkes.

Frustrated, I sat still for a long minute, tapping my lip and thinking. I could feel that I was fishing in the right area, but not the right pond.

And then I got another idea.

Typing quickly on my tablet, I did a search for high schools with a bobcat as a mascot. I found plenty, but there was a sense that *this* was the direction I needed to explore. So, with each and every high school in the Southwest that had a bobcat as a mascot I began to look into their girls' athletic teams.

I found Bunny at five in the morning.

Sydney Garhart, aka "Bunny Garhart" was a track and field star in her Memphis, Tennessee high school. She'd been a state champion in both the 100-meter and 400-meter hurdles, and her neighborhood paper had done a half-page article on her two years earlier.

The article mentioned that she'd been offered a full scholarship to several universities, including UT. She planned to study audiology. Sydney's younger sister was hearing impaired, and she wore hearing aids. Sydney wanted to become an audiologist to help other kids with similar impairments hear again.

My mind immediately went to the bunny from my vision. That stuffed bunny had had overly long ears, and when I thought more about it, I realized that sound waves travel through the air, and that's why she'd been chosen by our unsub.

The newspaper article also mentioned that Sydney's nickname, "Bunny" was given to her by her track and field coach way back when she was in middle school because of the way she hopped over the hurdles, and it'd stuck with her.

In the photograph accompanying the article, she'd been surrounded by trophies and medals and a small stuffed animal in the form of a rabbit sat perched on her shoulder.

I studied her photo and how alive and full of promise she'd been, and it struck me how dazzling her smile was. I felt my eyes sting with tears, and I stared somberly at her photo for a long, long time.

CHAPTER 12

At around quarter to six, I got up and made some coffee, hoping the aroma would wake Dutch. It did, and he padded out to the kitchen looking just as tired as when he went to bed four hours earlier. "Morning," he muttered.

I handed him a cup of black coffee in his favorite mug. "I found her," I said, after he'd taken a sip.

He blinked at me in confusion for a moment and then he said, "Sydney?"

I nodded and reached for my tablet. Handing it to him I waited until he'd read some of the article before I said, "She was studying audiology. She wanted to become an audiologist."

Dutch squinted at me curiously. "That's important?"

I nodded. "Sound waves travel through the air."

It took my husband a moment or two, but then recognition bloomed. "Simone was water, Ji was fire, and Sydney was air."

I nodded. "That leaves earth. He's planning on killing one more student before he moves on to something bigger."

Dutch set the tablet aside and leaned against the counter, crossing his arms which made his well-toned biceps bulge. I always appreciated that view, but my mind wasn't focused in that direction at the moment.

"Something bigger?"

I nodded grimly. "He's got something big planned, Dutch. Something to really make a statement."

"Like what?"

I shrugged. "I'm not sure, but there is this sense that he's got some sort of big finale planned. And I really, really don't like the vibe that I'm picking up from it."

Dutch studied me for several moments, and I waited him out. At last, he said, "Did you make any headway on her crime scene?"

I shook my head. "No. I know I'm right about the environment around her, but I can't figure out where that might be."

Dutch glanced at the clock on the microwave. "You said we'd find her right around nine-thirty a.m. today."

"Yep," I agreed. "I'm not sure it matters that I can't figure out where she is because someone's going to find her anyway."

"It'd be nice to get to the scene before anyone else who might corrupt it does."

I knew what he meant. If I was right and Sydney's body was going to be discovered in a little over four hours, then it was probably going to be discovered by a regular citizen and not someone in law enforcement, which meant the scene could be compromised, and we'd possibly lose some evidence that might point us in a direction.

"We'll just have to hope that whoever finds her has seen enough CSI shows to know they shouldn't mess with the scene."

Dutch grunted. "Have you told anyone else yet about finding her ID?"

"No one but you, cowboy."

He nodded. "It's still early. I'll give it a half hour before I call Brice and Baldwin."

"And Oscar, right?"

"Later," he said. "Baldwin's on the student roster search, so he should be updated before any of the other agents. Scott's sorting through Ji's classes and Simone's classes seeing if there's a common student to both girls."

"Has he had any luck?"

"Nope. So far, none of the students from Ji's classes match any of the student's from Simone's classes. On the off chance that this unsub began targeting these girls in previous semesters, Baldwin's also sorting through old class rosters. It's slow going, but we gotta be thorough."

"What about the Vans angle? Did Toscano's connection in D.C. pan out?"

Dutch rubbed his face with his hand, no doubt trying to rub away his exhaustion. "Their calculation is that the unsub is five-ten to six feet tall, and weighs about one-ninety. His shoe size is anything from a size ten to a twelve."

"Doesn't narrow it down as much as I wish it did," I said.

"Right. Still, he's recruited a grunt agent in D.C. to sort through sales records of local stores that sell Vans, hoping to get some kind of a list together."

"What about social media?" I asked next. "Did any of the girls know some of the same people?"

Dutch frowned. "Oscar's been working that angle. The girls had acquaintances from some of the same pools of people, but no one from their friends or followers' lists fit the description of our unsub."

"And still no luck tracing the number he called Toscano's phone from?"

"Zippo," Dutch said. "He's routing all of his calls from D.C., but those numbers just end up being reroutes from other countries."

My shoulders sagged. "Goddamn, this guy's *elusive!*"

"He is," he agreed. "But maybe there's a common name from Sydney's classes. It's our only shot at finding this guy quickly."

I sighed heavily.

"You tired?" he asked me.

"No. Wide awake. I'll probably crash at noon, though."

"Again," he said with a grin.

I rolled my eyes.

"Want to go out to breakfast?" he asked next.

"At this hour?"

"Magnolia Café," he countered.

I brightened. The Magnolia Café is world famous. And for good reason. Their food is delicious, creative, and consistently fantastic. "I'm in for a stack of gingerbread-banana-pecan pancakes."

"Get dressed, and let's roll," he said.

He didn't have to tell me twice.

We arrived at Magnolia and were met by Brice and Candice. "You called and asked them to join us?" I said when I saw them seated at a large booth at the back of the restaurant.

"I did," he said, taking my hand and leading me to the table.

Candice got out of her seat to hug me in a warm greeting. "How're you doin, Sundance?"

"Better than yesterday, but still traumatized to be honest."

"I bet," she agreed.

We ordered coffee to start, and just when it arrived, Oscar entered the café. "Hey," he said after limping across the floor and sliding in next to me. Pointing over his shoulder, he added, "Toscano's parking. He'll be in in a minute."

Sure enough, the seasoned agent came into the café looking a bit lost. We waved to him, and he ventured over. "I've heard about this place," he said, taking a seat next to Dutch. "I also hear the food is great."

"That it is," I told him.

He nodded at the waitress when she asked about coffee, and then he focused on me. "I understand you discovered Sydney's identity."

I nodded. "Sydney Garhart. She was a track star at her Memphis, Tennessee high school—the White Branch High School Bobcats. She was a state champion hurdler. An old coach gave her the nickname, 'Bunny', and it stuck. She was at UT on a full scholarship, and this would've been her junior year."

Toscano looked at me with pride. "Great job, Abby."

I offered him a small smile. "Thank you. It took me most of the night to track her down."

Brice glanced at his watch. "I'll make the call to her parents later this morning, after we confirm she's missing from her residence. I'm not going to tell her parents that we suspect their daughter has been murdered until we make a positive ID, but at least I can tell them that we suspect she's been abducted and prepare them for the worst."

"Should we call off the search for her body at Texas State?" Oscar asked. "Since they were the wrong bobcats."

Brice looked at me, and all I could do was shrug. "Might as well be thorough," I told him. "Since the search is already in full swing over there, it's probably a good thing to let them finish their sweep of the campus."

Brice nodded, then said, "Okay, no more shop talk. We all could use a break."

"What's the pool up to?" Dutch asked him.

"Three hundred," Brice said, with a hint of a grin.

My brow furrowed. "What pool?"

I glanced at Oscar, and he seemed as confused as I was, but everyone else at the table was smirking like they were in on a joke.

Candice said, "The pool for how long it'll take Oscar to work up the courage to propose to Nikki."

Chuckles sounded around the table, and I couldn't help but join in, especially when Oscar's face flushed bright red.

"Cox is already out," Brice said. I suspected he was the one in charge of the money. "He guessed Oscar was gonna propose in the hospital. And Williams guessed it'd be the day Oscar got shot, so he's also out."

"What about Baldwin?" Toscano asked. "Didn't he pick a date right around now?"

Brice nodded. "Oscar has until the end of the day to make Agent Baldwin three hundred dollars richer."

"Not funny," Oscar said, but he couldn't hide his grin, even in spite of his embarrassment.

"How come I didn't get in on that action?" I complained. I hate being left out of things.

Everyone at the table turned expectant eyes on me. "You're kidding, Sundance, right?" Candice said. And then she eyed Dutch suspiciously. "I'm surprised Dutch hasn't already consulted your intuition about the date."

Dutch held his palms up. "I told you I wouldn't," he said. "But, as her best friend, I'd think *you'd* be more likely to weasel that out of her, Fusco."

It was Candice's turn to hold her palms up. "Sundance can vouch for me. I haven't even hinted to her about Oscar's proposal."

I rolled my eyes and looked at Oscar. "Don't let these fools pressure you into picking a date until you're ready."

"I won't," he said. "Trust me. And you can also trust me that Baldwin isn't getting any richer on my account today."

A jolt of excitement went through the others.

"Who's in this pool?" I asked.

Brice made a circular motion. "All of us, Cox, Baldwin, Williams, Gaston—"

My jaw dropped. "Whoa! *Gaston* picked a date?"

"He did," Brice said. Pointing to Oscar he added, "And don't think about asking what date he picked. We don't need you to get in good with the director by giving away the winning date."

"Like I'd tell Gaston," Oscar said, crossing his arms and scowling.

I knew it was mostly for show, and I felt that Oscar actually enjoyed being the center of attention, even if was at his expense.

Brice also pointed to me. "You're not allowed to give anyone any predictions on this, Abby."

I laughed. "If anyone asks, Brice, I'm definitely going to point you fools in the wrong direction, just to get your goat."

Our breakfasts arrived, and the banter continued as we all tucked into our meals. I was so glad for the break from the horror of the previous morning. We'd all been affected by Sydney's murder, and I felt the whole team was benefiting from some lightheartedness away from witnessing the violence and inhumanity that made up a good portion of our jobs.

After I'd polished off my plate of pancakes, I sat back and patted my stomach, giving in to a satisfied sigh. The chatter around the table had devolved into talk of sports, and I'm more a fan of figure skating or rhythmic gymnastics than I am of baseball or hockey. So, I allowed my eye to wander around the restaurant, and my gaze landed on a woman carrying a small watering can, giving water to the various potted plants nestled neatly on the restaurant's windowsills.

Almost as soon as I noticed her, my intuition binged, and my mind's eye immediately went to the jungle vision I'd had for where Sydney's body would be found.

"Ohmigod!" I said, sitting forward and slapping my hands on the table.

Chatter at the table stopped abruptly, and all eyes focused on me.

My gaze went to Dutch when I said, "I know where she is."

My husband wadded up his napkin and took out his wallet. Removing several twenties from the billfold, he set the stack on the table and said, "Let's roll."

We arrived at the Research Greenhouse, at the College of Natural Sciences around 8:15 a.m. Dutch and Brice had made several calls on the way there, and campus police, Baldwin, and Cox met us at the curb.

An older gentleman in a lab coat with a halo of white hair and thick glasses was also present, and he held a keycard tightly in his hand.

We got out of our respective vehicles and gathered with those who were already there.

Introductions were made, and I learned that the man in the lab coat was Professor Bach. He taught bioscience at the university, and he was also the greenhouse manager. Essentially, he was the person in charge of who had access to the greenhouse spaces that were rented out to students and researchers for their various experiments in bioscience.

"As you requested, Agent Harrison, I haven't entered the greenhouse storage boxes myself, but I did conduct a search of the outer perimeter of the entire greenhouse and two of the large windows at the back of the building, between section GC1 and 2 have been tampered with. If someone wanted to trespass on these premises, that would be the only spot to do it from.

"It's out of security camera range, and those are the only two windows that weren't fitted with an alarm because they're fixed in position and do not open. Tampering with any of the other glass panes would've caused an alarm to go off."

I glanced at Candice who eyed me in return. "Someone knew their way around this place."

Brice glanced over his shoulder and motioned to Agent Cox. He nodded and set off to investigate the back of the building and secure the windows for the CSI techs once we'd confirmed that we'd found Sydney's body.

Brice then motioned to the main entrance and said, "After you, Professor."

The scientist got underway and led us inside. "GC1 is this way," he said, and began to set off to the right. Everyone but me followed.

Dutch and Candice glanced back at me, and I pointed to the left. "She's this way," I said, focusing on the specific tug in my solar plexus that was urging me to head to the left.

Dutch whistled to the group, and one by one, they looked over their shoulder at him. Pointing toward me, he said "Abby says it's that way."

My FBI group immediately changed direction and came back toward me, but the professor and the campus police unis continued to walk forward as if they weren't aware that we'd abandoned them.

"Professor Bach," Brice called as I set off and the group followed.

"What's going on?" I heard him say.

"We believe we'll find our victim this way."

"But the break in is this way," he argued.

I kept walking, allowing my radar to continue to point me toward the area where I knew we'd find Sydney.

"We'll check that out later," Brice said. "Please come this way with us so that we can access the area where we believe our vic is."

I continued to walk down the long hallway, my heels clicking against the polished cement floor.

"Abs," Dutch whispered, sidling up to me. "Slow down a little. The professor's an old guy. He can't keep up, plus you're making Oscar sweat."

I realized that I'd been walking at a good clip, and paused long enough for the professor, and the four unis accompanying him, to reach us.

Bach and Oscar were a bit out of breath when they came up to the group. "You're heading toward GC 2 and 3," Back said. "That's well away from the break-in."

I nodded. "Indulge me, Professor," I said. Then I motioned for him to come up next to me so that we could continue on.

We walked for what seemed like a long time. The greenhouse itself was an enormous circular structure, with twenty-foot ceilings, humid atmosphere, and bright florescent lighting. Through the windows, I could see the famous UT Clock Tower come into view. The very same clock tower that was used by a sniper to murder fifteen people and injure another thirty-one in 1966. I knew the case well, curiosity driving me to look it up around the time we'd moved to Austin.

An involuntary shudder traveled up my spine when I looked at the clock tower. There was the ring of déjà vu with it, and that bothered me, but I couldn't think about that at the moment. I had to keep my radar focused on finding Sydney.

Along our route, we passed several large black doors all with a controlled lock pad that I assumed only a key fob could unlock. I walked by them without pause until I got a strong pull in my solar plexus and felt the urge to stop and look right.

Pointing to the door I said, "There."

Brice nodded to the professor, who seemed to balk at the notion of opening the door.

"What's in there?" Brice asked, noting the professor's hesitation.

"Several plants of the genus Amorphophallus."

"Are they poisonous?" Dutch asked, also not understanding the professor's hesitation.

"Not necessarily," the professor replied, "but these plants are quite fragile, and very difficult to replace. They've all been domed with glass, so when you enter, please be careful of them, would you?"

"Of course," Brice said softly but firmly, motioning to the keypad.

The professor swiped his card against the black panel changing the red light on the panel to green and then the old man pulled the door open and immediately, every single one of us close to the entrance bent at the waist and gagged. "Ohmigod!" I exclaimed, using my sleeve to cover my nose. "What *is* that?"

Wafting out of the doorway was *the* most horrible smell I've ever gotten a whiff of, and that's saying a *lot* given how many dead bodies I've seen.

"Oh, my," the professor said, his expression immediately flashing to worry. "As I said, this room houses several plants in the Amorphophallus family. I'm sure you've all heard of the corpse flower?"

I stepped back away from the door, gagging and coughing, and Candice came with me. "You've got a corpse flower in there?" she asked him, her own nose covered with the back of her hand.

I assumed most people had heard of the corpse flower, an absolute giant of a plant that I believed bloomed only once in a while and when it did it gave off the smell of rotting flesh. I could absolutely believe, given the smell coming from the room, that the beastly plant was inside that room.

"Among others," Back said. "Although, it's not currently in bloom, but two of the Rafflesia plants are."

Everyone behind us was now getting a good whiff of the odor oozing out of the room, and all of us continued to back up several feet because the stench was just awful. And it was then that I fully understood why, when I'd tried to tune in on

Sydney's location I'd come away with the unmistakable sense of decay near where she'd died.

The professor was the only one of us not backing away from the door, and I noted that his brow was knit with concern. "You shouldn't be able to smell them," he muttered. "They're covered in glass domes specifically to prevent this from happening."

Bach began to step forward into the room when Brice took a few quick steps forward, reached out a hand and laid it on the old man's shoulder. "Steady, there, Professor. Let us clear the room before you contaminate the crime scene."

"I'd say it's already contaminated," Oscar said through a cough.

Brice mostly shut the door, leaving it open a crack and, after taking out his keys, he turned to Baldwin and tossed them to him. "Scott, can you grab some masks and the tube of StinkBalm out of the glovebox of my SUV?"

"Got it, boss," Baldwin said, looking only too happy to get away from the foul odor.

Candice and I moved even further from the doorway, both of us covering our faces with the bottom half of our shirts. "Wow," I said. "That makes me want to give up my pancakes, and you know how much I love Magnolia's pancakes!"

I couldn't be sure, but I suspected Candice was smirking at me from behind the cover of her shirt. "It's clever when you think about it," she said, pointing toward the room where Brice was standing guard while breathing shallowly.

"What's clever?"

"The unsub brought Sydney here to the greenhouse where the atmosphere is naturally warm and humid, hurrying decomp, and used the corpse flowers to cover up the smell."

I grimaced. It was awful to think of the poor young woman I'd seen on the screen the day before that way. "I can't decide if I'm hopeful we've found her or not," I admitted.

Candice nodded. "I get it. The poor thing never had a

chance."

Baldwin came back a few minutes later and passed around two tubes of StinkBalm for us, which we all applied liberally. It didn't completely mask the smell of decay, but it kept all of us from gagging. Then, the party donned gloves, footies, and masks and moved into the room, but I held back, like I'd done with Ji. I didn't want to see Sydney's face, frozen in death. Watching her in pain and terrified was enough for me.

Still, when the door was pulled open and everyone began to file inside, my gaze landed on various ferns, vines, and palm plants, cementing the feeling that Sydney had been taken to a jungle atmosphere. I quickly looked away, though, afraid of what I might see if I peered into the room too far.

Brice held the door open while Dutch, Oscar, the four unis, and Candice stepped through. He then glanced at me expectantly. "You comin'?"

I shook my head. "No, Brice. I can't."

"Okay," he said gently, his eyes filled with a sympathetic warmth that was a rare expression for him. "I'll send Candice out once we confirm this is the crime scene."

I nodded, and Brice followed the others into the room, the door closing slowly behind him.

I waited maybe all of three minutes before Candice came out, tugged off her mask and one look at the expression on her face left no room for doubt; Sydney's body was inside that room.

Without a word, my bestie came over to lean against me, shoulder to shoulder. "I fucking hate this case, Sundance," she whispered.

I held up one palm. "Preaching to the choir, Cassidy."

"How do we find this guy?"

I sighed heavily. "I wish I knew."

"What connects these girls to each other?" she asked next. "I mean, except for the earth, wind, water, fire element thing."

"Hate," I said simply. "This monster hates women, and he's made a ritual out of killing them."

"There has to be another commonality, Abby," she said. "These girls share only a few solid traits. How would anyone know that without knowing *them*?"

I rubbed my temples. "I don't know. I mean, it's almost like this guy got his info from other people and put together a target list based on that info."

Candice stared keenly at me. "Maybe that's exactly where he's finding them," she said.

"What do you mean?"

"Maybe this guy has *accomplices*."

"I sucked in a breath. "Ohmigod, Candice . . . *yes*. That's it! He's not acting alone!"

There was a knowing in my gut that said that there were other people involved in these murders. In my mind's eye, I saw the white, blood speckled lion again, emerging from the corner and flanking him were three other lions, all with menacing red eyes and white fur, but my vision was interrupted when the door in front of us opened abruptly, and one of the unis came out, talking on his cell phone. "Yes, sir. I think it's time to have a meeting with the dean. We've got a serial killer on campus, and we'll need to set up a task force ASAP."

Candice and I watched the officer pace in front of us, talking to someone higher up the food chain than himself. He was flushed and sweating, and I doubted it was only due to the warm humid environment of the room he'd just exited. In fact, to me, it was obvious that whatever the scene inside looked like, it was bad and not something campus police saw . . . well, ever, probably.

The officer stopped pacing to listen intently, and we continued to watch him silently. His gaze then shifted abruptly to me, and he said to the person on the phone, "Hey, hold on a sec, Cap." And then he crooked his finger at me.

I pointed to myself and mouthed, *Me?*

He nodded.

I glanced at Candice, unable to tell if this was trouble or

not. She had squared her shoulders but kept herself pressed against me. "Together," she whispered, acknowledging that we would both step forward.

I walked the ten paces to the uni, and he said, "Captain, I'll call you back in a minute with more intel." After hanging up the call, he looked at me in that way that most cops who're unfamiliar with my abilities do—accusingly. "How'd you know where to find her?" he demanded.

I sighed. "I'm a professional psychic, sir. I'm paid to find things that're hidden."

His gaze was focused and glaring. "I don't believe in psychics."

"Ah," I said with a roll of my eyes. "That's the first time anybody's ever said that to me."

"I'm serious," he said crisply.

"I'm not," I replied.

The officer squared his own shoulders, and I could see three chevrons on the collar of his uniform, making his rank a sergeant. Or, a guy used to asking questions and expecting straight answers.

Sergeant McSerious then placed his hands on his hips. "I'm going to ask you one more time; how did you know where to find the girl's body?"

I glanced at Candice. What was I supposed to answer? That I'd just had a good guess?

"Sergeant," Candice said softly. "Abby is—"

"Was I talking to you?!" he snapped angrily.

I blinked and made an O with my mouth in an, "Uh-oh," kind of way. This dude did *not* know who he was dealing with.

"Don't care if you were or you weren't. I'm answering," she replied calmly. A bit too calmly. She also took out her cell and fired off a quick text.

"I want *her* to answer," he said, jabbing a hard finger into my chest.

I was so shocked by the sudden display of aggression that I actually took a step back. And then I laughed, because it was just *so ridiculous!*

Sergeant McSerious's face flushed beet red with fury. "What's so funny?" he growled, looking at me like he very much wanted to throw me to the floor and slap some cuffs on me, just to teach me a lesson.

And I had no doubt that he'd probably done that to some or even many of the students he'd encountered who wouldn't take his bullying with a tremble and a cowering gaze.

Candice immediately stepped in front of me and stood up as tall as her five-foot-seven-and-a-half inch frame would allow. "Do. Not. Touch. Her," she said.

Sergeant McSerious snarled, then reached up and grabbed Candice roughly by the shoulder just as the door to the greenhouse opened and Dutch, Brice, and Baldwin came hurrying out.

But they were too late to stop what happened next. With a speed that'd be alarming if I hadn't seen it before, Candice—in one fluid move—had removed McSerious's hand from her shoulder and had him twisted around to face forward with his wrist twisted up behind his back bending him over in a submissive posture.

He tolerated that for all of a nanosecond before he reached for his pepper spray with his free hand, but Candice was quicker and looped her free arm through his, locking it behind him by bending her elbow. When he tried to violently shove her aside, she leaned back, pulling up on both his wrist and his elbow, and he was effectively neutralized.

"Whoa!" Brice yelled, rushing forward to stand in front of McSerious, who, swear to God was doing his level best to break free of Candice's grip, but she had him so firmly that he didn't really have a play.

"*This* guy," Candice said in that calm, lethal manner of hers, "thinks it's okay to physically shove a couple of FBI consultants around."

"*You're under arrest!*" McSerious yelled.

I put a hand to my mouth to stifle a giggle. It was such an absurd statement for a completely neutralized cop to make.

"Candice," Brice said, his expression tense and pained

190

while his gaze shifted from his wife to McSerious and back again. "Please?"

Candice scowled at him, but she also dropped McSerious's wrist and arm, stepping quickly away so that when he whirled around—which he did—she was ready for him again by taking up a defensive posture.

But when he was free to face her, the sergeant actually drew his gun, pointing it at Candice while spitting with fury. *"Get down on the fucking ground!"*

"Whoa, whoa, *whoa!*" Brice yelled again, while he and Dutch quickly moved around McSerious to stand in front of Candice with their palms raised and their bodies blocking her from his careful aim.

"Put the gun *down*, Sergeant," Dutch hissed.

"Move to the side!" McSerious yelled. But neither man moved.

By this time, three other unis had come out of the room and were forming a half circle around us, their hands on their weapons and their mouths slack-jawed, and Baldwin had also stepped protectively closer to me and Candice, his own hand on the gun holstered at his ribcage.

Hell, even Oscar, who'd been last out of the greenhouse, gimped over to stand on our other side, his shoulder against mine and his hand on his weapon while wearing a look that could kill. I had a feeling he was thinking he owed me one, and if push came to shove, he'd do the shoving, pushing me aside while he shot McSerious without a moment's hesitation.

As the situation escalated with no sign of a way to cool things down, I pulled out my cell phone and hit a number on my speed dial. As it began to ring, I tapped the speaker function and held the phone up toward McSerious.

Gaston answered on the first ring. "Director Gaston," came his crisp greeting.

"Sir," I said, my voice quivering with emotion. "We have a situation that's turning very ugly even as we speak. One of UT's campus police sergeants has assaulted both me and Candice after accusing me of being involved with Sydney's murder, and at this very moment, he's drawn his gun, and he's aiming it at Candice *and* Special Agents Harrison and Rivers!"

McSerious's wild eyes flickered to me and the phone I was holding.

The director was quiet for a beat before he said, "Put him on the line."

I clicked off the speaker function and held my phone a little further out toward McSerious, wiggling it like a worm on a hook. "The *Regional Director* of the FBI would like a word with you, Sergeant, and might I also say that, should you decline his call in order to further assault me and my team, your ass will . . . effectively be grass."

McSerious's gaze twitched from Brice and Dutch to my phone, then to Brice and Dutch again, and all the while his gun was drawn, aimed squarely at them, and the unis behind him were ready to back him up should the situation ratchet up another notch.

After an awkward pause, I pulled the phone back and put it to my ear. "Director, he doesn't seem to want to take your call."

"Put me on speaker again, Abigail."

I did as I was told and again held the phone out towards the sergeant.

"Sergeant," Gaston began, "this is the Southwest Regional Director for the FBI, Bill Gaston speaking. It's my understanding that you're currently aiming your weapon at two of my agents and my highly valued consultant, Ms. Fusco. Is that correct?"

McSerious's expression became even more alarmed. "Your *consultant* assaulted an officer, Director! And your agents are currently obstructing an arrest!"

Gaston said, "No need to yell, Sergeant. Who do you report to?"

"Captain Blake Firestone of the UTCP," he snarled, his gun still aimed at my husband and my best friends.

"Will you hold the line for a moment, Sergeant?" Gaston

said. Given the gravity of the situation, I marveled at how calm he seemed.

"They're all under arrest, sir!" he yelled.

"Hold the line," Gaston repeated, as if McSerious hadn't just shrieked at him, and then there was a beeping sound that told us we were on hold.

The ten of us stood there tensely, no one moving. Out of the corner of my eye, I could see a small crowd of students and other staff in lab coats begin to gather round at a safe distance. Every student had their phone out, filming the scene.

Great, I thought. *We're about to go viral.*

Seconds ticked by, and McSerious eyed both Dutch and Brice with such malice that I was actually a little afraid for them. The sergeant's gun, however, was still trained on the space between them where Candice stood with folded arms and an unflinching glare.

"I'm not going to tell you two again; *move,*" McSerious growled, obviously out of patience.

Neither Dutch nor Brice so much as twitched. In fact, both of them stood up a little taller in the face of the obvious threat. "And *I'm* not going to tell *you* again, Sergeant," Brice snarled. "Holster. Your. Weapon."

No one made a move to obey the other, and the unis gathered behind McSerious looked back and forth at each other, thoroughly anxious and unsure about what to do.

Meanwhile I continued to hold aloft my phone, and just as my arm was getting tired from being extended outward, Gaston came back on the line and said, "Sergeant Todd. I have your captain on the line. Go ahead, Captain Firestone."

"Sergeant Todd," Firestone said, his tone angry. "Report back to the station. *Immediately.*"

McSerious's eyes went wide, and he looked toward my phone incredulously. "Sir," he began. "I was assaulted by a civilian who is now hiding behind two federal agents. Tell *them* to stand down so that I can arrest her!"

"Report back to the station without arresting anyone on

scene!" Firestone snapped, the fury in his voice unmistakable. "And that's *an order*, Sergeant!"

McSerious's lips pressed into a hard, thin line, and he holstered his weapon, his hand shaking as he did so. Then he turned his gaze toward me, and I swear there was murder in his eyes. "This ain't over," he snarled.

"Oh, but it is," I replied, offering him a pleasant smile and a casual wave.

And, even as I spoke the words, I could feel the lightness in the pit of my stomach that confirmed that he was in deep doodoo and Candice and I were free of ever encountering this asshat again.

He snarled at me once more, then turned on his heel and began to walk away. One of the other unis tried to go with him, but McSerious snapped, "Stay, Sheffield!" The officer immediately stopped in his tracks. McSerious also paused and pointed in our general direction. "Keep your eye on the two women and be prepared to arrest them the moment you get word from me."

Hoo, boy, I thought. *And it ain't even noon.*

CHAPTER 13

For the rest of the morning and into the early afternoon, none of us saw hide nor hair of Sergeant McSerious. The only indication that he'd been rightfully put in his place was when the uniformed officer he'd identified as Sheffield got a call and abruptly stopped watching me and Candice like a hawk.

Meanwhile, Brice, Dutch, Oscar, and Baldwin all worked the crime scene alongside the remaining campus police and some CSI techs, and even though they covered the area meticulously, there was very little in the way of evidence.

Word traveled out to us that the shell casing from the bullet that killed Sydney couldn't be found and there were no prints on the door handle—it'd been wiped clean. Also, to everyone's relief, the glass dome covers of the two corpse plants were set back over the flowers after being dusted for prints, and the overpowering smell of rotting meat lifted to everyone's relief.

Meanwhile, Brice got footage from one of the security cameras, which he downloaded to his phone and brought over to show me and Candice.

"Not much to go on," he said as he held the phone while the video loaded then began to play.

We could see Sydney walking in front of a man wearing a black hoodie, with the hood pulled down, black sweatpants, a pair of Vans shoes, and donning black gloves.

In one hand he clearly held a gun, which he pointed at the small of Sydney's back. She walked stiffly, her hands slightly raised. No one else was in the hallway and the timestamp registered four a.m., which was why they were totally alone in the building.

"How'd they get into the room?" I asked, watching the part of the video where the pair approached the door and disappeared from view.

"One of Sydney's roommates is a PhD student of

Professor Broch's, helping him with a series of experiments on the corpse flowers. He had a keycard to the room."

"Did you check on the roommate's alibi?" Candice asked. "Maybe the roommate was in on it."

"I had William's check her out," Brice said. "He just called to confirm that he spoke with the roommate, Christiana Dietz, and it doesn't appear she's involved. Christiana has cerebral palsy, and she's confined to a wheelchair. She told Williams that her keycard was in a backpack on the back of her wheelchair that was stolen when she and Sydney were in line at a food truck, waiting to order the day before yesterday. And I've just confirmed that Christiana did file a police report about her stolen backpack."

"So the unsub was stalking Sydney long enough to know all about the roommate," I said. "Brice, he obviously followed them to the food truck and also probably got in line behind them, so maybe there's some video surveillance footage we can look through."

"A CPU detective already looked into it and didn't come up with any video footage nearby. The food truck was parked on the far end of campus in front of an open field, so we might be out of luck."

"We should still send one of our squad to check it out anyway," Candice insisted.

Brice smirked at her. "Gee, why didn't I think of that?"

Candice rolled her eyes, but then she smiled sweetly at him. "Sorry. I shouldn't try to tell you how to do your job."

"And still, you will," he said, but he reached out to grab her hand to show her there was no ill will.

"Hey," Oscar said, spotting us as he came out of the greenhouse. He limped over to where we stood, and the expression on his face suggested he had an update. "They're bringing her out now."

At that exact moment, the doors to the greenhouse opened, and two men pushing a stretcher wheeled out Sydney's body. She was encased in a charcoal gray body bag that effectively took away the feel that there was an actual person inside. Still, no one spoke as she was wheeled past us and over to the exit where the ME's van was parked.

Once she was out the door, Oscar turned again to us, and he seemed excited. Like a kid with a big secret.

"What?" I asked.

He lifted his latex-gloved hand, which was curled into a fist, but then he turned his hand over to expose his palm as he spread out his fingers to show us what he'd been holding onto. "Look what I found."

I sucked in a breath. "Is that the shell casing?"

He lifted his chin, clearly proud of himself. "Yep. It must've rolled under the planks of one of the planter boxes. That's probably why the unsub left it behind—he couldn't find it, and I only looked because I wanted to be extra thorough."

"How'd you get down on the floor with that thing?" I asked, pointing to his leg brace.

He chuckled. "I pulled a groin muscle but managed it okay."

I laughed too, picturing Oscar doing the splits to look under the wooden planks in the room.

Candice, however, was completely focused on the evidence bag in Oscar's outstretched palm. "A shell casing," she whispered, and I understood her excitement.

Shell casings are like finding a nugget of gold. There is so much they can tell us, from the type of gun used, to discovering traces of DNA, and sometimes even to the weapon itself as all bullets fired from a gun carry striations from the muzzle that are as unique as fingerprints.

"It's a 7.65 casing, and it's old," Oscar said, holding aloft the baggie with the casing to study it curiously.

"What do you mean, it's 'old'?" Candice asked.

"Vintage," Oscar said.

As he was the ballistics expert on the squad, I could tell there was more to the story by the look on Oscar's face.

"How do you know it's vintage?" I asked.

"I had a neighbor next door when I was growing up,

named Sam White. He was an old WW2 vet. He saw a lot of action in the war and was part of an elite ops group that was specifically charged with hunting down SS officers. He confided in me that the mission wasn't a capture assignment, it was an eliminations op.

"Anyway, Sam was apparently really good in the field, and I know that because, with every SS officer he shot, he took their Lugar as a personal trophy. SS officers were each given a Luger as part of their initiation into Hitler's police squad," he explained.

"So, one day, feeling nostalgic," he continued, "Sam invites me and my older brother down to his basement, and in a big glass case down there he had his collection of Lugers, and I swear there were at least three dozen of 'em. More importantly to this case, though, is that Sam also collected the SS's ammo."

Oscar paused to hold up the shell casing between his thumb and his index finger. "This is a nine mill, which is standard size for a Luger, but they don't make this kind of bullet casing anymore, so these are worth a lot of money on the web if you can convince somebody to sell you vintage ammo. Luger P08s are the weapon they were designed for."

"A Luger," I said, staring at the casing. "You think our unsub knows they're connected to Hitler's SS?"

"I'd bet my house on it," Oscar said.

"You think this guy's a white supremacist," Candice said. "Like he's affiliated with a specific hate group?"

"I do," he said.

I nodded too. "What hate groups do we have in this area, Oscar?"

He scoffed. "The list is long, Coop. Texas is a hotbed for white supremacists."

"Are any of our guys monitoring these groups?" Candice asked.

"Yep," he said. "There's a team at the Dallas bureau that's dedicated to tracking each hate group within the state and monitoring their members."

"Can we go talk to the Dallas bureau?" I asked.

"Sure, but it'd be quicker to call," Oscar said.

"Set up the Zoom," I told him. "I want to pick their brains."

"Will do," he promised, then pocketed the shell casing for safe keeping.

"What're you thinking, Sundance?" Candice asked.

"I'm thinking that there's something here to dig into." My mind drifted to the vision I'd had of the four white lions. "Oscar, do you know off hand if any of these groups have a white lion for a mascot?"

"I don't, Coop. We can ask the guys later when we get them in the meeting."

"Can you call someone over there now?" I asked him, feeling time was of the essence.

He offered me a lopsided smile. "Sure thing."

Oscar limped away to place his call, and Candice and I stood alone together again. "You think the lion from your vision is more significant than just a symbol of a murderer?"

"I do. Sometimes my radar speaks only in metaphors, but sometimes there's a subtle more literal meaning, and, because the bobcat mascot in my vision was a symbol for Sydney, I'm wondering if the lions might also be some kind of mascot."

"Lions meaning the accomplices," she said with a nod.

"Exactly. I'm wondering if this guy might be the head of a group, or, more specifically, the head of a white supremacist group."

"It's definitely worth a look," she said.

As if on cue, Oscar returned and said, "We've got the meeting, but we gottta leave now. The team leader at the Dallas office only has an hour to spare today."

I made an enthusiastic swirling motion with my finger. "Let's go!"

"Go where?" I heard my husband call.

Looking over my shoulder I saw him coming out of the greenhouse. "We've got a meeting with the Dallas Hate Crime team," I told him.

Dutch nodded. "Good group. It's headed by a friend of mine from my rookie days at Quantico."

"Trish Kirkpatrick was with you at Quantico?" Oscar asked.

My ears perked up at the sound of a woman's name. Not that I'm the jealous type or anything . . . (cough, cough).

"Yeah," Dutch said. "She already had a stellar career in Southern California when I met her. She had a way of infiltrating these white supremacist groups and getting some great intel from them without them ever suspecting her. She had a close call, though, right before she was accepted into the Academy, and it shook her up for a while. To my knowledge, she hasn't tried to infiltrate a group since, and these days, I'm pretty sure she leaves the heavy lifting to the agents reporting to her."

"Oh, wow," I said, like I was fully invested in this woman's credentials. "That's really impressive to be able to infiltrate a hate group like that. How old is she?"

Dutch shrugged. "Late thirties. But she looks much younger. And way too innocent looking to be a plant for the FBI, which is what made her so effective back in her fieldwork days."

"Uh-huh," I said, giving a big ol' nod and a forced smile. "She sounds really smart too."

"She is," my husband said. "Got top grades in most of the classes we had together, back in the day."

"Uh-huh," I repeated. My gaze flickered to Candice who was watching me intently like she knew the green-eyed kraken was about to come unleashed. "You guys hung out a lot *back in the day?*"

"A fair amount. She helped me study for some of the more technical classes, and I helped her get in shape for the physical tests."

"I see . . ." I said.

"Abs," Candice said softly. "We should probably get go—"

"Is she *pretty?*" I demanded in a far sharper tone than I'd intended.

At this moment, Dutch seemed to realize he'd walked right into a trap. His eyes widened, and he began to look around him like a drowning man searching for a life preserver.

"Was she . . .? Edgar, I . . ."

I crossed my arms and began tapping my feet. "That's a yes," I snapped.

Oscar laid a hand on my shoulder. "We should go," he said. "Remember. The team only has an hour."

I shrugged him off. "Is she *single?*" I asked my husband next.

"Abs," he said with a sigh.

"*That's* a yes!"

"Sundance," Candice tried. I ignored her. The kraken had awakened.

"What physical tests did you get her in shape for, Dutch?" I demanded next.

"It was a long time ago, Edgar. Let it go," he snapped, and there was something so distinctly defensive and layered in guilt about his energy that I understood immediately what he and *Trish* had "worked" on.

"You fucking bastard," I whispered.

Dutch had spent twenty-one weeks at Quantico when he'd trained to become an FBI agent. After he graduated, he'd been assigned a female partner who'd made no bones about the line she was willing to cross to get close to Dutch, but I never really suspected he'd cheated on me with her. Okay, so maybe for a *minute* I had, but when he told me he'd been completely faithful to me during that time, I'd believed him.

"It's not what you think," he said lamely, and he tried to grab my arm to bring me toward him, but I pulled away.

"Do. Not. Fucking. Touch me!"

"Can we discuss this somewhere else?" he said when several people looked toward us.

I turned on my heel. "Go to hell!"

Candice caught up to me in the parking lot. Oscar was

nowhere in sight, but he was walking with that awful leg brace, so he was likely still making his way out of the building.

"Hey, Sundance," she said oh, so casually.

"I *don't* want to talk about it, Candice."

"Understood. So, let me do all the talking."

I glared at her.

She was unfazed. "Dutch trained at the academy, what? Twelve years ago?"

"Immaterial!" I snapped with a wave of my hand.

"Why?"

"Because all these years, he's been *lying* to me!"

"Has he?"

I stared at her with wide eyes and a gaping mouth. "Yes!"

She nodded. "I see. And your lie detector never went off?"

I opened my mouth to offer a snippy retort, but dammit . . . she had a point. "He lied by omission! That's still a lie!"

Candice pressed her lips into a tight smile. "While you were stomping away, Dutch pulled me aside and said that all that he and this other rookie—"

"Trish, Candice. Her name is *Trish Kirkpatrick*."

"—ever did was kiss. It was a one-time thing, and the second he came to his senses, he realized how much he cared about you and didn't want to blow it, so he cooled it with her."

I glared hard at her. "Why are you taking *his* side?!"

"Because this is a stupid thing to be this upset over, Sundance." I winced, and my eyes watered. "Hey," she said, putting a hand on my shoulder. "I know you're upset. You feel betrayed and exposed, but my friend, it was *twelve* years ago. The time to be this upset would've been back then. In the years since, you and Dutch have built a whole life together. He didn't cheat on *this* version of you. He cheated—and I'm using that term very loosely—on the version of you that he'd only been dating a few months."

I didn't say anything for a long time. Long enough for Oscar to finally join us in the parking lot. "Hey," he said, panting a little. "What's the plan?"

Candice turned expectant eyes to me. "It's your call, my friend."

I sighed heavily and shook my head. Rejection is my Achilles' heel. By confessing to have had a thing for this rookie agent, Dutch was admitting that, at some point in our relationship, he'd rejected me, and that hurt. A *lot.*

Still, Candice was right. The incident was over a decade old, and during a time when neither Dutch nor I had even discussed exclusivity. In my defense, however, I'd always thought it'd been implied.

But then another more difficult thought occurred to me: Not long after Dutch had become a field agent, we'd had a pretty big misunderstanding on Valentine's Day, and I'd fled to Denver for a friend's wedding. There, I'd reunited with an old flame, and things had gone a lot further than just kissing.

I'd confessed this to Dutch, and he'd never once held it against me.

Nor had he held it against me when I'd had to pretend to be super into another man during a top-secret mission we'd been on together. So, I kind of owed him for all the things he *hadn't* said during those two times.

With another sigh I said, "Let's go talk to Trish."

Oscar looked relieved, and Candice smiled.

I rolled my eyes and headed over to Candice's SUV.

Candice drove like she always did, and Oscar and I could only hold on tight as she wove through traffic like Vin Diesel on another *Fast and Furious* mission. We arrived back at the office in record time, and Oscar got right to work linking us to the bureau in Dallas.

When their video came on the screen, all my jealous fears and worries evaporated. In front of us was a pretty woman with long brown hair, light blue eyes, a heart-shaped face, pale skin, and the belly of someone seven or eight months pregnant.

In other words, I was struck by how much she resembled me—except for the preggers part. So, it was somewhat obvious to me that when Dutch had been at Quantico for those nearly six months, he'd missed me. And I knew it was more than that Dutch had a "type". I'd met his ex-wife who looked *nothing* like me. And I'd picked through his old yearbook, and I'd seen a few of his high school girlfriends, who didn't resemble me at all either.

But this woman, she could've been my doppelgänger. And, weird as that may seem, it brought a little relief to my injured, insecure fee-fees.

"Hello," she said when the audio feed kicked in. "I'm Special Agent Kirkpatrick."

Oscar nodded to her and pointed to himself. "Agent Hernandez and these are two of our consultants, Candice Fusco and Abby C—"

"Rivers," I said quickly. "I'm Abigail Rivers, Agent Kirkpatrick. I believe you know my husband, Agent Dutch Rivers?"

Kirkpatrick seemed to be caught a little off guard. She stared at me intently for a moment, no doubt seeing our resemblance and said, "Hello, Mrs. Rivers. It's nice to meet you. I knew Dutch back at the academy when we were both rookies."

"I'm aware," I said, and there was no doubt that I understood *exactly* how she "knew" Dutch.

Kirkpatrick subconsciously rubbed her belly. She was dressed in maternity clothes, but they were chic and well-tailored to her proportions. On her left hand was a two-plus karat, diamond engagement ring with a matching baguette encrusted wedding band, and both a diamond bolo bracelet and a two-toned Rolex watch on her wrist.

She'd either married up or they were paying FBI agents more than I thought.

She offered me a small smile, but it didn't seem to hold any spite or malice, so I backed off a little and dipped my chin in acknowledgement.

Focusing again on Oscar, Kirkpatrick said, "How can I help you?"

Oscar filled her in on the string of murders we were looking into and our belief that they were connected to a hate group; specifically, to one that may have a white lion for a mascot.

At the mention of the white lion, Kirkpatrick's attention seemed to focus a little more intently. When Oscar was finished, she asked, "How did you arrive at the white lion's connection to the unsub?"

Oscar became suddenly mute and made a point not to turn his head to look at me. Candice did the same.

I felt my cheeks heat, knowing that we'd come to a moment of truth. And I couldn't blame them for pausing before answering either. I never really know how to explain to an authoritative figure that I'm legitimately psychic. Culturally, most people like me are seen as a joke, or worse, that we're crazy. But twenty years as a professional doing this kind of work, and producing the kinds of results I produce, have definitely beaten the odds of chance. Convincing someone with no real interaction with an intuitive of my skill level is a whole other story.

"You may have heard rumors that our bureau uses a psychic," Oscar began.

Kirkpatrick snorted derisively. "You're kidding me, right? Your *psychic* came up with this? Don't tell me you believe this horseshit, Agent Hernandez."

Oscar's shoulders squared, and he leaned in toward the monitor's camera. "I'd appreciate it, Agent Kirkpatrick, if you didn't insult our greatest asset."

Kirkpatrick's gaze landed on Candice, and there was a whole lotta judgment in that look. No doubt she thought Candice was the professional psychic. And I'm sure she thought that way because she'd "known" Dutch and couldn't imagine him romantically associated with someone like me.

Shaking her head, Kirkpatrick said, "Six months ago a seven-year-old kid went missing, and for weeks, we had no leads. Then, his family shows up with this fortune teller in tow and tells us the psychic had a vision, and she knows exactly where the kid is.

"Because we had no other leads, we let her talk, and she tells us the kid is dead, and he's been buried in a dried-up riverbed, just south of Denton. She says she can guide us to the remains, and wouldn't you know it, she does just that. We start digging exactly where she's pointing and surprise, surprise—we find the kid's corpse.

"No sooner do we mark off the crime scene than she's asking the kid's parents about the reward money. They'd put up fifty grand. We found that a little suspicious, so we start looking into her. We find out her son's a registered sex offender who got popped a decade ago selling kiddie porn, and he's got no alibi for the day the little boy was abducted.

"He confessed an hour after we had him in for questioning. Told his mom what he'd done and she cooked up this whole scheme to throw us off the scent and get paid well for doing it. We saw right through her."

I'd heard about the case she was talking about, and, at the time, it'd really upset me. I hated hearing stories about scam artists trying to pass themselves off as professional psychics.

Candice eyed Kirkpatrick testily. "Dutch spoke very highly of you, you know."

Kirkpatrick blushed demurely, and I could feel that flicker of jealousy waking up in my insides again.

Candice continued. "Which is why I know it'll be a disappointment to him when I tell him how rudely you just insulted his *wife*."

Kirkpatrick's brow furrowed for a moment, and then her eyes darted to me, and it was clear that she finally understood that *I* was the psychic working for the Austin bureau.

Her blush deepened, and it was anything but demure. "I— I'm sorry," she said, clearly flustered. "I didn't realize—"

"Of course you didn't," I told her, and it felt pretty damn good to have the upper hand here. "As for my credentials and track record, I suppose that if you didn't trust *me*, you'd at least trust our numbers. I know Gaston sends you guys the same monthly report he sends to all the Texas bureaus, right?

The one that lists each bureau's percentage of cases solved?"

Kirkpatrick looked at me without blinking. That told me she'd seen the report.

Consistently, our numbers blew all the other bureaus' stats out of the water—and we were working almost exclusively on cold cases, which made our percentages all the more impressive.

Turning her attention back to Oscar she said, "Forty years ago, a guy named Louis Beam Junior—a white supremacist—wrote a manifesto called 'The Leaderless Resistance'. In it, he said that the future of white power lies not in one or twenty organized white supremacist groups, but tens of thousands of what he called 'lone lions'. Individuals not acting on behalf of a group they were affiliated with, but individually capable of carrying out acts of terrorism on their own.

"He somewhat rightly predicted that this was how the white power movement could gain traction and avoid government crackdowns where whole groups of people could be swept up in investigations and indictments. The theory failed to gain traction until the age of social media. Since then, these lone lion domestic terrorists have caused a world of hurt, and what's made them so successful has been our inability to track and trace them because, if they aren't tied to a specific hate group, how do we even find them? These guys operate in the shadows. Sure, we can find dialogue of some of them on various white-supremacist platforms, but these bastards never use their real names, and it takes time and subpoenas to come up with an IP address for any of these individuals, and there are so many of them that our resources are overwhelmed."

"Has any of the dialogue you've been monitoring involved killing female minority students at UT or even more generally, killing minority students?" Candice asked.

Kirkpatrick shifted in her seat, and she added a wince. She looked very close to her due date, and I suspected her back must ach from the pressure of the baby on her kidneys. "I have two guys on my team who've been heavily involved in monitoring the WS chatrooms. I'll talk to them and see if they've picked up anything, but, even if they could point to a specific conversation, it's exceptionally hard to tell who's going to follow through on any of the violence being fantasized about. Most of these guys are just bluster and beer."

"Can *we* talk to your two team members?" Oscar asked. "I'd like Abby to weigh in on anything they can point us to."

Kirkpatrick's gaze again flickered to me, and I could tell she was trying to reconcile her experience with a grifter, posing as a psychic, versus the woman in front of her who was married to a man she'd spent twenty-one weeks with, and had apparently gotten to know very well.

"Sure," she said stiffly. "Why not. I'll talk to them first, though, and prep them. I don't know how they're going to feel about interacting with . . . a . . . um . . . person like Mrs. Rivers."

I couldn't help but roll my eyes. "Please tell them I don't bite."

"Much," Candice murmured.

I slapped her knee under the table, and she smiled innocently at me.

"I'll still want to speak with them and prepare them," Kirkpatrick said, and her tone was firm.

"We'd appreciate it," Oscar said. "We'll wait to hear from either you or them."

We ended the call, and Candice clapped her hands and said, "Well, *that* was fun!"

I got up from my chair and began to walk out of the conference room.

"Where you goin', Coop?" Oscar asked.

I paused to look at my watch. Dammit. It was just a little after eleven a.m., too early for a prickly pear margarita—my go-to drink when life became a pain in the ass. "In search of chocolate," I said.

Candice was by my side in a flash. "I have a better idea," she said, her eyes dancing with enthusiasm, which I hated her for.

"What?"

"You'll see," she said, taking hold of my arm. "I'll drive."

"My odds of survival go way down when you're behind the wheel, you know."

It was Candice's turn to roll her eyes. "Whatever," she sang and continued to pull on my arm.

Grudgingly, I allowed her to lead me out of the room, and hopefully to something delicious, loaded with carbs, and guaranteed to make me feel better.

I could not have been more wrong.

CHAPTER 14

"*Why?*" I shouted as Candice pointed to the barbell loaded with more than half my bodyweight.

I was dripping with sweat, panting like a dog, and my legs were trembling, threatening to give out on me.

"Come on!" Candice yelled in reply. "You can do it, Abs! Two more reps and you're done!"

"No! I'm not doing them!"

Across the gym, the owner of the CrossFit "box" Candice had dragged me to looked on with concern. We were the only two other people there, and neither one of us was a member, but Candice had paid a fee for the "privilege" of working out during their open-gym hours.

"Sundance," she said, pushing the barbell closer to me with her foot. "Come on. You can do hard things."

I shook my head and glared at her. That was her favorite mantra of late. Anytime I complained about anything difficult going on in my life, she was there with that line, tossing it out like confetti at a birthday party.

"I *know*! But the fact that they're hard is *why* I don't *want* to do them!"

"Two. More. Reps. Let's go!"

"As a bestie, you suck," I growled, bending over to grip the barbell. With *considerable* effort, I heaved it up onto the front of my shoulders and then with a slight squat and a jump, managed to heft it off my shoulders while ducking under it to catch the barbell overhead.

I then slammed it down to the mat-covered floor where it made a satisfying *boom-ba-boom-boom!* sound.

Candice clapped her hands. "That's the spirit!"

I bent over again and gripped the barbell. "I . . .," I said, pulling it from the floor, "hate . . ." I added when I had the barbell once again on my shoulders, "*YOU!*" I shouted, completing the lift and then throwing the thing to the floor again.

Candice clapped again and came in for a sweaty hug. "See?" she said. "You did it!"

"Get off me, you swamp beast," I growled, laying my tired head on her shoulder. Now that the workout was over, I had to grudgingly admit that getting through it felt pretty good.

When she'd first pulled into the parking lot of the CrossFit gym, I'd thrown a big old fit. But Candice was having none of it. She threw an extra pair of leggings, gym shoes, and a tank top at me, then confiscated my phone and left me in the car with the windows rolled up while she sashayed her way into the building.

It was a sunny day, and it got hot in that car quick. So, I'd sworn like a sailor then got out and trailed after her. After changing into her spare gear, I'd joined Candice on the gym floor, hoping she'd be satisfied if I merely spent ten minutes on the rower.

She wasn't.

It was the most miserable forty minutes of my life, and if you've followed my life, you know exactly how miserable that would be.

After putting all our gear away and collecting our things, Candice waved at the gym owner, and we were once again back in the car. "I need a shower," I moaned, leaning back in my seat. "And a massage. And maybe even an ambulance."

"How about I treat you to a plate of nachos instead?"

I thought about that for exactly two nanoseconds. "Okay," I said. "But I'm not sharing."

"Didn't expect you to," she said with a laugh.

She started the car just as a buzzing sound reverberated through her gym bag in the back. "That's my phone," I said, making no move to retrieve it and eyeing her expectantly.

In return, Candice looked at me skeptically. "Really?" she said. When I didn't move, she added, "Ohmigod, you're such a child!" But she did fetch my phone for me and tossed it into my lap just as it was on its last ring.

"Hey, Oscar," I said, picking up the line and putting it on

speaker.

"Coop! Where've you two been? I've been calling both of your phones for the past twenty minutes."

"Candice decided what I needed most was a gauntlet of pain."

There was a pause, then, "She took you to CrossFit, didn't she?"

I made a face at Candice, and she grinned in return. "She did, and dude! I barely survived!"

"I've seen those guns she calls arms, and I don't doubt it."

Candice was cut like a Greek goddess. It was just one more annoying thing about her. "So what's up?" I asked, wanting to get off the topic.

"I heard from Kirkpatrick. And from your husband. Looks like she called him right after she got off the call with us, and he gave her the lowdown on your abilities. She was singing a more tolerant tune when she called me back, and she's sending down one of the two agents she was talking about. He should be here in about forty minutes."

"Perfect," I said as my stomach rumbled. "We'll have enough time to get nachos."

"Get them to go," he insisted. "And maybe take a shower before you head back here."

I looked down at the tank top I was wearing, which was still soaked in sweat, and then caught a glimpse of myself in the side mirror. "Roger that," I said. "I'll shower at Candice's cuz it's closer, and we'll see you in a few."

"Oh, hey!" he said before I could click off. "Pick me up a pulled pork burrito."

"You got it," I said. "Anything else? Candice is buying so I'd take advantage while you can."

Candice shot a little side-eye my way.

"In that case," Oscar said, "Make it a burrito, an order of the fish tacos, an extra side of guac and salsa, and a large Coke."

"You got it, buddy!" I sang, clicking off the call and smiling triumphantly at my sidekick. She may have gotten my goat at the gym, but I'd just gotten hers right back.

In response, Candice turned her head to look at me with an evil grin, and then she stomped on the accelerator, and I didn't say another word for the rest of the ride. Okay, well, I *did* scream once when we swerved to avoid colliding with a tractor trailer, but other than that I was deathly silent, settling for gripping the overhead handrail and praying a *lot!*

A while later, loaded down with to-go bags and the mouthwatering smell of hot cheese and corn chips, we arrived back at the bureau.

The team was back too. Oscar, Dutch, and Brice were standing in a half circle, talking with a handsome, and well-muscled guy, who looked to be in his late thirties.

As we approached the group, Dutch caught my eye and nodded. I totally ignored him.

Oscar limped forward to us, rubbing his hands together greedily. "Which bag is mine?" he asked, pointing to the several that we each carried.

"These," I said, indicating my entire armload.

Oscar carefully took them from me and winked at Candice as he passed her on the way to his desk. "You owe me, Hernandez," she said softly.

"Put it on my tab," he replied with a laugh.

We set our bags down on my desk, then went to greet the Dallas agent.

I let Candice walk in front of me to avoid making direct eye contact with Dutch.

As she approached, Brice smiled at her and said to the Dallas Agent, "Agent Christian, I'd like to introduce my wife, Candice Fusco, and our ace in the hole, Abbigail Cooper."

The agent turned to us and smiled, revealing dazzlingly white teeth. "Candice," he said, extending his hand to her. "Travis Christian. Nice to meet you."

"Hello, Travis," she said warmly. "Nice to meet you as well, and thanks for coming down."

"Happy to help." Turning next to me, his smile lost much of the luster. "Abbigail. Nice to meet you."

"Likewise," I said, offering him the same forced, lackluster smile in return.

It was obvious, pretty immediately, that we both considered the other an adversary.

"I've never worked with one of you people before," he said.

"A woman?" I asked.

He and the others chuckled, but there was a look in Travis's eyes, like he didn't appreciate the sarcasm.

"Funny. Good to know you have a sense of humor. I was expecting someone a little more . . . sensitive."

"Start lobbing lame psychic jokes at me, and I can get a little testy," I replied.

Still, I offered him my hand, trying to make peace, and in turn, he accepted it, but then he squeezed it in that way that guys do when they're trying to show you how firm a handshake they have or how big their dicks are. I always forget which.

When he let go, I resisted the urge to run to the fridge and cover my hand in ice, settling for simply letting it fall to my side, where it throbbed for the next ten minutes.

Candice could read me pretty well, and I knew she could tell I was hiding some irritation, so she said, "Why don't we all convene in the conference room? We brought plenty of food if anyone's hungry."

I cut my gaze to her, giving her a look to kill.

She smiled and added, "Of course, Abby's nachos are off limits. But I got two extra orders, just in case, so we'll be good."

I dropped the death ray eyes and headed over to my desk to grab my food before anyone else tried to swipe it, then led the way into the conference room. We all gathered around the table, and beverages were offered and passed around, along with paper plates, utensils, and napkins, and soon enough we were having ourselves a fiesta.

"Wow," Agent Handshake said. "These nachos are good."

"Right?" I said, again trying my best to be a good little

sport. "Bomb Tacos has the *best* nachos on the planet."

Agent Handshake grimaced and moved his head side to side like he wasn't sure about *that.* "Like I said, they are good, but I've had better. We've got a place in Dallas that'd blow these out of the water."

A hush fell over the conference room. Evvvveryone knew how much I loved the nachos from Bomb and how insulting them was a slight I wasn't about to let go.

True to form, I narrowed my eyes and forced a toothy smile. "Well, maybe next time you can grab a to-go order before you come this way. It'll save you the trouble of eating our swill. Which we offered to you for free."

Dutch cleared his throat and looked pointedly at me. I continued to ignore him.

Agent Handshake seemed surprised by my retort, and he scoffed. "Sorry. Didn't mean to insult anybody."

"Sure, sure," I told him in that easy breezy tone that really says, "Fuck you, you prick."

Candice coughed lightly and eyed her husband like, *Do something!*

Brice gave the tiniest shrug like, *What do you expect me to do? You know how she is!*

It was Oscar who jumped in. "We appreciate you taking the time to come down here and advise us, Travis. Anything you can tell us about these lone lions would be great."

Handshake wiped his hands on his napkin and finished chewing the mouthful of apparently substandard nachos before he said, "The movement got started forty years ago by a guy named Louis Beam. He had this idea of connecting individual 'lions' as he'd call them, all across the country via the internet to form a seemingly disconnected pride. I think he liked the double entendre, because his manifesto is chock full of that word.

"Anyway, he was definitely a pioneer ahead of his time by about twenty years on this. He'd take his dial-up computer all around the nation, stopping to meet with the leaders of small supremacist cells and show them how they could recruit members and spread the message of hate from the comfort of their dining room table. The idea of a one-man army all around the country causing havoc not as a group, but as lone individuals who didn't need to be in close proximity of each other to feel connected, was incredibly effective. If these guys acted independently—if they caused terror and violence in a thousand different places all over the country, then they wouldn't risk exposing a larger cluster to a bunch of sweeping indictments that'd take the whole cell down in the process.

"Beam's sole purpose was to incite a race war, and, as we now know, his tactics of on-line recruitment and racist hate-filled speech spread like wildfire. The same methods of recruitment he began back in nineteen-eighty-two are the same ones being deployed by every terrorist organization out there, from ISIS to the Proud Boys, and everyone in between.

"And, as we've seen lately, particularly here in the US, these tactics have been *effective*. Yeah, there're still many cells that are more organized with members clustered together, but there're far more individuals out there acting independently to bring violence and hate to their local communities. These are the lions Beam first imagined."

Candice said, "So, these lions aren't members of any one organization? They don't affiliate with any specific group?"

"A lot of them don't, but the irony from the research we've done in the past decade tells us that community is still important to these guys, and most of them do end up recruiting at least a few local members into these small cells of three to ten people. Timothy McVeigh was one of the first of these guys, and he recruited Terry Nichols and Michael Fortier into his cell."

"Could that've been merely because the bomb McVeigh used to blow up the Murrah Building was bigger than one guy could carry into a truck?" Oscar asked.

Handshake nodded and appeared chagrined. "Loading five-thousand pounds of ammonium nitrate and nitromethane is a daunting task for one guy. Splitting the heavy lifting three ways probably sounded good to him when he thought up the plan."

"Are any of the groups you're monitoring right now capable of putting together a bomb of similar magnitude?" Brice asked.

Scott shrugged. "Nitrate and methane are much better regulated these days, and we've got a built-in watch list when anyone without specific agricultural credentials orders a little too much, but there're so many other ways to spread terror.

"Take Vegas, for example," he said. "You put a guy on the top floor of a large hotel with enough guns and ammo for a small army, and within ten minutes sixty people are dead and over four hundred others are seriously injured. Not quite up to the Oklahoma City bomb standards, but it didn't need to be. It just needed to cause terror among a large segment of the population, and it did."

"I didn't realize Paddock was a white supremacist," I said.

"Who knows what he was?" Handshake snapped, the attitude creeping back into his voice. Clearly, he wasn't in the running for the *Abby Cooper's Number-One Fan!* award.

Meh. I'd live.

"A cowardly, piece of shit mass murderer," Candice said softly. "That's what he was."

Brice reached out and squeezed her hand. Candice had deep roots in Vegas, and one of her very dear friends—an old college roommate named Tiffany—had been one of the 59 people murdered that night. The poor girl had made it to the hospital, but by the time she'd gotten there, every operating room and surgeon was occupied trying to save other victims.

We learned later that Tiffany had been shot through the liver and the triage team had black-tagged her. She'd needed immediate surgery to survive, and as that was impossible, they'd done their best to make her comfortable, but there was little they could do otherwise.

She'd died an hour later, alone on a stretcher, conscious and bleeding internally until she'd succumbed.

It took Candice an exceptionally long time to come back from hearing the details about her friend's death, and for a while there, I'd been worried about her.

Handshake didn't know any of that, though, but I was still a little ticked off at him for bringing it up.

He seemed to notice Brice offering his wife comfort, and read between the lines. "Anyway," he said. "This serial killer you're trying to hunt down has all the markings of one of these lions. I've got twenty-five to thirty of these guys on my radar, but no one I've identified has been boasting about taking out students at UT."

"If you had to give him a profile, what would you say?" Oscar asked.

Handshake took a sip of his water before he replied. "I think he's probably in his late teens or early twenties. White—obviously, and likely Arian. I'd also say he's sexually repressed, had a troubled childhood, and sees himself as a savior . . . a nearly god-like figure.

"I'll guess that he dresses himself with a militaristic flair—maybe not fatigues, but more like Neo in the Matrix, and he has an overly inflated view of himself and his physical prowess. I'd also say he's a malignant narcissist, misogynist, racist, bigot, and in general hates anyone who doesn't share his rigid viewpoint that white, cis men are at the top of the social structure, and are under threat of extinction from minority, foreign, and feminist forces. The narrative in his head is that he and others like him are at war, and all bets are off. I think he scours white supremacy sites online, but rarely participates in the conversation. And, I'd wager that he's highly intelligent, strategic, technologically sophisticated, and often underestimated. He most likely came from a broken home, and at least one of his parents is concerned about how quickly he's become radicalized, but they're too afraid of him to alert the authorities."

"Do you believe he's a student at UT?" Oscar asked.

Handshake shook his head. "I think it's likely he's currently enrolled, but I also believe he works hard not to attract too much attention on campus to his warped world view."

I nodded as Handshake spoke. My radar agreed with everything he was saying.

"Any suggestions on how we can catch this guy?"

Handshake sighed. "You're going to have to hunt him down one clue at a time. I'd start with the university and see if they have any records of a white, male student threatening violence on another, minority student—likely a female. I'd then widen the search to include any professors that've been threatened or intimidated by a student who fits the description I described."

Brice looked at me and Candice. "Rivers and I have a meeting with the university president and the chief of campus police at three o'clock today. We'll be asking to sift through their student records, looking for anyone who's made threats or has had a history of mental illness, but I've already gotten some pushback from that office. The UT president is uncomfortable having the FBI look through any of the students' personal records without a warrant."

"Can we get one?" Candice asked.

"Doubtful," Brice said. "Without a name for us to specifically target, a judge isn't likely to grant a sweeping warrant to cover all of UT's student records."

"So, the president is okay with the murders of three of his students on university grounds and more likely to follow?" I asked, incredulously.

"I didn't say that, Cooper. He's as disturbed as anyone about what's been happening to these women, but he's suggesting he's suspicious of our intentions—"

"Who isn't," Candice scoffed.

Brice continued as if she hadn't commented. "—and without a named person of interest, he's reluctant to hand over the files."

"But we already got a big roster of female students when we were trying to find Ji. What's the damned difference?" I asked.

"Identification is different than investigation," Brice said simply. "I doubt we'll get anywhere even if the chief of campus police is cooperative."

I shook my head and rolled my eyes. "You're telling me that we'll need to bring the name of our unsub to him in order to search for said unsub?"

Brice nodded with a tired sigh. "Yep."

"So we're screwed," Candice said. "How the hell are we going to find this guy if we can't dig into the student files for someone matching the description Agent Christian provided?"

"We're not screwed," I said as my radar flashed the Greek symbol Omega in my mind and followed that with the image of a newspaper. "We need to interview the editor of the UT newspaper, and maybe a couple of the heads of UT's fraternities and sororities—what're they called?"

"The Panhellenic Council," Candice said. "Why, Sundance?"

"Because if anyone's plugged into campus gossip, it's the editor of the student newspaper—"

"The Daily Texan," Dutch said. We all looked at him. "It's the name of the student newspaper."

I almost thanked him, but then I reminded myself that I was still a little miffed, so I simply continued. "And we need to check out the sororities because if this guy was in a fraternity—" I paused to look at Handshake to get his take on that likelihood, and he seemed to think about it for a moment before he offered a slight nod, and I continued. "Then he probably attended a sorority party or two, and maybe he espoused his views to some of the sisters and-or he was rejected by a couple of the young ladies, and he seemed to take it a little too personally."

"I like that angle," Oscar said, and to my surprise, Agent Handshake was also nodding a little more enthusiastically this time.

"Great plan, Edgar," Dutch said, smiling at me.

I had to hand it to the guy; even when I was so pointedly and rudely ignoring him, he kept giving me chances to bring peace to the table. I relented and offered him a small smile in return. "Thanks, cowboy."

Candice got up from the conference table. Looking at me and Oscar, she said, "Shall we?"

I closed the lid on my half-eaten serving of nachos, which would no doubt end up being devoured for dinner. "We shall," I said.

Oscar too got up stiffly, and I knew his leg was probably throbbing from all the walking he'd done today.

As we began to head toward the exit, Agent Handshake said, "Hey, mind if I come with you?"

I was about to reply with a firm, *No!* when Candice said, "Sure, Travis. We could use your expertise for these interviews."

"Great," he said while I glared at Candice.

Traitor! I mouthed.

She patted my shoulder and whispered, "There, there, Sundance. You'll survive."

CHAPTER 15

We headed to the offices of the Daily Texan first. And I'm using the term, "office" loosely here, because the place was little more than a somewhat enclosed space in the basement of the William Randal Hurst building—or HSM as the students called it.

Candice had called ahead and got us an immediate interview with both the editor in chief and the managing editor.

"I'll bet they want to pick our brains about the murders on campus," I said after she'd hung up the call.

"Definitely," Candice agreed.

"We'll need to tread carefully," Oscar said from the backseat. "We don't want to give up any detail that could compromise the investigation."

"Noted," I told him.

"I can take the lead on questioning," Handshake said.

I turned my face toward Candice. When she glanced at me, I rolled my eyes, and I'm pretty sure it wasn't lost on the guy in the back.

"Terrific," Candice said to him, never breaking eye contact with me. "Abby and I will let you and Oscar take point on the interview, and if Abby or I need to jump in with a follow-up, we will."

I scowled at her and turned my face back toward the windshield choosing to stay silent for the rest of the ride.

We got to the HSM building in good time, but, by the look of the packed campus, it was going to take us awhile to find a parking slot. Candice let Oscar and Handshake out in front of the building, but ordering me to stay and use my radar to find a spot.

This was a little trick she seemed to deploy more and more lately, and I might've thought it annoying if it weren't such a fun challenge. "Turn right," I said, pointing to the first intersection.

"Gotcha," she said, turning right without question.

"It's on this street," I told her confidently.

We cruised slowly down the road and my radar kept pinging that we were very close to an available parking space. "I don't see anything," she said while we both scanned both sides of the street like a pair of starving vultures, looking for some easy pickings.

As we continued to move forward, well past the area I'd indicated, she said, "Did we miss it?"

My brow furrowed. "Make a U-turn."

She did and we went back the way we'd come only to end up at the same intersection from where we'd started our search. "Abs, there's no spot—"

"There!" I exclaimed. A woman had appeared, and was rushing to her car, which was parked right in front of the building we wanted to get into. Candice chuckled and put on her turn signal.

A minute later we were parked and hustling out of the car.

"God I love that radar of yours," Candice said.

"You want it?" I laughed.

"Uh . . . *tempting* as that might be, no way do I want to see some of the stuff you see."

I sighed. "It's not always the picnic it's made out to be."

"I can only imagine."

We hustled inside the building and followed the line of students down the stairs, along a bright hallway and stopped at the doors for the Daily Texan.

Through the glass pane, we could see Oscar and Handshake already speaking to a young man with pale skin and jet-black hair.

"Hey," Candice said when we sidled up next to them.

"That was quick," Oscar said.

Candice nudged me with her shoulder. "Abby's radar really comes in handy when you're hunting for a good parking place."

Handshake eyed me curiously. "Where'd you park?"

"The spot *literally* in front of the door," my sidekick said.

Handshake didn't seem impressed. In his defense, he was an arrogant prick, so I doubted much impressed him.

"Where're we at?" Candice asked, her gaze landing on the young man in front of us.

"Candice Fusco, Abby Cooper, meet Noah Sumner," Oscar said, making the introductions.

Candice extended her hand first. "Noah," she said warmly. "We spoke on the phone."

"Hi," he said nervously. And then his gaze shifted to me, and he said, "Are you the police psychic?"

I was slightly taken aback that he knew about me, but quickly recovered. "I've been known to assist in an investigation or two," I told him, taking the hand he offered me and shaking it.

"That is so cool!" he said. "I read about you in the Statesman a couple of weeks ago."

"Ah," I said, and felt my cheeks heat up. The Austin American Statesman had done a brief article about me a few weeks back. I had refused to grant them an interview, and they'd gotten precious little out of anyone else in the bureau, but that hadn't stopped them from running a story about me, especially after they'd reached out to other bureaus and police agencies I'd worked with, who'd coughed up a fair amount of detail and adding words of praise.

"I'd love to do an interview with you, Ms. Cooper," Noah said.

I smiled tightly. I don't give interviews because I don't like the attention, and by "attention" I really mean the assholes that can't wait to get to the bottom of an online article to leave a really hateful comment about me and my "supposed" abilities. I had enough enemies without encouraging a few more from the young fraternity bros on UT's campus.

"Sure," I said to Noah, going for the path of least resistance. "I'll reach out after this investigation, and we'll set something up, okay?" I lied.

He flashed me a bright smile. "Awesome!"

Handshake took it upon himself at that moment to clear his throat impatiently, and I eyed him, thinking that he was growing on me less and less by the minute.

I made a motion with my hand like, "After you," and he focused his attention on the young editor. "We're here because we'd like your help, Noah," Handshake began.

"Right," Noah said. "But I don't know how I can help you, sir."

"Well, as the editor here, I'm guessing you're one of the best people to ask about different fringe groups on campus."

"Fringe groups?" Noah repeated. "What do you mean by *fringe?*"

"Groups that might only allow white men to join," Candice said bluntly. "White supremacist in nature."

Noah shook his head. "Nah. There's no way anything like that formally exists here on campus. UT's president would put a stop to it right away, not to mention the student body here in Austin wouldn't tolerate anything like that. This campus is super diverse, and we'd shut that down quick."

"What about informally?" Candice asked.

Again, Noah shook his head. "We'll get the occasional story of someone getting too drunk at a party and calling someone the N word, but usually it's nothing more than that."

My gaze became unfocused as something familiar lit up in my mind. I saw the Greek Omega symbol again, but this time, my vision morphed into the view of a tropical island somewhere in the South Pacific. I interpreted that somewhat literally when I asked Noah, "Are any of the fraternities planning a trip to an island in the South Pacific?"

He looked at me blankly for a few seconds. "You mean, for like, spring break?"

"Yeah," I said. "Are any of the fraternities headed to Bali or . . ." I paused to study the image in my mind's eye again. The island felt small in size, and although I'd never been further west than Hawaii, I simply *knew* that this location was a tropical island near Australia.

The name of the island suddenly blossomed fully in my mind. "Fiji," I said. "Are any of the fraternities planning a spring break trip to Fiji?"

Noah's jaw dropped. "Whoa," he said. "You're talking about Phi Gamma Delta."

Handshake's attention pivoted to me, and I could tell that I'd shocked him.

"Phi Gamma Delta is headed to Fiji?" Candice asked, and I knew she didn't understand why that was important, but she also knew that confirmations were things that some of my larger insights were based on.

Noah shook his head. "No. I mean, I don't know if they're headed to Fiji, but that's their nickname."

"What's their nickname?" Oscar pressed.

"Phi Gamma Delta's nickname is Fiji," Handshake said.

Noah pumped his head up and down, his eyes wide as he continued to stare directly at me. "That's right. And they're a fraternity with a somewhat blemished history of racism. Their unofficial mascot is called, 'Fiji Man', a dark-skinned guy in a grass skirt with a bone through his nose."

"Wow," I said, my own eyes going wide. "That is *beyond* offensive."

"Right?" Noah said. "They're prohibited from displaying it, but I'm pretty sure a few of the members they still try to get away with it at one of their Fiji Islander parties. No one ever formally complains, but we've all heard rumors."

I looked at Candice and Oscar pointedly, while avoiding eye contact with Handshake. They both nodded, and it pleased me that they understood me without a single word spoken.

Candice lifted her index finger and made a swirling motion. "Let's roll," she said.

"Wait . . . you're leaving?" Noah asked.

"Sorry, kid," Oscar said. "We've got interviews to conduct. Thanks for your time, though."

I followed behind Candice, and we were almost to the door when Noah called out, "Miss Cooper! You're still gonna let me interview you, right?"

I glanced at the kid over my shoulder. "Of course!" I told him, then held up my pinkie finger. "Pinkie swear."

We made it back out to the hallway, and Candice glanced at me with a smirk. "Liar."

"Yeah, yeah," I said. "He'll get over it."

Candice set the pace, and we walked quickly down the hallway toward the stairs. I knew she was as anxious as I was to interview the frat boys from "Fiji".

"Coop! Fusco! Wait up!" Oscar yelled.

We both stopped and looked back. Oscar was limping as fast as his leg brace would let him, and I was suddenly worried that he'd do some damage to that artery if he didn't slow down. "We'll wait," I told him so that he'd stop rushing toward us.

Between us and Oscar was Handshake. He was eyeing me like a puzzle he couldn't quite figure out.

It didn't bother me. I get that a lot, actually.

He reached our side and waited next to us while we waited for Oscar. The poor guy was trying to take slow, measured steps, but I could tell he still felt the pressure to hurry.

I smiled at him and held my hand up to let him know it was okay, which was when I became aware that someone was watching me.

Glancing over Oscar's shoulder I saw a figure in a black hoodie and jeans, standing off to the side of the students walking past him. The hood was pulled down low, so I couldn't clearly see his face, but I *knew* he was staring directly at me.

He put a hand to his head, and at that exact moment, my phone rang. I looked at the display, and it read, *Unknown*.

Glancing back at the figure down the hallway, I lifted the phone to my own ear and answered the call. "Hello?"

"Hello, Abby," he said.

A chill ran down my spine.

"Did you enjoy the present I left for you in the greenhouse?"

"Abs?" Candice said. "Everything okay?"

She was, no doubt, looking at my face which had almost certainly gone pale.

Without answering her, I lowered my phone and took off at a full sprint, heading directly for the hooded figure.

He saw me coming and also lowered his phone before turning and taking off like a rocket.

I passed a confused looking Oscar and didn't pause to explain, I simply aimed for the fleeing man and hoped I could gain ground on him before he made it out of the building.

I should've known better. I'm a forty-five-year-old woman who'd barely survived her morning workout, trying to run down a twenty-something young man in the physical prime of his life.

He left me in the dust.

Still, that didn't stop me from continuing the chase.

He led us down the corridor to another set of stairs. Panting hard, I caught a glimpse of him as he leapt up the steps, taking them two or three at a time, and I knew that a set of exit doors must be at the top of the staircase. I thought that if I could only make it up them fast enough, I might get a feel for which direction he took off in, and maybe we'd get lucky and spot him on a traffic cam or something.

Weaving around a crowd of students, I hit the stairs and also tried to climb them two at a time. That was a no go, and I tripped midway up, nearly doing a face-plant, but managed to catch myself just in time. Pushing off from the stairs again, I worked on pumping my legs as fast as I could and finally reached the top.

My lungs heaving while I scanned the area. As I'd guessed, there were a set of exit doors just beyond the stairwell, but there was no clear sign of the unsub, however, there *were* dozens of students inside and out wearing dark hoodies. The area at the top of the stairs on this end of the building was a wide-open space with plenty of corridors feeding off of it and another staircase right behind the one I'd emerged from.

He could've gone anywhere from here, and I knew I had

no chance to run him down or even figure out which way he'd gone. It was a fifty-fifty split on whether or not he'd even exited the building.

"Fuck!" I yelled, doubling over to rest my palms on my knees, and that's when I became aware of Candice, coming to a stop at my side.

"Which way did he go?" she asked, panting hard herself.

I almost felt smug at the fact that she was also out of breath.

"I don't know," I said, standing tall again.

She turned wide eyes at me. "Our unsub?"

I nodded.

"Then he knows we were here," she added.

"Yes. Yes, he does."

"He's been following us?"

"I'd count on it. He wants to know how close we are to catching him. This is a game of cat and mouse to him, and he thinks he's one step ahead."

"Shit," she said. "So far, he is one step ahead of us."

I sighed heavily. "Should we go find the—"

"Hey!" we heard, and Candice and I turned to look where the call was coming from. Handshake was hurrying toward us. "What's going on?" he demanded.

"Abby saw the unsub."

Handshake eyed her in puzzlement, then he turned his gaze to me. "How do you know?"

I held up my phone to show the call from an unknown number. "He called while he was watching us. I was looking in his direction when he placed the call, and my intuition said that it was him. When I began running toward him, he took off."

Handshake appeared even more confused. "So, you don't *really* know it was him," he said.

"Yes. Yes, I do, Agent Christian. It was him."

He raised a skeptical eyebrow, and it annoyed me because that's usually *my* move. "He could've easily been a student, placing a call that just happened to coincide with a caller on your phone, and when you started running toward him, he got spooked and fled."

"Why would he get spooked in the first place?" Candice demanded.

"I don't know, but if I were him, and I saw a strange woman running right toward me with an angry look on her face, I'd probably take off running for it."

I glared at him. "Wanna play that out?" I asked, my hands balling into fists. God, I *hate* skeptical, arrogant assholes like him.

He smirked at me, which just ratcheted up my irritation. "Pass," he said.

"It was him," I insisted. "You can believe me or not. I don't care."

"Come on," Candice said, moving back toward the stairs. "We should find Oscar before he thinks we've abandoned him."

Oscar had made it halfway down the hall by the time we found him. "Where'd you go?" he demanded, breathing hard and clearly irritated that all three of us had left him behind.

"Abby saw the unsub," Candice told him.

Oscar's eyes bugged wide. "You did?" he asked me.

"Yeah."

He looked past me toward the hallway leading to the stairs. "I take it you didn't catch him."

"Nope," I said. "He's a fast one."

Oscar's attention then moved to Handshake, who was looking particularly annoyed. To Candice he asked, "What's with him?"

"He doesn't believe Abby saw our unsub."

Oscar's gaze swiveled back over to Handshake, and it was his turn to look annoyed. "If Cooper says she saw the unsub, then she *saw* the unsub, Agent Christian."

Handshake didn't reply, but I could tell he had a perfectly snide comment he was just itching to make, and none of us missed the slight roll of his eyes.

Oscar's attention turned back to me. "Can you describe

the guy?"

I shook my head. "He was wearing a hoodie that put his face in shadow. I didn't get any detail other than he was a white male, thin build, maybe five-eleven to six feet tall."

Oscar nodded, and then he looked toward the ceiling of the hallway. I looked up too, and I knew pretty quickly what he was looking for.

"No cameras," I said.

"Nope," Oscar agreed. "Maybe there're some outside that'll catch his exit."

I frowned. I had a feeling that, even if there were security cameras on the outside of the building, finding a tall, lean, young man in a hoodie was going to yield far too many candidates. "Oscar, I'm not sure if he's even made it out of the building yet." And then I pointed around the hallway as students walked past hustling to get to their next class, to lunch, or back to their dorms. From that observation alone I could count off twelve young men in hoodies, four of whom had the hood pulled up over their heads, obscuring their faces.

"So what do you want to do?" he asked me.

"Let's stick with our original plan to interview the members of Phi Beta Fiji," I said.

Candice smirked. "Phi Gamma Delta," she corrected.

I waved my hand airily. "Betato, Gammato, Candice."

She chuckled. "We're back this way," she said, pointing over her shoulder.

We walked slowly so that Oscar could keep up. Still, the poor guy was huffing and puffing pretty good by the time we reached Candice's car, where Oscar seemed to hesitate getting in.

I didn't blame him.

Candice seemed to read his mind, because she pulled open her car door and snapped, "Oh, for Christ's sake, Oscar, I'll drive the speed limit, okay?"

His gaze traveled to me, and I thought that maybe he was thinking that if we were about to be killed by riding in

Candice's car, I'd speak up.

I shrugged, gave a lopsided smile, and got in. He followed suit a moment later.

True to her word, Candice *did* drive the posted speed limit for once, although she completely blew threw a crosswalk where several students had already stepped onto the black and white lines, but why quibble when we ended up alive and in one piece at Fiji house.

The fraternity was large, old, and weathered. Built in a Colonial Revival style, it reminded me of a plantation house that had definitely seen better days. Next to the main building was a sign bearing an artist's mockup of a massive renovation with no date posted about when construction would start. I had a feeling the building commission was still busy milking alumni for contributions.

We found a spot to park not far away, and the four of us got out and approached the building. I didn't much care for the vibe coming from the house—old houses can carry a *lot* of residual energy from all the souls that've lived—and sometimes died—there. As a rule, I try to avoid older buildings as much as possible because they always seem to overwhelm my radar.

Still, I followed dutifully behind the others, keeping pace with Oscar as Handshake and Candace took point.

"Is your phone on or off, Coop?" he asked me.

I glanced at him then at my phone. "It's on."

"Think that's a good idea?"

I grimaced. "I'm damned if I do and damned if I don't, buddy."

"If he can reach you, he can hold you hostage as a host for his next execution."

"I know."

"What's the upside to keeping your phone on, then?"

I paused to look frankly at him. "I *want* him to contact me. I want him to take the kinds of chances he just took to get close to me. He *thinks* he's torturing me, and to be fair, he is, but he's also putting himself closer to being caught, and,

Oscar, we've *got* to catch this son of a bitch."

He nodded. "Okay, but maybe let me hold your phone and answer the call if he calls again."

"Why?"

"To deny him the hit he thinks he's gonna get, Coop. This guy loves to see you rattled. It elevates his pleasure when causing pain. If I answer, he's denied the adrenaline, and he might come even closer and take an even bigger risk."

Without any further questioning, I handed Oscar my phone. "If Dutch calls, don't answer it. Just hand it back over."

"Got it."

"His name comes up as 'SSMS'."

Oscar cocked a questioning eyebrow.

"Super sexy main squeeze," I translated.

Oscar's face reddened. "Jesus, Coop . . ." he said on a sigh. "There're just some things I don't wanna know."

"Wanna know what your nickname is?" I teased.

"No!"

I giggled. "You'll ask me someday. You wait. You'll see. Curiosity is gonna get you to ask."

"Doubtful," he said, pocketing the phone.

We headed up the stairs to stand behind Candice and Handshake, who knocked on the front door.

It was opened by a short, elderly woman with cotton candy-colored hair. Definitely not what I was expecting.

"Hello," she said, eyeing Handshake like he was the leader of our little group. "Can I help you?"

Handshake did the honors of flashing his badge. "Special Agent Travis Christian, ma'am," he said with authority.

The woman ogled his badge like a scared squirrel. Her hand went to the necklace around her neck, which she tugged on nervously. "You're here about the girls, aren't you?"

I think we all blinked a time or two before Candice said, "Yes. How did you know?"

"It's all anyone can talk about on campus," she said. "I don't care if it's the middle of midterms. The president should've suspended classes and sent everyone home."

I agreed with her completely.

"Are you the house director?" Candice asked.

"Yes," she said, then offered Candice her hand. "Stephanie DeVoe, everyone calls me Stevie though. I've been the house director here for the last thirty years."

"Thirty years?" Oscar said appreciatively. "Impressive." He then offered his own badge and introduced himself, me, and Candice, something Handshake had failed to do. "Can we talk to you and a some of the fraternity members, ma'am?"

Stevie stood aside. "Of course. Come in, please."

We entered into the large front hall which was much cleaner and well-kept than I'd expected. "This way," she said, and we followed along, passing a living room area with black leather sofas and lots of bright orange accents.

Stevie came to a stop in a smaller seating area that resembled a den. There was a smattering of young men in and around the area—most of whom gave the four of us some curious looks, but none of them seemed overly interested in our sudden appearance inside their frat house.

"Have a seat," Stevie said, indicating several of the club chairs in one area of the room. "Would any of you like coffee or tea?"

"No, thank you, ma'am," Oscar said. I liked that he was taking the lead here, mostly because it seemed to irk Handshake.

Oscar grunted as he sat down, and Stevie pointed to his leg brace. "Did you hurt your leg?" she asked, and she still seemed a little nervous and flustered, because her voice wobbled a bit.

Oscar smiled. "Nothing that won't heal soon, ma'am."

Stevie moved over to an ottoman and pulled it forward to set it under Oscar's leg. His face again turned red, and he thanked her.

I liked that she was so naturally nurturing. I hoped she'd be able to give us a hint about the unsub. Stevie was the last to sit down, and she clasped her hands together and said, "What did you want to know?"

Handshake opened his mouth to speak, but I beat him to it. "Ms. DeVoe, as you may or may not have heard, all of the young women executed on campus were smart, accomplished, women of color."

Her brow knit together, and I knew immediately she could tell where I was headed.

"It's our belief that the person responsible is a student on campus," I continued. "A white male in his early twenties, who might allow his racist views to come out publicly. And we think there might be a link between him and this fraternity."

Stevie's hand went back to tugging on her necklace. "Why would you think there's a connection between what that horrible person is doing to those girls and this house?"

Stevie was naturally defensive of the young men under her charge, but there was just something that bothered me. Maybe it was the look in her eyes that suggested her defensiveness was a bluff. Whatever it was, I didn't like it.

"We're merely asking questions," I told her. "After all, the nickname of this fraternity is Fiji, correct? And the unofficial mascot is Fiji Man, right?"

I wanted her to know that we knew of the fraternity's history of insensitivity.

A blush touched Stevie's cheeks. "This chapter has worked very hard to repair its former transgressions. I can assure you that no member here would even *think* of advancing such a shameful of racist agenda."

Liar, liar, pants on fire said my radar.

I turned my head to look pointedly at Candice, just to let her know that Stevie's pants were metaphorically smokin'.

"Ms. DeVoe," Candice said, "are you certain that no member of this house has expressed views that are even a little . . . inappropriate?"

"No. Absolutely not!" she insisted.

My lie detector wasn't buying it.

"Stevie?" a new voice asked. I looked over my shoulder and saw a young man standing in the doorway. Tall with light brown hair and deep-set eyes with a square jaw, he was just the kind of guy I would've been attracted to in college. "Is everything okay?"

"Yes, Chase," she told him. "Of course." An awkward silence ensued while Chase continued to stand in the doorway, staring at us like he expected to be in on the conversation. Stevie finally said to us, "Chase Frazier is this year's president of Phi Gamma Delta."

"Chase," Candice said, waving to him, "will you join us, please? We're from the FBI, and we have some questions about the brothers of Fiji."

Chase's eyes narrowed. He looked suspicious of the invitation, which, I couldn't really blame him for, given the fact that four people from the FBI were sitting in the den of his fraternity house.

To Stevie, he asked, "Do I need to get my dad on the phone?"

"No, dear," she said. "At least not yet."

"Let me guess," I said, pointing my radar at the young man. "Your dad's a lawyer."

"He is," Chase replied.

"You don't have to answer our questions," Handshake offered, and I glared at him. "But we would like to ask them, and you can answer or not answer any question we throw at you."

Chase moved into the room and took a seat opposite Handshake. "Fire away," he said, doing his best to appear casual.

"We're investigating the murder of three female students here on campus," Oscar said before Handshake could ask the first question.

Chase nodded. "I heard about that."

He said it like it was a rumor he'd overheard, rather than a series of three horrific crimes committed by a monster that was the only thing anyone was talking about on campus.

"We believe the person responsible is likely a white male, a student, and we have reason to believe these are hate crimes."

"Hate crimes?" he repeated. And there was just something about the way he said that. Like he'd been rehearsing the line. "What does any of that have to do with Fiji?"

"The profile of the individual we're looking for suggests he might be a member of a fraternity, and we believe he's also a white supremacist."

Chase dropped his gaze to the floor, as if he were deep in thought. Shaking his head he said, "None of the brothers here would do anything like that. We're all about inclusion."

My own gaze darted around the room and out into the hallway which had a good view of the front living room where a dozen young men sat talking or studying. Not a single soul had skin any darker than olive.

"How many members are people of color?" I asked Chase, just to push the point.

He blinked. "I . . . I mean, there's Rich Punjab," he said. "And Pete Yang."

I wanted to laugh. "Rich" and "Pete" didn't sound very diversified if you asked me.

But Chase was still searching his memory banks for another brother of color. He did a lot of fast blinking but didn't offer up another name. "This was a bad year for recruitment. Our numbers are down from years past."

Candice and I traded skeptical eyebrows. It didn't matter if *this* year's recruitment was down. It mattered what the past *four* years had shown.

Oscar asked the next question, but my gaze had moved from Candice to over her shoulder toward a bulletin board at the side of the stairwell leading to the upper floors. And on that bulletin board was a flyer that seemed to be calling for my attention.

Motioning to Oscar that I wanted my phone, he reached into his back pocket and got it out, handing it to me with a frown. I knew he was worried the unsub was going to call and I'd pick up, but I had a more urgent need for my phone at the moment. Getting up from my chair, I moved over to the flyer to read it more closely. Behind me the conversation paused briefly, but then it resumed, with Handshake taking over the questions.

Once I was standing in front of the flyer, I read,

Hey, Fijis!

Your Invited to a Hot Shower Party with Kappa Alpha Theta!

I noted right away that the party had taken place in the past. In fact, it'd been two nights before Simone had called in to the *Toscano Files*. After very subtly taking a picture of the flyer with my phone, I glanced back over my shoulder. Chase had just answered a question Handshake had asked, and his gaze found me. There was no hiding how nervous he appeared seeing me at the billboard.

I smiled sweetly and returned to my seat, waiting out the next six or seven questions from Handshake, in which both Chase and Stevie continued to insist that the young men at Fiji were angels from heaven and perfectly innocent of any impure thought.

In other words, the bullshit in the room was at least waist deep.

Finally, Handshake stood, and the rest of us got up as well. "Thank you for your time," he said to Stevie and Chase.

"Of course!" Stevie said as we began to leave the den, while Chase stood sentinel by the chair he'd occupied and watched us walk out.

I walked slowly so that Oscar didn't feel like he had to hurry, and as we approached Chris on our way to pass him, the young man's eyes narrowed, and I again smiled pleasantly at him. To me, he was nothing but a boy at the peak of his power. He'd probably brag about being president of Fiji for the rest of his life. It was actually a little sad.

Pausing for a moment, I pointed to the bulletin board. Oscar followed my finger and also paused next to me. "A hot shower party?" I asked.

Chase grinned, but there was sweat on his brow, and I

didn't think it was from the Texas heat. "Yeah. Wild time."

"I bet." I said, and I continued to stand there expectantly, just to see if Chase would offer up a little more. Oscar held vigil with me, and I knew he was picking up on the subtle fact that there was more to the story.

Under the pressure of our collective stares, Chase cleared his throat and eventually said, "For hot shower parties, we get dressed up in towels, wear shower caps, and bring some bath toys. It's juvenile, but fun."

"Ah," I said with a chuckle, giving Oscar a playful slap on the shoulder. "College. I have many memories of fun parties myself from back in the day."

Oscar laughed lightly too. "The good old days," he said.

I nodded like the three of us were having an easy breezy conversation when all three of us were well aware of the subtext. "Anyway, thanks again. Good luck on your midterms," I told Chase.

He nodded, and his shoulders relaxed with relief. It was what I'd been hoping for. I needed him to not think about following up on something I knew full well he was hiding.

We caught up to the Candice and Handshake outside, and right away, Oscar asked, "What'd you pick up in there, Coop?"

I motioned to where Candice's car was parked. "Let's get to the car first."

Candice offered me a curious look before she led us to her car, and we piled in. "Spill it, Sundance," she said.

I took a deep breath. Revealing what I was about to confess brought me a sense of shame that I knew I wasn't responsible for, but still, it wasn't something I'd shared with anyone. Not even Dutch. "I have a cousin," I began.

"I thought you had at least a half dozen," Candice said.

"Yeah, I do. What I mean is, I have a cousin I don't speak to, and will never speak to again."

"Why?" Oscar asked.

I took another deep breath. "Because he's a white supremacist."

"Whoa," Candice said. "Really? I mean, I've heard you talk about your parents and how bigoted they are, but I didn't know you had a cousin who was involved in that movement."

I shook my head and dropped my gaze to my lap. "The thing is, I used to really love this cousin. He was so cool. Just a great kid, or so I thought. And then, one weekend about fifteen years ago, I was on the West Coast visiting my medium friend, Theresa, and my cousin and I got together for lunch, during which he took a call from a buddy of his. I couldn't hear the whole conversation, but I do remember my cousin smiling and saying loudly into the phone, 'I could use a little *hot shower!*' And he repeated it a few times, which was enough for me to understand it was a chant between him and his buddy, and that *hot shower* was code for something else."

Oscar glanced at the fraternity house, then turned back to me. "Did you find out what it's code for?"

"I asked Chad—my cousin—about it when he got off the phone, and he laughed and said that it was code for 'white power'. The two sound enough alike to get away with saying it in public. That was the last time I ever spoke to him."

"I'm still not following," Handshake said.

I held up my phone so that they could all see the photo I'd taken of the flyer.

"Whoa," Candice said.

Handshake said nothing, but his brow was deeply furrowed.

Then Oscar said, "I'm guessing you don't think it's a coincidence."

In answer, I said, "My cousin belonged to a fraternity when he was in school. I don't know for certain which one, but I'm suspicious that it might've been Fiji."

The three of them simultaneously looked back at the frat house we'd just vacated. "We aren't going to get a confession out of Chase or Stevie," Candice said.

"No," I agreed. "But we *might* be able to learn a little more from Kappa Alpha Theta."

Candice smirked. "Good thinking. Let's head over there

and see what they have to say."

I put my hand on her arm. "I think only you and I should go."

A pregnant pause followed. Neither Candice nor I were FBI agents, and we both lacked an official badge, so getting info out of the young women might be a little tricky.

"Coop's right," Oscar said. "The sorority girls are far more likely to open up to you two ladies than to us."

I nodded and sent him a grateful look.

"I'll drop you boys off back at the office," Candice said. "It's only ten minutes away and we can be back here in twenty."

"Good plan," Oscar said. Turning to me he added, "Want me to keep your phone, Coop?"

I shook my head, feeling that I needed to keep it with me. "No. But I promise not to answer any unknown callers."

"Good," he said, but I wasn't quite sure he believed me.

Candice set off and I thought to myself that I hoped we could interview the women at Theta and be back at the office for the rest of the afternoon within an hour.

Little did I know that my plan for the day was about to go completely off the rails.

CHAPTER 16

The Kappa Alpha Theta house was another Colonial Revival structure. Situated just off the street and partially hidden behind two walls and a wrought iron gate, the place had a soft pink, two-story central house, with two one-story wings attached.

There wasn't much in the way of available parking places, which forced Candice to wind around the surrounding blocks until my radar found us a spot. Before we got out of the car, Candice held me back by putting her hand on my arm, then she took out her phone and conducted a search, on what I didn't then know, but eventually she nodded, and we got out and hoofed it over to the sorority. We arrived at the house with its big Greek letters displayed prominently next to the door, then we passed through the tall black iron gate to the front entrance, above which was a large banner that welcomed us to Theta.

"Let me talk first and follow my lead, okay, Sundance?" Candice said as she walked up the steps to the front door.

"Copy that, Cassidy," I said.

My partner knocked, and while we waited for the door to be answered, we could hear the chatter of students inside.

The door was opened by a gorgeous blonde, with bright blue eyes, a delicate nose, and a perky mouth. "Hi!" she said jovially. "Can I help you?"

"Good afternoon," Candice said. "I'm Bridgette Gloss, class of 1994, and this is my fellow Theta sister, Annette Armstrong, also class of '94. We're in town for a conference, and thought we'd drop in to see our old house and hang with our younger sisters for a bit."

Blondie's expression went from friendly to excited. "Ohmigod! We *love* it when sister alumni drop by! Y'all come on in!" she said, waving us across the threshold.

We came into another large foyer which led directly to a

staircase and up to the second story and the sorority's sleeping quarters. As I looked around, trying to appear as if I recognized my surroundings, I noticed how neat and tidy the place was. This was in large contrast to my own college experience where, for four years, I lived in an atmosphere that can affectionately best be described as, "Dorothy's house—post tornado."

Once we were inside, the blonde shut the door and turned to us, beaming that bright white smile. Offering us her hand, she said, "I'm Brandy Herschel."

"Hi, Brandy," I said, taking her hand while also pointing my radar at her. She was an interesting mix of bubbly energy mixed with an undercurrent of anxiety. She was, no doubt, stressed about her midterms.

"Wow," Candice said as she stood next to me and looked all around the area. "So much has changed, and, at the same time, it's still really familiar."

I mimicked her by looking all around too and nodding appreciatively.

Candice pointed to the walls, which were painted a light peach. "Remember when the walls were celery green?"

I chuckled. "I do. We had a few jokes about covering them in vegetable dip for a late-night snack."

Brandy and Candice laughed, then Brandy said, "Come on into the living room and meet the girls," she said.

We followed after her and entered a charming, spacious room with lots of cream hues and light pastel accents.

Sitting in the living room area was a sea of platinum blonde hair, light eyes, and bare tan legs. It was like a Swedish convention had come to town and decided to sit a spell at Theta house.

"Hey, y'all! Meet two sisters from the class of '94!" Brandy exclaimed. I had a suspicion that she'd been on the cheer team in high school.

Lips parted around the room, exposing beaming, bright white teeth, but for many of the girls there was an unnatural vacant look to their eyes. It was an odd effect, actually. It made me recall the movie *The Stepford Wives*.

Candice, in full "Bridgette Gloss" role, waved at the girls and said, "Hi! I'm Bridgette and this is Annette. We're so excited to come by and hang with y'all for a little while."

A few sorority members nodded, but the rest continued to look at us expectantly, like we were the entertainment for their afternoon.

"What do y'all do?" asked one of the girls.

"We're both in marketing," Candice said, thinking quickly. "We work for a large advertising firm in Chicago."

"Chicago?!" one girl exclaimed. "I would *love* to live and work there!"

I smiled wide at her. "Make sure to give us your email, sister, and we'll help make some connections for you after you graduate."

The girl squealed and tapped her feet excitedly.

Candice sat down on one of the only open loveseats and motioned for me to sit next to her. I did and remained quiet as she began to subtly grill the girls.

"So! Tell me about these crazy scary murders on campus," she said. "Annette and I caught a bit of the story on the news last night."

"Ohmigod," said one girl to our left. "We have all been so freaked out! We've been walking each other to classes and picking up our sisters after dark. I swear, if it weren't midterms, I'd have headed home to Dallas after the first girl was found!"

One girl, however, tucked away in a lone chair in the corner said, "He's not after blondes though. All the girls that've been killed have been more . . . ethnic."

I felt the hair on the back of my neck stand up on end. Her comment made me bristle. A few of the girls looked nervously at the speaker, and then over to us to see if we'd call out the insensitivity of the comment.

I waited to see what Candice would say or do, and she simply shuddered and said, "Still, it's just so creepy! You need to be careful, sisters. This nut job could change up the profile of the next girl he grabs."

The chick in the corner sighed heavily and rolled her eyes.

I cocked my head at her and asked, "You don't agree?"

Tapping her chest, she said, "I'm a criminal justice major with a minor in psychology, so I can tell you that he's not going to do that. He'll stick with girls of color if he gets another chance to kidnap someone."

"Criminal justice with a minor in psychology? That's impressive," Candice said.

Corner chick nodded. "I'm going to be an FBI profiler. The pay is lousy, but I figure I can work that job for a few years, then write a book and a screenplay about all the criminals I profiled."

My brows arched in surprise. Becoming an FBI profiler was no easy task, and it certainly took more than a BS in criminal justice and a minor in psychology, but I had to appear as if I believed she could do just that. "I love that plan," I told her.

She smiled in a way that told me she thought herself special. "Thanks."

"Are y'all still going to some great parties?" Candice asked next. "When we were students, we lived for the parties that Fiji threw. They were always a wild time!"

A cascade of groans ensued, but Brandy's voice rose above the fray, "Fiji's parties are so lame. They threw a hot shower party last weekend and sent us a message that, and I quote, 'Gentlemen prefer blondes.'"

The girls laughed, but I could tell many of them were uncomfortable with the informal request from Fiji.

"What's a hot shower party?" I asked.

More groans ensued. "They wanted us to come wrapped in a bath towel," one girl said. "I mean, why not just throw a beach party if you're looking for us to come half naked?"

Lots of blonde heads nodded.

"There're some cute boys there, for sure, but most of the brothers are such narcissists," said Corner Girl.

"Did you go to the party?" Candice asked her.

"I did," she said. "Most of us went, but a lot of us left early."

"Why?" my sidekick pressed.

"Some of the brothers got really inappropriate with Chloe."

I looked around the room. More nodding heads, but no one was looking anywhere else except to the girl in the corner, which told me that Chloe wasn't here.

"Did they hurt her?" Candice asked with concern.

"No," Brandy said. "Well, not physically. They were just really rude to her."

"In what way?" I asked.

A somewhat uncomfortable silence followed. Finally, Brandy said, "Chloe's mixed race. A couple of the brothers were picking on her for it. They told her to go back to Theta house, dye her hair blonde and bleach her skin, then she could come back to the party."

My eyes widened as my radar binged. "Wow," I said. "That's so *blatantly* racist!"

That won me lots of nods. "They'll deny it if they ever get called on it," Brandy continued. "But Chloe wouldn't lie about something like that."

"What's Chloe's last name?" I asked, like our line of questioning was perfectly normal.

"Hill," Brandy said. "Chloe Hill."

"Do you know which boys said that to her?" Candice asked next.

Brandy shook her head and looked around the room at her sisters to see if any of them knew. Everyone was shaking their heads.

Candice eyed me, and we traded looks of concern. Then she then turned back to the group. "Is Chloe here?"

Brows furrowed, and I knew the sorority sisters were curious why she was pressing the point, but Candice didn't explain, which I think was a good thing because one of the girls eventually said, "She's at the Tower,"

"The tower, like the UT tower?" I asked. My pulse started

to race when I remembered that I'd caught a glimpse of the famous clock tower earlier, and it had sent a chill down my spine.

At the time, I'd thought it was because of the famous mass shooting there by Charles Whitman in the midsixties, but now I was wondering if there was a more prophetic reason for the chills.

But as I looked at the girls in the room, I could tell I'd said the wrong thing. They were looking at me like I'd just asked a dumb question that I should already know the answer to.

Candice rolled her eyes and covered for me. "Annette, remember? The tower was going through that major renovation when we were students here. We never saw it completed, but I heard they'd turned the building into a great place to study."

Her answer seemed to satisfy the girls, because their odd looks at me turned to smiles directed at Candice.

"Oh, yeah!" I said, smacking my head. "We should head over there and check it out, Bridgette. I'd love to see it."

Candice got up and said, "Maybe we could find Chloe and offer her our support. She might need a little alumni sisterhood love after experiencing that kind of hateful racism."

I nodded like that was the best idea ever. "Do y'all know where she usually studies?"

"Second floor," corner girl said. "In the library."

I stood up too, and we were about to take our leave when Brandy said, "Wait, y'all are leaving? Don't you want a tour of the house? We've had a lot of updates in the last couple of years. You might really like them."

Candice and I exchanged side glances. I could tell the girls were getting a little suspicious of our odd behavior.

"Sounds wonderful!" Candice said. Then she motioned to Brandy and added, "Lead the way."

Inwardly I groaned. My gut suggested we didn't really have time for a tour. Something was off, and I didn't like it, so the second we moved on from the dining area, where we both made sure to "Oooo," and "Ahhhhh," I pretended to receive a phone call, when really, I'd hit the speed dial for my hubby.

"Sorry!" I said to Brandy and the five or so other girls with us, wiggling my phone. "I have to take this."

Moving off to the side while the others chatted and waited for me, I heard Dutch say, "Hey, dollface. What's up?"

"Hi, Dutch!" I said all perky-like. "What's goin' on?"

There was a pause on Dutch's end of the call, and he said, "Uh, babe. You called me."

"Oh, no! Malware! Did it hit every computer on the network?"

Another pause and Dutch said, "Edgar, are you in trouble?"

"No, no, don't worry about that. Of course you should've reached out to us at the conference. We're actually taking a break right now, but we can head back to the hotel and send you a copy of that file. Just make sure to have Brice text Candice to get her out of that meeting, okay?"

"I'm covering for you, right?"

"Yes. Absolutely," I said.

"Got it. And Brice needs to text Candice right now?"

"Definitely."

"Gotcha," my husband said. "Anything else?"

"No. I'll be in touch once we're ready to send the file, okay?"

"Okay," he said. "Call me later and explain, would you?"

"Of course. Chat soon!"

After hanging up, I looked over at Candice, and she did a masterful job of appearing alarmed. "Did I hear we got hit with malware?" she asked.

I nodded and went for more of an irritated look. "We did. Gibs opened up the wrong email, and it spread like wildfire. That was Dutch. He wants us to send over a copy of the Safe Haven file to his personal computer. I've got a copy stored on my computer back at the hotel, and as long as I don't log into the network, I should be able to get it to him by our deadline."

Candice's phone pinged and she lifted it to read the incoming text that I knew Brice had just sent her. "The office is freaking out. We should go right now," she said.

I nodded again, and then we both made a show of appearing sad that we had to cut our visit short, promising to return if we got another break during the conference.

Brandy and another young woman accompanied us to the door. "Thank you for coming!" Brandy said. She seemed to be a lovely girl, and I felt a little bad that she thought we were going to make some connections for her after she graduated. The guilt got the better of me, and I said, "Brandy, give me your digits, and if I can make a connection for you in the future, I will."

The young woman danced on the balls of her feet a little as she recited her number, which I entered into my contacts with the odd feeling that it wasn't a totally fruitless act.

Candice stepped out of the house first, and I was right behind her. We moved fast down the drive, out of the gate and began to jog the two blocks to where we'd parked.

Once we got to her car, my sidekick clicked the locks and we got in, but just as I was putting on my seatbelt, I took notice of a folded piece of paper, tucked into the corner of the windshield. "Wait!" I said as Candice punched the start button and was about to pull out of the spot.

"What?"

In answer, I rolled down the window, folded my jacket sleeve over my hand and reached my arm out and around to grab the note. Even before I unfolded it, I knew the note contained something bad. Careful to keep the fabric of my jacket between my fingers and the paper, I peeled back the folds, revealing a message written in crimson. It read:

Too bad

So Sad

Your too late!

"Fuck," Candice whispered, looking over my shoulder. "He's taken another girl."

I nodded, feeling a sense of both dread and rage course

through me.

Candice continued to study the note for another moment, then she pointed to it and said. "He uses Y-O-U-R instead of Y-O-U-'-R-E."

Something clicked into place in my mind, and I dropped the note into my lap to lift up my phone, pull up my photo's app, and immediately go to the one I'd taken of the flyer from Fiji House. "Look!" I said, holding the image aloft so Candice could see it. "It's the same misspelling!" For emphasis, I pointed to the line on the flyer that read,

Your invited to a Hot Shower Party at Fiji House . . .

"He's definitely a Fiji," Candice said softly.

Another thought occurred to me, and I pulled my phone back to trace my finger over my contacts' list and pull up the new number I'd entered just minutes before.

It rang twice before Brandy picked up. "Hello?" she said tentatively.

"Brandy," I said, relieved she'd answered. "It's Ab-Annette." I'd almost blown my cover.

"Annette?"

"Yes," I said, impatient to get to the point. "I need to ask you; what's Chloe's major?"

"What's *Chloe's* major?" she asked, and I knew she was thinking it was odd that I was calling to ask her about the sorority sister I hadn't yet met.

"Yes," I said, barely holding back the urge to yell at her to just answer the question.

"Uh . . . it's Geophysics. Chloe's really smart."

I dropped my head and closed my eyes. "Dammit," I muttered.

"Excuse me?" she said.

"Sorry. Listen, Brandy, I gotta go, but I'll be in touch soon, okay?"

"Um . . . oh—"

I hung up on Brandy before she could finish her sentence, and I didn't care if I was being rude. Turning to Candice, who was staring at me with concern, I said, "I'm gonna ask you this only once, and probably not ever again, but I need you to drive like a bat outta hell Candice. We gotta get to the UT Tower, *now!*"

Candice slid her sunglasses on, turned the wheel of the car, and hit the gas. Hard.

We jolted out of the space, and I swear she was at sixty miles an hour before I had time to blink twice. While she weaved in and out of traffic like Mario Andretti, I looked away from the windshield and tried to keep my shaking hand steady as I pulled up Dutch's number on my cell and called him.

"Edgar," he said, answering on the third ring.

"I need every available LEO at the UT Tower! Immediately!" The adrenaline of the past few seconds had hit my veins like liquid hydrogen.

I heard Dutch snap his fingers three times, and I knew from experience he was getting everyone else's attention. "Talk to me," he said.

"He's got another girl, Dutch! Chloe Hill! Tell Toscano *not* to answer his phone! In fact, tell him to turn it off!" I was terrified the piece of shit frat boy was going to get ahold of one of us and force us to listen to him murder Chloe.

"Toscano!" Dutch yelled. "Turn off your phone! Now!"

Just like I'd anticipated, my call waiting beeped with an unknown number. "Son of a bitch!"

"What?" Dutch and Candice said together.

I sent the call to voicemail and told my husband, "He's trying to call me. I gotta turn mine off too! Call Candice if you need me!"

With that, I hung up and turned off my phone, then clutched it in my hand when Candice took a sharp turn, tires squealing.

Sucking in a breath as we rounded the corner and barely missed a student on a bicycle, I didn't move another inch until Candice braked hard right in front of the UT Tower.

As we jumped out of the car, which was double-parked, students began to pour out of the surrounding buildings, and all of a sudden, a siren blared loudly across the campus. It didn't sound like it was coming from an emergency vehicle—it sounded much louder, and coming from overhead.

"ALERT, ALERT, ALERT!" came a robotic voice over the loudspeaker. "CAMPUS POLICE HAVE A REPORT OF AN ACTIVE SHOOTER NEAR THE UT TOWER! PLEASE SEEK SHELTER IMMEDIATELY AND AVOID THIS AREA! LOCK ALL WINDOWS AND DOORS! CALL 911 IF YOU SEE SUSPICIOUS ACTIVITY! ALERT! ALERT! ALERT!"

Within seconds the students all around us began to panic. It was like the opposite of a flash mob. People scattered and began to run out of the building we were trying to enter. Candice and I were hard pressed to make headway toward the doors. We got bumped and jostled, and I was pushed to the far left, away from her. I fought to try to get back to her side, but just as I tried to push back to the right, a student dropped at my feet, and nearly simultaneously a shot rang out, the echo bouncing between buildings.

Collective screams undulated across the swelling mass of students, many of them trying to change direction midstride, while dozens more turned abruptly around and pushed their way back outside. Sirens erupted again, this time from all corners of the campus.

I bent down to help the girl at my feet up, but as I grabbed her under the arm, my hand slipped off her skin and came away wet. I stared at the dark blood covering my hand, and it was a moment before my brain could compute what'd happened. The girl had been shot through the shoulder and her frightened eyes were staring up at me.

As I reached for her again, there was a small explosion of concrete right in front of me. I felt the sting of sharp pieces of cement cut my neck. Almost within the same moment, the loud bang of a gunshot reverberated against the buildings.

Purely on instinct I darted to my left, crouching down, and was pushed and jostled by even more students in a total panic as they tried to get to cover.

Adding to the chaos, there were screams all around me, some as close as right next to my ear, but even they couldn't rise above the sound of yet another gunshot. In front of me, a young man crumpled to his knees, his hands covering his stomach before he pitched forward to lay his head on the ground.

I let out my own startled cry, realizing in that moment that the gunman was either aiming at me and missing, or aiming at the students around me. My head turned wildly as I looked for Candice, but she was nowhere in sight. She'd been lost to the chaos of bodies fleeing to and fro.

Another explosion of cement to my right sent me scuttling even further sideways.

More terrified cries of panic filled the air, drowning out even the approaching campus police with their sirens blaring.

"GET DOWN!" someone screamed.

It might've been me.

In the next moment, someone grabbed my hand and pulled me hard to the left, just as I was bumped by another student and nearly fell. In the confusion of limbs and bodies clamoring to find cover, I couldn't see who had hold of me, but I assumed it was Candice, however, when I finally got a look at my own hand, I saw that it was wrapped in the dark skin of a young man.

"*This way!*" he shouted.

Another shot rang out, and panicked students began dropping to the ground, covering their heads with their hands, in a desperate attempt to get low enough not to be an obvious target for the gunman.

The young man holding onto me leapt over the prone, terrified students, pulling me with him, and I had no choice but to jump over them too.

I tried to tug away from the student pulling me through the crowd, thinking he was definitely putting himself in danger by dragging me along, but he wouldn't let go.

"*There!*" he shouted, pointing ahead to a doorway just off the main entrance. It looked like a maintenance access.

Somewhere behind me I thought I heard someone shout my name, but it was impossible to tell because of the chaos.

In front of us, a blast of mortar and brick shot out from just to the right of the door we were running toward, striking me hard in the forehead and chin.

The ricochet cut into my skin, and I hissed, stumbling again, bringing my free hand up to my forehead.

The kid in front of me had ducked too, and I suspected he got even more shrapnel than I had, but he didn't waver when he reached the door and pulled it open.

He was pulling me toward the opening when two other women and a young man ducked inside first. We all seemed to stumble inside together, and the student who'd had hold of my hand, let go, so this time as I tumbled forward, I actually fell, slamming hard onto the concrete just as another sharp sound echoed from the door's exterior. I flinched and looked over my shoulder, only then noticing a convex bump the size and shape of a bullet lodged midway up the steel door.

I rolled over onto my ass and surveyed my surroundings. There were five of us huddled inside the small room which also held a concrete spiral staircase leading up to what I assumed was the clock at the top of the tower.

All of us were panting from exertion and fear, and the two girls were openly sobbing. The kid who'd saved me was moving toward them, checking to see if they were okay, and I had to appreciate him all the more because he had a deep cut above his right eyebrow and a line of blood dribbled down his cheek while the girls appeared to be okay . . . physically at least.

My gaze drifted over toward the door again, and I stared at the bullet that'd been stopped midflight, telling myself that the steel barrier was enough to keep us safe, but in my mind, I wasn't buying it.

Pointing to the stairwell, I said to the young man who'd pulled me in here, "Where does that lead?"

He shook his head. "No idea. You okay?"

I nodded, wiping at my forehead and seeing more blood

on my hand.

"I think he was shooting at you," the kid said, his brown eyes wide and frightened. "I saw kind in front of you get hit, and I felt like you were next."

I nodded again. "I probably was."

"Who's shooting at you?" he asked, his voice hard, like he kind of wanted to blame me.

He'd have to get in line. I was certain I'd be blaming myself for weeks and months to come. "The guy who's been killing the girls on campus."

"The girls from the podcasts?" a girl across from me asked.

"Yeah. I think so. He's got it out for me."

"Why?" she asked, tears dribbling down her cheeks.

"What did you do?" asked the young man next to her.

I stared at them for a long moment and finally said, "He wants to torture me, and because he's a sick and twisted son of a bitch, I hope like hell he gets blasted by a hundred rounds of ammo, anytime now."

The young man who'd pulled us to safety went over to the door and put his ear to it. We hadn't heard anything more since we made it inside the alcove. He listened for a minute, then looked back at us. "I don't hear anything. Maybe I should go for help? If this guy is hunting you, then you'll need the campus police to protect you."

I stood up and pulled down the zipper to my jacket, exposing the holster and weapon at my waist. "You're not going out there. It's way too risky. I can handle anyone who tries to get in here. Lock the door, and we should be okay."

The kid eyed my gun warily, so I zipped my jacket back up and added, "I'm a consultant for the FBI, and my husband is a special agent with the bureau. I've been helping him work these murders, and we all thought it best for me to wear a weapon . . . just in case."

The kid seemed to relax a fraction, and he reached up to turn the dead bolt on the door, but he couldn't get it to turn. "Shit!" he said, hissing as he tried to twist the lock. "It won't budge."

"What?" I said, walking over to him and trying the lock myself. He was right. It wouldn't move even a centimeter.

"We should barricade the door," one of the girls said, her voice quaking with fear.

I looked around our area but there was nothing to use to barricade the door. I didn't know where the shooter was firing from, but I suspected it wasn't from the Tower building. It was likely from another building with a clear view of me and Candice emerging from her car, and I wondered if I'd been wrong about Chloe being taken. Maybe it was all just an elaborate setup to get me in position to blow me away. I was lucky that he seemed to be a bad shot, but there was a giant load of guilt on my shoulders for the other students who'd been shot in my stead.

Still, I couldn't focus on that right now. The girl in front of me was right, we needed to barricade the door until we were sure the coast was clear.

"Candice!" I gasped, suddenly thinking about my sidekick.

"Who?" the girl who'd suggested barricading the door asked.

I shook my head. "My partner. We got separated. I don't know if she's safe."

Reaching toward my back pocket, I lifted out my phone and tapped at it. The screen remained black.

"What the . . .?" I said, and then I remembered that I'd shut my phone down. I stared at it for a moment, wondering if I should turn it back on or not. I didn't know if the psycho murdering people was trying to call me on it or not, and if I saw his number flash across the screen, I knew myself well enough to know that I'd answer it and scream at him.

It'd be the perfect excuse to kill Chloe if he had her, and my gut told me he did, even though he was also shooting the shit out of the campus from some nearby building.

The young man who'd saved us began to walk away from me, moving over to the staircase.

"Where're you going?"

"I gotta get something to barricade the door," he said. He then began to climb the steps.

I moved over to the staircase too. Looking at the three other students I said, "Don't let *anyone* past that door."

They all nodded and hurried to put their backs against the door to brace it should the shooter come looking for me.

I didn't know how the killer would get past the police responding to the scene, then again, I had to remember that we believed he had accomplices, so anything was possible.

I followed the kid up the first few stairs and said, "I'm Abby, by the way."

He looked over his shoulder. "Malik."

I offered him a weak smile, and he returned it. "Thanks for saving me back there, Malik," I said.

He shrugged nonchalantly. "It's cool."

We climbed up and up to the first doorway off the stairwell, which I figured was about two or three floors up, it was hard to tell. Malik moved over to try the door, but it was locked tight.

Without a word we went back to climbing the stairs again, winding our way up and, about the fourth or fifth floor, I had to pause to catch my breath. Malik appeared relieved to have an excuse to catch his as well.

We got underway again, and as we climbed a little slower now, I said, "How did you know the door would open?"

"Huh?" he asked, looking at me over his shoulder again.

"The door to this stairwell. How did you know it'd open?"

"I got a text."

We were a few steps away from another landing with yet another door.

"You got a text?" I asked, stopping for a second to grip the railing and catch my breath again.

"Yeah," he said, pausing to address me. "It was really weird. It came in about a minute before the shooting started."

A prickly feeling lit up the hairs on the back of my neck. "Show me."

Malik lifted his phone out of his back pocket, tapped at

the screen and swiveled it toward me.

The text read:

Wait for the show by the west exit.
That woman in the photo will be there.
Grab her & get to the maintenance entrance to the left.
It'll be open.

I scrolled down past the message and saw a photo of myself, taken from the hallway just outside the school newspaper's office.

I looked up at Malik. "Fuck," I whispered, because in that moment I knew what was about to happen next.

Glancing up at the landing and the door just a few steps away, I noticed a white piece of paper tacked to the door's window. In big black script it read:

This way for a hot shower!

Malik's gaze traveled with mine, and I could see the puzzlement in his expression. "Hot shower?" he said.

"Shhh!" I hissed, putting a finger to my lips. In the softest whisper I could manage I said, "Malik, we gotta get outta here!"

He was staring at me in confusion, so I reached up and grabbed his arm tugging him back down a stair. He reflexively resisted my pull, and it was that tiny delay that sealed what happened next. The door banged open, and onto the landing paraded a tall, blond, light-eyed guy, dressed in camouflage, Kevlar, and looking like he was about to meet up with a special forces unit to resupply them with all the weapons he carried on his person.

He was flanked by two others dressed the same.

The leader took one look at Malik, lifted a Luger pistol, and shot him in the chest.

I gasped and tried to catch Malik as he fell back, but his weight carried me off my feet and we went tumbling backward, down the stairs. I felt my right wrist snap as I crashed onto a stair, and a bolt of lightning lit my entire arm on fire.

The pain was excruciating, and I heard myself cry out. I continued to tumble another stair or two before I managed to stop myself, but Malik's body traveled down several more stairs. I caught a glimpse of his still form before my wits returned, and I attempted to unzip my jacket to grab my gun, but my wrist wouldn't cooperate. The pain was so intense my vision blurred, and I saw stars.

Footsteps sounded above me, and I shifted slightly to reach my left hand to the zipper, thinking if I could just pull the gun free, I might be able to get off three quick rounds. I'd never shot a gun with my left hand before, but these were desperate times, and whatever I did manage to get off would at least be at close range. I didn't have to be off by much to kill these pieces of shit.

I tugged on the zipper, but it held tight. I was lying on my right side, and when I looked down, I could see that I was at an odd angle that was forcing the fabric to fold in on itself, and the zipper couldn't get enough tension to slide down.

I shifted again, but I was too slow in the whole process, and the fucker who shot Malik was practically on top of me. "Hey, Abby," he said, pointing the WWII era gun straight at me.

I was hissing with pain and fury. "Fuck you," I growled.

He laughed. "I'll pass. You're a little old for me."

The guys behind him chuckled and elbowed each other. I didn't care because I wasn't focused on my fee-fees at the moment. I was focused on a plan to kill these motherfuckers before they killed me.

"Thanks for coming to our podcast," the leader said.

I stared at him, imagining all the ways a bullet could mess up that smile.

There was a sudden buzzing sound, and the guy with the Luger reached for his phone, lifting it off a holster at his side. He clicked the speaker function when he answered the call. A male voice spoke in between panting breaths. "They're . . . on top of me, John!"

"You've served your country well, patriot," John said. "A grateful nation thanks you for your sacrifice."

"Tell my mom—" said the caller, but his voice was interrupted by an insanely loud, BANG! And then all we heard were more gunshots and the commotion of shouts from police, with one in particular rising above the fray, yelling, "Shooter is down! I repeat! The shooter is down!"

John clicked off the call with a sick, satisfied smile and pocketed it, then he raised the gun in his hand slightly, angling it right at my forehead.

To be honest, I've stared down the barrel of many a gun in my time—hell, I've even been shot once or twice—but I don't know that I ever felt as close to death as I did in the moments after that phone call. Staring into John's eyes I could see him wavering. Shoot me now? Or shoot me in front of an audience?

It was all I could do not to blink as I met his gaze with my lip curled into a snarl. "You. Disgust. Me," I told him.

The motherfucker actually smiled. Then he relaxed his grip on the gun, using it to wave at me. "Grab her. Bring her with us."

I tensed as the two assholes flanking John stepped forward to reach down and yank me up to my feet. I cried out sharply because my wrist was jostled, and the pain was insane.

"Jesus, lady nut up!" one of them snapped.

I was panting hard, trying to think my way out of this. I'd lost my phone on the stairs, and my gun was currently out of reach because I couldn't get to it without exposing that I had it. They'd likely find it anyway once they patted me down, but then it occurred to me that they *hadn't* patted me down— they'd simply reached for me and were dragging me up the rest of the stairs and through the door. That's when the tiny spark of an idea came to me. If it didn't even occur to them that I might be packing, I could possibly get away with getting the jump on them, as long as I was able to get to my gun without them noticing.

"I think my rib is broken!" I gasped, doing my best to pull

my left elbow towards my gun holster, trying to hide its bulge from view.

The guy grabbing my left arm didn't say anything, but he did let a little of the tension out of my arm, which was a really good sign.

If I could just appear to be cowering from an injured rib, I might at some point be able to sneak my left hand inside my jacket to retrieve the gun. It wasn't much of a plan, but it was something.

The two guys carried forward into an empty corridor. We trailed behind the leader all the way down the hallway to the far end, passing closed doors where I suspected students were hiding in terror after barricading themselves inside.

As far as I could suss out, the plan these guys had concocted was a pretty damn good one. The cops would think that they'd eliminated the shooter and also conclude that he was the serial killer who'd been murdering the girls on campus. They'd probably assume he was alone, and the only one they had to worry about. Still, they'd definitely keep searching the area for accomplices, but probably not in earnest, and that search alone would take hours and hours, given how large the campus was.

So the shooter was actually just a sacrificial lamb to buy these three other assholes time. No one in law enforcement was likely to get to where we were until well after dark, which was long enough to pull off a podcast where they shot me live on camera before they fled, fading away into obscurity. I doubted they had the cajones to appear on camera. No, they'd keep to the shadows and pull the trigger without a hint of who they might be, and the only lead we currently had to their identities was that they might be members of Fiji House.

I had to hope that Candice, Oscar, Dutch, and Brice would figure out who they were sooner or later. If I didn't live through this, I hoped to be able to watch the gun show from the Other Side.

At the end of the corridor, John opened a door to a room with a bright florescent bulb. The room itself was small and sparse—likely an individual study room. The only things in it were a table, a couple of chairs, and the young woman I knew might very well be Chloe, sitting in the corner with her hands bound behind her back and a gag stuck in her mouth.

I felt fury ripple through me. She had a very swollen black eye, a fat lip, and her hair had clearly been yanked and pulled out in some places.

They'd roughed her up pretty good, and I was too angry to even scream obscenities at them. Instead, as the door closed behind us, I made sure to look directly at Chloe so that she could see that she had an ally in this room. Someone who was going to fight to the death to try and save us both.

John pulled out a chair and sat down. Belatedly, I saw that on the table were two microphones, a camera, a set of headphones and a computer.

John motioned for me to sit, and I felt the two thugs to the side of me release their grip on my arms.

I held myself in a hunched position, cradling my right wrist with my left hand which served to hide the bulge of my gun and give further credence to the belief that I'd broken a rib or two on the stairs.

To keep up appearances, as I moved toward the table and the set of chairs, I made sure to wince with each step and hissed loudly as I slid into the seat. I did all of this as slowly as possible so I could allow my mind to map out exactly what moves to make to free my gun and blow John away before the other two blew *me* away.

Once I was settled, one of the goons who'd brought me in—let's call him Lizard Breath—moved to the laptop on the table and took it with him over to a chair that was placed against the wall. He studied the laptop for a moment before getting up and coming over to the camera, which he aimed at my side of the table and away from John, then he positioned one of the microphones closer to me and moved the other a little closer to John on the opposite side of the table.

The other goon—let's call him Donkey Face—moved to Chloe and pulled out her gag. She was panting heavily, and I was a little worried she'd pass out, but when her gaze shifted over to me, I could see the fire and fury in her eyes.

That girl still had plenty of fight left in her.

Good.

I held her gaze, hoping she could see my strength too, but then Donkey Face jerked her to her feet and pulled her over to the table to be shoved into the seat next to me.

Lizard Breath adjusted the camera facing us one more time, making sure Chloe and I were centered and focused for the view from the camera. Then he went back to his chair, placed the laptop on his knees and said, "We're good to go, John."

John made a motion to Donkey Face, and he stepped outside, closing the door behind him.

I had a feeling he wasn't going anywhere. He was on lookout duty, which meant that, with him out of the room, another domino fell in my favor.

Before the camera started to roll, I made a show of bending forward and coughing as wetly as I could muster, while also pulling down the zipper on my jacket. Clutching my left elbow against my ribcage I said, "I'm having trouble breathing."

"You won't have long to worry about it," John said, with that same sick smile spreading across his lips.

I don't know that I've *ever* wanted to annihilate someone as much as I wanted to do him in at that moment.

And I probably would've except that Lizard Breath pointed to John and yelled, "Action!" like he was Martin-fucking-Scorsese. The little prick.

John leaned in toward the microphone. "Hey, fellow patriots. I'm coming to you live from the UT campus, where our brother-in-arms, Jason, with the courage of a warrior and the heart of a true patriot, took up arms to take out a bunch of Black lives that no longer matter." John paused to snicker, and Lizard Breath chuckled too. "Jason gave his life to the cause, and he dies a hero and a legend."

I leaned in toward the microphone in front of me, (pulling

again on the zipper of my jacket) and made a series of gagging noises.

John shoved his chair back, his rage igniting faster than I would've guessed, and he punched me hard in the face. I recoiled back and fell out of the chair. Chloe cried out, but then she cowered when John made a move like he was about to punch her too.

"Fuck!" I yelled from the floor as much out of pain as it was for a distraction because I was able to slip my left hand into the inside of my jacket and wrap my hand around my gun without anyone noticing.

"Get up," John demanded. And then behind me I heard him fumble with the camera, probably making sure to tilt it toward me on the ground. "This is how we treat traitors and false prophets," he said. "Some of you might recognize the whore who claims to be able to predict the future. Abigail Cooper. Some psychic," he scoffed. "She couldn't even predict that today's the day she's gonna die."

I glanced over my shoulder at John, and a light bulb went off in my mind.

He was right. I *hadn't* predicted that today would be the day I'd die, which, for someone who'd had her radar up and active for the last several days, wasn't something I was likely to miss.

And I took that to mean that today wasn't going to be my last.

It was going to be John's.

"Get up," he snapped while I continued to crouch there.

I shifted to my knees, knowing that if I had a chance to take him out, it'd have to be now. My brain buzzed with the few options available to me, and I lined up the one that might allow me and Chloe to live.

Groaning again, I moved my torso in such a way that I pushed the chair I'd been sitting in against the door. I then swiveled as if I was going to use it to help me get up. The biggest impediment to my plan to take out the two assholes in the room was that I'd have to keep Donkey Face from busting in and shooting me shortly thereafter. I thought I could take down John and Lizard Breath, but with my injured wrist, I didn't know if I could take out Donkey Face too.

Like his two accomplices, Donkey Face was armed to the hilt, so it wasn't something I wanted to risk my life with, so I'd have to do something to prevent him from getting in the room.

Coming fresh into my mind was a YouTube video I'd watched only a few weeks ago on how to effectively barricade a door using only the leg of a chair. All you had to do was lift the chair, place the leg between the handle and the door, then twist the chair slightly to anchor it in place. Easy peasy.

But doing that would mean that, with my busted wrist, I'd have to pick the chair up, place the leg just right and twist it while *also* reaching for my gun. That was a whole lot of movement with my right hand that appealed to me almost as little as getting shot in the face.

Still, I knew I had to try, so I gritted my teeth, bent forward, put my right elbow on the chair seat to hide the action of pulling my gun free. The gun in my holster was positioned for a right-handed retrieval, so, when I lifted it free using my left hand, it'd be facing backward from the way I needed to use it. I'd have to flip it around carefully and get a grip on it while also putting a finger on the trigger, ready to shoot.

"Get up!" John snapped.

I coughed wetly again and lifted a knee, playing up the whole, "I'm injured!" act. Pushing my left arm inside my jacket, I got my hand on the gun and, miraculously, managed to pull it out of the holster. Using the inside of my jacket to hold the gun while I flipped it around, I started to get up to my feet, praying I could get a grip on it as I rose up.

In another small miracle, I felt the grip slide into my palm, but I couldn't get my index finger into the trigger guard, but my middle finger managed the movement, which, honestly? Was somewhat poetic.

Standing tall with my back to John and Lizard Breath, I

bent down again and gripped the back of the chair with my right hand, hissing and clenching my jaw from the pain. Sweat poured down from my brow as I began to lift it, eyeing the door handle and praying that I could heft the chair high enough to get the leg into that small gap between the lever of the handle and the wood frame of the door.

"What're you doing?" John asked.

I didn't answer him. I simply continued to lift the chair.

It surprised me when he laughed. "She thinks she's gonna throw the chair at us," he said to Lizard Breath.

Lizard Breath chuckled too. "Shoot her," he said.

I was panting with the effort not to drop the chair, the pain in my wrist again blurring my vision and causing a cluster of stars to sparkle behind my eyes.

Finally, it was high enough, and I angled it slightly, watching with relief as the leg slid into place. I then twisted it, locking out Donkey Face.

Behind me, John and Lizard Breath laughed some more. They thought my effort to barricade the door was hilarious. "Oh, no, we're trapped!" John mocked, and he and his buddy laughed even louder.

I suspect it stopped being funny when I whirled around and started shooting, pulling the trigger in rapid succession. I'd been aiming for John's head, but the action of shooting a gun with my left hand was so foreign, and the ricochet so jolting that I only managed to shoot him in the chest.

Still, he reeled backward, hitting the wall hard and sinking to the floor. Out of the corner of my eye I saw Lizard Breath jump to his feet, dropping the laptop as he reached for his gun. But then Chloe bolted up from her seated position, aiming her head right at Lizard Breath. Her head connected with his chin, snapping his own head back, where it struck the wall, and he dropped like a sack of flour.

I'd stopped pulling the trigger on my gun when John disappeared behind the table. Kicking one of the legs to shove the table out of the way, I saw that he lay panting and in pain, but was otherwise unharmed because all of my bullets had hit him in the Kevlar vest he wore.

He grimaced and lifted his Luger, ready to blow me away. My middle finger was quicker and my aim truer this time.

His head snapped back and there was a spray of blood that shot up against the white wall. My last bullet had found its mark, right between his eyes.

The ordeal wasn't over, though, because behind me there was the hammering of Donkey Face's foot against the door. I knew he could see through the window what was happening inside, and even though he couldn't get in, he'd resort to using firepower at any moment.

"*Chloe!*" I screamed. "*Get down!*"

Sure enough, in the next instant, the window of the door shattered into thousands of pieces and Donkey Face shoved his gun through the opening, aiming it directly at me.

I stared down the muzzle of the gun that would surely kill me and thought about how sad it was that after all that, these assholes were gonna win anyway.

I closed my eyes, wondering how much pain I'd experience before I actually died, and heard the sound three rapidly fired gunshots from nearby. Then came the sound of a loud thud of a body hitting the floor.

Opening my eyes, my gaze met Chloe's. She was crouched down against the wall behind the door, staring back at me as if I could tell her how we'd both just survived certain death.

A voice beyond the door shouted, "*Sundance?!*"

My eyes misted, and I choked on a sob. The relief flooding through me was overwhelming.

"In here!" I called back, my voice breaking on the words.

There was a slight commotion, and then Candice's voice was closer to us. "I got you, girl."

I stood up and turned my face to the window. "Hey," I said, spotting her standing just outside, her body in a defensive stance and her gun held tightly while aimed at the ground. Glancing at the floor, I saw Donkey Face, lying on his side, a large pool of blood forming at his head.

"You okay?" she asked, her chest heaving as much from

adrenaline as exertion.

I grinned wide, overwhelmed with so many emotions of relief and gratitude. "I'll live," I told her, barely able to believe it myself.

She kicked the gun that Donkey Face had been holding away from his hand and said, "Thank God, Sundance. Your husband would've killed me if I didn't bring you back alive."

I laughed and cried at the same time, then my knees gave out, and I sank to the floor, where Chloe inched forward and leaned in for a hug, her shoulders shuddering with sobs of relief. I held her tight and whispered, "You're safe, honey. You're safe."

CHAPTER 17

Dutch, Brice, Oscar, and Handshake all arrived just as Chloe and I were helping Candice secure Lizard Breath's hands. We used his shoelaces and made sure he was completely unarmed by stripping him down to his underwear, forcing him to be marched out in front of all the cameras that would capture his perp walk, which was a bit of sweet justice, if you ask me.

Later, as we were being debriefed by both campus police, Dutch, and Brice we learned a great deal, and I was able to fill in all the blanks.

The three dead men were Jason Fuchs, John Muller, and Brett Lange. The group's lone survivor, and the guy who was going to be tried for all the girls' murders, was Scott Albrecht.

They were what you'd expect from young white supremacists; Arian in appearance, full of themselves, racist, bigoted, and misogynistic assholes without a critical-thinking brain cell between them.

I was actually relishing that three out of four were dead, and I looked forward to the day when Scott would feel the pinch of a needle that'd end his life too, because my radar told me that'd be his end.

Along with the innocent three young women that'd been executed live on our podcast, Jason, the shooter from the rooftop of another building, had murdered two other girls and wounded six additional students and one professor.

It gutted me that we hadn't figured all this out sooner and spared everyone such tragedy, but sometimes, as hard as we try, we just can't get there fast enough.

Still, there was one bit of good news; Malik, the young man who'd saved my life by ushering me into the stairwell, had survived his gunshot wound—but barely. He'd been saved by the three brave students we'd left on the ground floor of the stairwell. They'd heard a gunshot from up the stairs, and, after a period of time, they'd crept up the stairwell to investigate. When they found Malik, they'd managed to put enough pressure on his chest wound to keep him alive until help could arrive, which was very shortly after Candice had reached me and Chloe.

I visited Malik in the hospital a few days later, and I learned that he'd suffered a collapsed lung, two broken ribs, a shattered shoulder blade, and some major muscle damage, but it looked like he'd be able to make a full recovery. Coincidentally (or not) the doctor who'd treated him in the ED had been Dr. Tonya Shaw—Simone's big sister.

As for Chloe, she was definitely traumatized, but getting help from a great therapist. I talked with her at length when we were on our way by ambulance to the hospital for my broken wrist and her various cuts and bruises. I did my best to assure her that it was possible to overcome such a terrifying ordeal—I'd done it over and over again, after all. Since then, I've checked in on her regularly, even after she returned home to take her final semester remotely so that she could still graduate on time.

In the ensuing days after the mass shooting, we learned a lot more about the four assholes who'd caused so much tragedy. Muller was the ringleader, and he'd come up with the name of their little group—they called themselves the "White Pride" and their symbol was a white lion.

Agent Handshake from Dallas had been particularly surprised by all the clues that I'd personally been able to piece together in the case, and I'm not gonna say that the Dallas bureau is now a fan of yours truly, but I do think there's a bit of respect there at least.

Anyway, as I'd already correctly surmised, the victims hadn't been chosen at random: Simone, Ji-Hye, Sidney, and Chloe were all selected because of their field of study. John had imbued quite a bit of folklore into his twisted version of reality, and he believed that sacrificing the girls and tying them to the four ancient elements would somehow bring about a blessing to him, his Pride brothers, and their mission.

He'd outlined that mission in a manifesto that was found

neatly set out on his desk back at the Fiji House fraternity, which our team raided once we'd identified him and the others. None of us could make a lot of sense out of the seventeen pages of ramblings, and it mostly sounded like the lunatic ravings of a self-indulgent, narcissistic, petulant, spoiled, man-baby, but what could you expect from a lunatic, self-indulgent, narcissistic, petulant, spoiled, man-baby?

Our team also went on to interview every fraternity member of Fiji, but we couldn't get any of them to confess they'd known what John and his other "Pride" brothers were up to. And we also couldn't get any of them to confess that they understood the true meaning behind, "Hot Shower," either.

Still, I heard a rumor in the days following that Fiji House was under review by the Interfraternity Council at UT, and sanctions along with other disciplinary measures were being considered. We also learned that their House Director, Stevie DeVoe, had abruptly retired. I'm not positive she knew the danger that John and his buddies posed, but I'm not positive that she didn't know, either.

A few days after some of the dust had settled, I bumped into Toscano on my way into the office as he was on his way out, towing a suitcase behind him.

"Cooper," he said warmly.

"Toscano," I said with a smile. "You leaving us?"

"I am," he said. "Headed back to D.C. for another go at the podcast."

His eyes were pinched at the corners when he said that, and it made me curious. "You don't look too enthused," I told him.

He sighed heavily. "Yeah, I know. Cards on the table, kiddo, this whole thing really shook me up. I started the podcast to put some good out into the world, to tell the story of these victims and their crimes and hopefully bring some closure to these open cold cases, but now . . ."

"I get it, Mike. But what's the alternative? You retire, go radio silent . . . then what? The assholes win?"

He offered me a chagrined half smile. "I'm worried that a copycat is gonna want to get famous by doing something similar."

I stared at him for a long moment, aiming my radar at his future. "There's nothing in the ether to suggest that that's gonna happen, my friend. In fact, there's far more energy around another cold case or two being solved because of the Toscano Files."

His expression shifted to hopeful. "Yeah?"

"Yeah, buddy. And it also looks like you're more popular than ever. I see a gold star above your head—that's my symbol for fame. Your platform is going to continue to grow."

He broke out into a grin. "Promise to be my guest host every once in a while?"

I laughed. "We'll see. First, I need to take a *much-needed* vacation with my hubby, then I need a little time paying attention to my private clients, *then* maybe I'll be free to pop in and say hello to your audience." Moving forward to hug him, I added, "In the meantime, you big softie, I'll be listening, okay?"

He hugged me back and chuckled. "Thanks, girl."

After Mike left, I headed to my desk and saw a stack of files on it. My shoulders drooped. The last thing I wanted to do was point my radar at yet another crime. Glancing around the room, I searched for Oscar, who I knew I could talk into going out for coffee. Proper procrastination requires a sidekick and caffeine. But Oscar was nowhere in sight.

"Hey, Baldwin," I called, seeing him at his desk, hunched over his computer.

He swiveled in his chair toward me. "What's up?"

"Have you seen Oscar?"

Baldwin looked around the room. "Not since yesterday. Why, you sensing something bad?"

"No," I said quickly. I didn't need to raise any alarm bells. "I just wanted to go on a coffee run and was hoping to talk him into going with me."

"Call him," he said, then swiveled back to his computer.

I lifted out my phone, (which was no easy task wearing a cast, I might add) and stared at my list of contacts, wondering if roping Oscar into yet another morning of playing hooky was a good idea. After all, I talked him into playing hooky with me *a lot*, and unlike me, he got a yearly evaluation from Brice, who, no doubt, took note of all the times Oscar and I skipped out during work hours.

Deciding it probably wasn't a good idea, I put my phone down and was about to settle for the black tar in the coffee pot near the break room when Oscar breezed into the office, looking out of breath and glancing worriedly at his watch.

"Hey," he said, hustling past me to his seat. "Sorry I'm late."

"No problem," I said, smiling at him. Then I picked up my desk phone and called Brice who was in his office, looking over a file. "What's up?" he asked answering the call.

"You're the one keeping tabs on the office pool, right?"

He looked up at me from his desk and said, "Yeah . . .?"

"Did anyone have last night?"

Brice laughed. "Your husband had a block of time from Monday through today."

"Brice,"

"Cooper?"

"Pay the man."

Brice's eyes went wide, and he immediately set the phone down and walked over to Dutch's office. I saw him say something from the doorway, and Dutch's head shot up, looking first at me, then over at Oscar, who had no idea anyone was talking about him.

Brice and Dutch then came out onto the floor and headed straight for Oscar's desk. He saw them coming and stiffened. "What's happening?" he asked nervously.

"Congratulations!" Brice and Dutch yelled, moving in to clap him on the back.

Every person in the office immediately looked up from

their work and over at Oscar, whose face had flushed crimson. He then turned to look at me and shook his head. "Coop," he said, rolling his eyes.

"About damn time you proposed to that woman!" I told him.

He laughed, then the whole office exploded in joyful celebration, and just like that, I managed to get everyone to play   a   little   hooky   with   me   after   all.

ABOUT THE AUTHOR

Victoria Laurie is the *New York Times* best-selling author of the critically acclaimed, national best-selling YA thriller *Wh∊n*. She also writes extensively in the adult paranormal mystery genre.
In real life Victoria is also a world-renowned psychic-medium. She currently lives and works in a quaint little suburb in the Midwest where she provides food, love, and shelter to a lippy parrot named Doc and a ginger-colored pup named Ember. To find out more about Victoria, her books, and availability for private psychic readings, please visit victorialaurie.com.

Made in the USA
Columbia, SC
31 May 2023

17574507R00154